INDESTRUCTIBLE

The Indestructible Trilogy: Book One

Emma L. Adams

This book was written, produced and edited in the UK, where some spelling, grammar and word usage will vary from US English.

Copyright © 2016 Emma L. Adams

All rights reserved.

CHAPTER ONE

It begins with a flare, and a tremor that rocks the earth.

Screams ring in my ears, drowned out by the explosion. I throw myself flat, eyes squeezed shut against the glaring light. I always thought I'd stand and stare my own death in the face, but right now, I don't have time to do anything but curl in on myself and wait for it to end.

Time passes. Maybe a minute. Maybe longer. The ground remains firm beneath me, as I lie in a foetal position, hands pressed to my face, but I'm not dead.

I'm not dead.

My eyes flicker open. Ashes drift past my face, fluttering against my skin. For a moment, ashes are all I see. Ashes… and a mile-wide stretch of burned ground.

The camp's gone.

I'm not dead.

The two thoughts mingle in confusion, then collide. My eyes open properly as I shift onto my side. Hard ground scrapes against bare skin—my clothes must have burned right off me.

My hands are slightly reddened, grazed where they scraped against rock as I flung myself to the ground. But I'm unhurt. Somehow. I felt that blast vibrate through my bones, shatter everything around me. I smelled the burning and heard the screams.

The screams.

Oh God. Oh my God.

They're gone.

I sit up, properly, stirring a dervish of ashes. The ground is bare. No bodies, not even a trace.

Oh, God. I press the heels of my hands to my eyes, like if I shut out the sight, it'll bring them back. Opal. Randy. Zeph. Shuddering breaths rack my body. My hands are damp when I move them back. I'm actually crying, for the first time since my sister died.

The same sight awaits as before, wavering before my eyes—dead ground. No life. I stir through ashes with both hands, fighting back a scream. How could I have survived? I should have been vaporised along with the others. My teeth chatter against each other, and some part of my brain tells me I'm going into shock.

I brush away the tears with the back of my hand, trying to steady my breathing. The smell of burning lingers, but the ringing in my ears has already faded to a dull buzzing sound.

Get up, Leah. You need to get up. Get to shelter.

The voice of common sense, the one that's kept me alive this long—it's right. Impossible, or not, I'm alive. And I need to get as far away from the Burned Spot as possible.

Yet I can't bring myself to walk away. My throat tightens as I stare around the campsite. There's no way to tell if anyone escaped, but they can't have. It happened too quickly. Only the rocks we sat on are mostly intact. Red-grey, barren ground stretches endlessly in every direction. Maybe this is the afterlife. For all I know, it looks the same as our world does now. But I'm breathing, my ankle's throbbing where I twisted it when I fell, and the panic rising in my chest feels all too real.

Now there's nothing to hide behind, I'm an easy target. I need to move. There's no sign of any settlements around, but we were heading west. There were rumours of a town over that way, and right now, rumours are all I have left to go by. *They'd tell you to run. Randy would tell you to run.*

A heat haze blurs the road ahead, a path cleared where thick pines once clustered. I liked the forest, liked the shelter, but even that didn't survive the explosion. My feet kick up dust dervishes, stinging already as rocks dig into my heels. I wrap my arms around myself as heat seeps from the air, goose bumps rising on my arms. My scalp prickles. The blast burned most of my hair away. My back feels bare without my backpack, and my parched throat reminds me that even my water-flask is gone. The one Opal gave me.

Opal's dead now.

No tears come to my eyes this time, but my throat feels like I've swallowed glass fragments. I won't survive long without water. Even if I'm made of different stuff to normal people.

Pyro.

The word rings through my head, like the echo of an energy blast. I've heard it before, but not for a while.

One time, we spent a few days in a town that had escaped the worst of the attacks, because it lay in the shadow of a mountain. The leader—presumably chosen by the people—didn't trust us, and we stayed only long enough to stock up on supplies. But the night before we left, another group of strangers came to the town. They were all dressed in red coats, like they were part of some kind of weird cult. Their hoods were pulled low, and everyone avoided them even though they were polite and left as soon as they had what they'd come for. Whispers followed them, and somehow made it to our group.

Pyros. They could summon fire from the depths of the earth, and walk away from an energy blast like it was nothing. That was all I managed to get out of Zeph before Randy yelled at him to be quiet. No one ever spoke about it again. We had better things to worry about, like surviving, avoiding the fiends. Running, always moving.

But I listened to their late-night conversations when they thought I was asleep, even when I first joined the camp after Mum and Dad died. I saw Randy polishing his gun, always sitting guard, pretending to watch out for the fiends. Like a gun would do any good against one of those monstrosities.

Randy's dead, too.

I still can't seem to accept it. My feet drag, like I'm hoping if I walk slowly enough, they'll catch up to me. Like I'll find Opal running alongside me, talking even though we weren't supposed to.

In just a few seconds, the blast took everyone, obliterated them without a trace. I'm alone.

The ground scrapes against my bare feet; the air is chilly and biting. I'm going to catch a cold if I don't find shelter. But I've reached the edge of the Burned Spot. Weeds and grass start to appear amongst the parched soil, shrubs poking out the ground. I'm heading the right way. I make out the shapes of mountains, white tips stark against the burnished sky. Even at night, it's blood-red, the moon shining like a pale eye. The red sky is so beautiful, it's easy to forget it's another sign the world as we knew it has ended.

My pace kicks up as I see the house. Abandoned, of course. Solar panels on the roof and neat little windows. The door is slightly open, but not like it's been kicked in.

The river nearby is my first stop. I scoop water in my hands, gasping as the cool water pours down my throat. Then I wash the grit and sand from my face. I try to avoid looking at my reflection in the sluggishly-moving water, but get the blurred impression of a stranger. Without the dark, curly hair that used to bounce past my shoulders, my sunburnt face is thrown into focus. I run my hands over my scalp, shuddering. The skin on my hands stays a burnished red colour even after washing them. But I'm still alive, still breathing, unharmed by the explosion.

And alone, with no one to tell me *why*.

It's been two years since Lissa died. Two years since I told myself I'd never cry for another person again. But I can't wrap my head around the idea that Randy and the others are gone. Even Opal. It's like if I run far enough, I'll find them again, out of range of the explosion, with answers. But that's stupid. Of course it is. You'd have to run faster than a human can to outrace an energy blast.

The door creaks slowly inwards as I enter the hallway. I'm lucky. This house was vacated fairly recently. The smells of decay and neglect haven't descended yet. I spot a throw over a chair in the living room and snatch it up, wrapping it around myself as I search for anything to salvage. My skin prickles. Something's not right. The dust has barely settled on the mantelpiece and the tall oak bookshelves. Did the people who lived here run when they saw the explosion in the distance? That seems a likely explanation, but something about the silence bothers me all the same.

First, clothes. I step out into the hallway again and jog up the stairs. I'm beyond feeling guilty for stealing, but the sight of the outfits in the wardrobe in the master bedroom—I'm guessing this house must have belonged to a couple—makes my chest tighten. They're so… pristine. Just normal clothes. Well, what used to count as normal. How can so little have changed in here when two years have altered the outside world beyond recognition?

Lissa would have loved this. My sister cried when we couldn't get nice clothes anymore, when the big shopping centres shut down—the ones that survived, that is. She didn't really understand what was happening. Well, how do you explain to a seven-year-old when you have no clue what's going on yourself?

I pick out the most worn-looking jeans and plainest T-shirt, which are a touch too big, but good enough. I even find a pair of lace-up running shoes, and a cap to cover my bald head. Maybe my hair will have grown back by the time I find somewhere to settle. If I find somewhere that accepts strangers.

But if this couple lasted so long out here on their own, logic suggests there's a larger settlement nearby. Unless they were just really, really prepared. I've been with the camp so long I almost forgot some people took their chances and stayed put. A lot of people stocked up when the energy blasts began and all the news reports started coming in about whole cities losing power overnight, and raided the supermarkets and bought solar panels just in case the blackouts came. Which they did, of course. Not that a sustainable power supply did any good against the fiends.

How did this place escape?

"This isn't right," I mutter, pulling the hat low over my face. At least it'll protect me from sunburn. I take a jacket for the cold. It's black and made of a velvety material I haven't seen in years. It's the only coat in the room that doesn't absolutely swamp me. I make a quick trip to the bathroom, averting my eyes from my reflection in the mirror over the sink as I splash more water over my face. My skin still stings, like a mild burn. I almost laugh at that. A mild burn, when everyone else was obliterated.

A sob heaves my chest, and I brace my arms against the sink. *Get hold of yourself!*

I snap upright as a tremendous roar shatters the silence. My heart starts pounding. *God, I'm an idiot.*

I should have known. The house was only abandoned recently, and there could have been only one of two reasons for that. One, the energy blast scared them away. But this house and the people who lived here have survived two years of explosions and horrors. Which leads to the second possibility.

Fiends.

My throat closes. The noise came from right over the roof. They've found me already. They'll have followed my trail. Like sharks can smell a drop of blood in water, the fiends can sniff out if a human's so much as tip-toed through a place. The blasts draw them like flies, and I haven't walked far enough away.

Another roar joins the first. *Great, there's more than one of them.*

I tread softly back into the landing, like it'll make a difference. I'm going to die, there's no doubt of it—I'm unarmed, not that any ordinary weapon can harm the fiends anyway. I brace myself against the wall as the first tremor shakes the house. My bones jar against each other, my teeth rattling in my skull.

The splintering sound of glass breaking. One of them has thrown itself against a window. The bedroom window. Gripping the wall so hard my fingers leave dents in the plaster, I start to make my way downstairs. Slowly. I feel every time one of the fiends slams into the side of the house, rattling the floorboards beneath my feet. I want to be on the ground, not that it'll do any good once they get in the house.

My heart pounds in my chest, as if it knows each beat might be the last. My palms are slippery, my throat dry. By the way the walls move, I can tell there are at least two fiends close to the house. My legs tremble and I nearly fall, two steps from the bottom of the stairs.

Wood splinters fly everywhere as the fiend bursts through the front door. Taller than the doorway, wider and more muscular than a human man on steroids, it squeezes into the hallway, directly across from me. Its scarred russet-brown skin is like hardened lava. Teeth as long as my arms protrude from its jaw. Its eyes are sunken in its head, but its senses are already trained on me.

I panic and run past, into the living room, even though it's too late to hide. The fiend lumbers after me, kicking furniture aside. Its feet are the size of small boulders, long nails ripping up the carpet. Heart in my mouth, I back away, searching desperately for something to grab. A last-ditch effort to defend myself.

The window shatters. Glass rains over my head, and a second fiend wrenches its way into the room. A screech tears through its throat, and it closes in on me. Its partner moves closer, head scraping plaster from the ceiling.

Nowhere to run.

My heart pounds. I grab wildly for the nearest object—a telephone sitting on the table, which surely couldn't have been in use—and hold it out in front of me. My muscles lock, arms trembling as I raise my pathetic weapon.

Tears sting my eyes. No one will find me here. No one will even know I'm gone. But I'll fight to the last second.

With a final screech, the fiends leap at me.

CHAPTER TWO

The first blow sends me sprawling, the useless phone slipping from my hand. I can't breathe. The fiend knocked the wind out of me, and my eyesight blurs my attackers into one gigantic being. They're toying with me. Their hands can rip me limb from limb, but instead they're going to drag this out until I'm begging for death.

A bright light fills my vision, and before I can register what's happening, my body moves by itself. I clench my hand, and as another fist swings at my head, my skin ignites. The fiend's still moving, but it's like the world's shifted into slow motion. I easily dodge the fiend's attack, my hand forming a fist.

The light's coming from me. From my own hand. On instinct, I take a swing at the fiend.

My fist blazes with light, the colour of fire. The punch to the fiend's ugly face actually knocks the monster back.

It's like I'm watching someone else. *That didn't happen. That didn't just happen.* For a moment, I just stare at my fist as the light fades away. It was a trick. Surely. Adrenaline, or panic, or hallucination…

The fiend shakes its head as though stunned, and I'm slammed back into the present moment. *Something* happened, and instinct wins out against logic. I push myself up, trying to get my breath back before the fiend can get another blow in.

But I've overlooked its companion. The second fiend roars, its breath harsh, like heat from a furnace. This time, no sudden bright light saves me, and I'm forced to duck its swinging fists. Though I avoid the brunt of the hit, half the wall collapses and I throw my arms over my head to protect myself. A ringing erupts in my ears as plaster cracks, bricks crumble, pieces of the ceiling fall down. I brace myself for the final blow, but it never comes. After a couple of seconds, I lift my head.

I'm crouched in a bed of plaster and brick dust, but I'm not dead, and the fiends have turned their backs on me.

Two figures stand outside the wrecked window, slightly blurred, though I can see they're wearing long, red coats with the hoods pulled down over their faces. If they're speaking, I can't hear a word over the roaring in my ears. But they've drawn the fiends' attention away from me. I struggle upright, legs unsteady but working. A long piece of splintered wood—a piece of a floorboard—catches my eye, and I snatch it up. If I can just get past the fiends while they're distracted…

My feet slide in the wreckage of the floor and the two fiends turn back to face me, fists clenching, muscled bodies coiled. I tense, gripping the wooden weapon tightly. My hearing's coming back, and the growl of the fiend raises the hairs on my arms.

Then the two figures in red leap in through the broken window. One of them delivers a blow to the fiend that actually sends it flying back, like a rag doll. The second fiend lets out a screech as its brother flies across the room, and hits the opposite wall. A picture frame crashes to the ground. The fiend rises, but it's hurt. Its partner lunges at the red-coated stranger, but a blade flashes and bright red blood sprays into the air. The stranger's holding a long knife—or that's what it looks like. It moves too fast for me to be sure, its wielder slicing at the fiend with a ferocity that leaves me shaking, convinced it's a trick. Convinced my brain's finally tripped out on me and I'm going to spend my last few seconds of life watching these images play out like a movie back in the old world.

The fiend has had enough. Limping after its partner, it stumbles through the window and out into the night.

The second red-coated stranger shakes his head at his partner, and his hood slips, revealing a mop of fair hair. He's human, not much older than I am by the look of things—twenty at most. Normal-looking, apart from the long red coat.

Pyro.

"Really, Cas," he says. "What did I say about minimising damage?"

"You said minimise the *casualties,*" says the other. He pushes his hood back, too, revealing buzzed-short dark brown hair. His eyes rove around the room as though checking for hidden enemies. I try to get a look at the knife, but he slips it back inside his coat.

"You ruined a perfectly good picture frame," said the first guy.

His partner says nothing, but walks through the room, searching out every corner.

"Cas, for God's sake. I think it'd be obvious if there were any more of those things here," says the blond guy.

"They were all over this place a few minutes ago. Something drew them away."

"Enough." The first guy finally turns towards me. Ordinarily, I'd have made a move by now—either taken my chances out in the night, or announced my presence, but this is the second impossible thing that's happened tonight and my brain's decided it's had enough. I'm half-convinced the energy explosion knocked my mind out of whack—that, or I'm having a really vivid dream.

I say the first words that come to mind: "Who are you? What the hell is going on?"

The second guy—Cas, I guess his name is—looks at me. I freeze a little inside. His eyes are like a predator's, cold and intense and calculating.

"I could ask you the same question," he says, softly. "You should be dead."

I've been thinking the same thing for hours. But I won't say it aloud. I meet his stare with one of my own. Getting intimidated won't do me any favours.

"Come on, leave the kid alone," says the first guy. "Are you okay?" he says to me.

I nod. "Yeah. I think. Who are you?"

He laughs. "You're all right. I'm Nolan. That jerk-ass is Cas. And you are…?"

"Leah," I say.

"Bit of a mundane name for a survivor like you," says Nolan. "Wow." He flashes a glance at his partner. "You want to explain to the boss?"

"She's not coming with us," Cas says flatly.

I shrink inside, but I won't let it show. "I never said I was," I retort.

"You…" Nolan sighs, shaking his head at Cas. "The first thing you need to do is ignore everything Cas says. Everything."

"We're wasting time," says Cas. "More of those things will be on the way, if they aren't already here. How the hell did you survive out here all alone?" He uses an accusing tone, as though my survival is a trick.

I narrow my eyes at him. "I didn't. I found this place like this. I don't know who lived here."

"Well, they'll be pissed at you, Cas," says Nolan. "You destroyed their living room." He surveys the damage to the wall. I was lucky. If that fiend had hit me, I'd have been knocked right through the brick to the other side.

"Whatever," said Cas. "Let's get out of here."

Wait! I want to say. I want to ask how they fought the fiends. I want to ask how I can possibly be alive. I want to curl up and cry for my friends and beg for answers. But I can't do any of those things. Whatever freakish power just exploded from me, the world isn't the same as it was before, and depending on strangers is a good way to end up dead.

"Hold up," said Nolan. "You okay to walk?" he asks me.

Cas makes an impatient noise. "I told you, she's not coming."

"She's one of us," says Nolan.

One of us. "One of you?" I ask, uncomprehending. "You're—what *are* you? How—?" I cut myself off before all the questions start spilling out. Admitting my ignorance will put me at their mercy. I'm already indebted to them for saving my life.

"Sweet hells, she doesn't know," said Nolan. "Where did you come from?"

I decide to chance it. "Over that way." I point in a vague direction. "My camp got caught in an energy blast."

The house suddenly seems very quiet. Nolan sucks in a breath. Even Cas turns back to face me, his eyes narrow slits.

"You're lying," he says.

"I'm not."

"You survived an energy blast?" says Nolan.

I nod.

"Wow. You're like one in a million, girl."

I don't know what he means. I try to look aloof, but I'm aware that my cap has slipped, and my bald head is in danger of being exposed. The idea of Cas seeing is somehow unappealing.

Ridiculous. Like I should give a crap, really. I have more important things to wonder about—like what in the hell just happened.

"Come on," says Nolan. "You'll be safe with us."

Cas starts to speak, but Nolan cuts him off. "You won't survive alone, not with those things out there. We're heading to a town just down the road."

So there was a settlement, after all. That's where I intended to go anyway, so I just nod.

"Not very talkative, are you?" says Nolan. "No matter. Let's get out of here."

Cas has already jumped through the hole in the wall. Nolan shakes his head after him.

"He has no manners. We'll go out the door. Less broken glass that way."

A few slivers have already embedded in my skin, but the pain's only starting to register now. Tiny bits of glass caused more damage than being thrown at a brick wall. Ridiculous.

I say nothing as I follow Nolan into the hallway. His remark about not being talkative hit a nerve. I used to chat as much as the next girl, but that was when raising your voice wasn't risking your life. With Randy and the gang, survival meant keeping your mouth shut and your ears open.

I miss him. Who'd have thought it? The grumpy old guy was only looking out for us. Cas reminds me of him in a way, except if anyone was left behind, I'll bet Cas would just leave them to rot.

I'll just stick with them till we reach town, I tell myself.

To my astonishment, the fiends really have gone. Nothing waits outside but the road ahead and the burning sky. Cas is already far ahead, his boots kicking up dust and rocks on the path. I glance at Nolan. With those strange red cloaks, they look more like members of a cult than ever. Then again, it's not the strangest thing that's happened tonight.

I'm more tired than I thought, because I can barely keep up. Nolan slows his pace to walk beside me. Unexpectedly thoughtful, unless he thinks I'm valuable in some way. I concentrate on not tripping over my own feet in the too-big shoes I took from the house, wondering where the couple who lived there are now. I hope the fiends didn't catch them.

The red sky is darkening. Not because night time is finally showing itself, but because there's a storm on the way. Bruise-purple clouds gather overhead, and the rumble of thunder makes the air vibrate. At least it isn't an energy blast this time.

The hazy outline of a town appears on the horizon. Spindly trees reach from the ground like clawed hands. Cas slows his pace as we get close enough to see that there's a fence around the outside. Metal, linked chains. A barrier against outsiders.

"What d'you think?" Nolan murmurs to Cas as we catch up to him just outside the place where a gate's been fitted into the fence. Topped with spikes.

"Not friendly," says Cas. "But what did you expect?"

Nolan shrugs. "The last town wasn't fortified."

"It wasn't near the divide," says Cas.

The divide? He must mean the fault line, the place the first earthquake split the earth, cutting England in two. I've been on the road for so long, I've no idea whereabouts we are. Global maps don't matter when the whole world is falling apart. I know the camp's been moving north, keeping as far as possible from the coasts in case another tsunami hits, crossing a strange landscape of untouched countryside interspersed with Burned Spots where the energy blasts hit. The blasts first struck the cities, mostly, places with high populations. The small Oxfordshire town I used to live in was mostly safe from the first wave of disasters, not close enough to the coast or the fault line to suffer anything more than small tremors.

Then the fiends came.

My mind pushes the memory away. It's not important now. What matters is survival, from one day to the next. That much I learned from Randy and the others.

"I'm going," I tell them. "My camp was coming here anyway."

Cas gives me a flat stare. "Go ahead."

But I don't move. Several people approach the gate from the other side. I tense automatically, wishing I'd searched the house for weapons. Even my pocket-knife would do. *Stupid. How could you forget?*

Two men peer at us through the gate. "Strangers aren't welcome here," one of them says.

Cas rolls his eyes. "Told you so."

"We aren't here to cause trouble," says Nolan. "We just need somewhere to stay until the storm passes, and to pick up supplies."

"There's no room for you here," the man says. "We won't open our gates to strangers, not when there's all kinds of unnaturals running around. Those fiends aren't going to take *us*."

"We saw some," says Nolan. "Not far from here. We can help."

"You brought them to our doorstep?"

The others move closer. They have guns, and a clicking sound tells me at least one of them is pointed right at us.

"Okay, okay." Nolan raises his hands. "Actually, we came to fight them off. I hadn't reckoned on you being unhospitable, especially—"

"When we're the ones saving your worthless lives," says Cas.

You could hear a pin drop. Or several barrels click.

"What did you just say?"

"Cas," says Nolan, warningly.

One of the men sticks the barrel of his gun through the bars of the gate. Cas raises his eyebrows.

"I wouldn't do anything hasty," he says, quietly.

I shiver. His tone is smooth as steel, and even the guy with the gun looks momentarily cowed. But he recovers, shifting his weapon.

"Your kind aren't welcome here," he says.

I can sense that he won't budge. None of the men are even looking at me. But they won't trust me as long as I'm with the men in the red coats.

"Go. And don't come back."

"Fine, then," says Cas. "You—"

"Cas!" says Nolan. He turns back to the gate. "Sorry. We'll leave." He gives me a guilty look, as though wondering if I'm going to try my luck with the guards.

But something about the walled-in town repels me. Maybe it's the memory of the explosion, fresh in my mind. In a place like this, there'd be nowhere to run.

I survived when I shouldn't have. Why? I want answers. I want to know what I am. Right now, sticking with these two's the best chance I've got.

We take to the road again. It runs alongside the town's fence, which makes me edgy for some reason. I'm as scared of what's on the other side as I am of what's out here.

This is the world we live in now. People put their own survival first. The men in the red coats appeared the same time as the fiends did, so they're untrustworthy by default. That's all I could glean from Randy's and the other adults' urgent whispers the day we saw the men in town. It might even have been Cas and Nolan we'd seen. Not that it matters now. I have to rely on two outlandishly-dressed strangers. Surviving the impossible has become part of my existence.

A roaring noise tears through the otherwise still air, makes me spin on the spot, my heart freefalling.

The fiends are back.

CHAPTER THREE

Cas's blade flashes as he pulls it from a sheath at his waist, beneath the bright red coat. I wonder fleetingly why the two of them are dressed so conspicuously if they want to avoid attention, then something more important hits me. *Why didn't I grab a weapon?*

The men at the gate have gone. They must have slipped away the instant the cries sounded.

Nolan curses. "We'll have to draw them away."

"Gladly," says Cas.

"But..." Nolan glances at me. I try not to let my fear show, but my legs itch to run as far as humanly possible.

"She's none of my concern."

Another screech rips through the air. I give Cas a defiant stare. *Go on, then. You're going to let the fiends tear apart an innocent girl? Can you live with that?* Most likely, yes. My body trembles, but survival means more to me than pride.

"Fine, you heartless asshole," Nolan says. "You can have your battle. I'm taking her somewhere safe."

Ordinarily, I'd tell him I could speak for myself, but my low-level fear rises as I glance behind and see at least four distinct shapes in the distance. We're outnumbered even if these two have crazy superpowers. Even if *I* do. I back up several steps.

Nolan sees where I'm looking and his eyes widen. "Hell," he says. "Our two fiends brought their friends."

"And I'm not sticking around here to die," I say.

"Fine," Cas says. "I'll draw them away from the town. You take the girl that way. Away from the divide."

Normally I'd object to him calling me 'the girl', too, but he's already running towards the fiends. They're close enough for me to make out their outlines now. Cas runs faster than I've ever seen a human move. He's already closed half the distance between us.

"Come on," Nolan mutters, beckoning me. "He'll be all right."

Strangely, I believe him. After all, Cas made short work of those two fiends earlier. These men are something else. But the feeling of being hunted descends on me again.

I follow Nolan around the town's outskirts, until we find another road. We've made the right choice. A forest sits ahead, thick branches spread wide as though forming a net to keep the monsters out. A hiding place.

We keep moving, treading through the thick undergrowth. That a place like this can still exist is a strange feeling. The world's cities were engulfed in flame, but the forests survived. Branches arch over my head. Nolan's on edge, constantly looking behind us. His red cloak swishes behind him. I want to ask so many questions, but the habit of keeping quiet and listening out is ingrained in me by now. I want to hear if the fiends are close by.

A rustling sounds in the canopy overhead. My heartbeat kicks up. *It's just a bird,* I tell myself. But the layered branches could hide anything, and the idea that I'm unarmed, in the company of a stranger, knots my muscles with tension. When another, louder rustling echoes in the branches, I snatch up a fallen branch with a pointed end.

Nolan raises his eyebrows. "You do know that won't be any use against one of those fiends, don't you?"

"I'm not an idiot," I say.

No weapons can harm the fiends. *But Cas's knife did.*

"I know you might not trust me," says Nolan, "but I really do want to help you. You…you might be exactly what we're looking for."

I watch his expression. He looks sincere, but I don't put down the branch.

"Why's that?" I ask. "Who exactly are you, anyway?"

"It's… complicated." He gives me a look, like he's assessing me. "You heard that man at the town. People don't trust us." He glances up at the canopy. Strips of moonlight peek through gaps in the branches, painting the scene in monochrome. It gives the illusion that the world outside might look the same as it did before the sky turned to fire and the earth to ashes.

"Why don't they trust you?"

"We aren't like the rest of you. Humans," he clarifies. "That's not to say we're not… human. But normal people don't see us that way."

"And why's that?"

"We can do things normal people can't."

Like Randy said. Summon fire…

"Like the fiends?" I say.

He gives me an assessing look. "Not like the fiends. We were around before they were."

"You're not telling me anything," I say.

"We don't give up our secrets easily." A slight smile curves his lips. "But then, neither do you."

I can't argue with that.

"Tell me a little about yourself, at least," he says. "Where were you born?"

I hesitate. *Don't talk to strangers.* But telling people my home town hardly matters now. Not when it doesn't exist anymore.

"A small town. You won't have heard of it. It was in Gloucestershire. Where are we now?"

"Scotland."

I stare around. "Seriously?" I suppose that explains the mountains.

"Yeah, near the border. Not that we have an up-to-date map."

No one does anymore. There used to be satellites that could let you track your location from your mobile phone or computer. But they're just bits of junk floating in space now. The energy waves short-circuit most technology, and the earthquakes and other natural disasters took care of the rest.

"Where are we going?" I ask, inwardly cringing that I'm implying I'm depending on him in any way.

"To our camp. It's hidden. Cas will meet us there."

He's still not telling me everything. Maybe he's as distrustful of me as I am of him. Randy was the same. In the two years we travelled around, I never really learned much about him. Other survivors were eager to share their life stories, but he acted as though the world had always been this way, like survival mattered more than memories. I never decided whether I agreed or not. I *wanted* to hang onto the past, of course, but old pain doesn't matter when you're starving and hunted. Now, it makes questioning Nolan difficult because I've tamped down any curiosity for so long, I don't even know what questions to ask.

"Why did you come to the house?" I say.

Nolan flashes me a glance. "We were chasing the fiends," he says.

I'd thought as much. "You can kill them."

"We can."

"If I go with you, can you teach me how to kill them?" I watch his face carefully.

"If you want to learn, then yes," he says.

This changes things. Not that I had anywhere else to go anyway, but the idea of actually being able to kill the monsters…

I picture myself wielding a knife like Cas, slicing the monsters apart. Fighting back. Not running. Something kindles inside me, amongst the ashes the loss of my companions has left behind.

Hope.

"You want to kill them," says Nolan. "Did… did they kill someone important to you?"

The words stick in my throat. I don't talk about her. I haven't said her name aloud in over a year. I clench my hand, fresh anger at the fiends rising. I *will* stay alive. For her.

"My sister. She was only seven."

"I'm sorry."

I say nothing, letting silence slide between us again. He slows his pace, head tilted as though listening for something. All I hear is the branches whispering to each other, the crackle of leaves beneath our feet. He gaze sweeps from side to side. He's anxious.

More rustling overhead. My fingers dig into the bark of the branch. I stop.

A figure drops to the ground behind us. Cas.

"What's happening?" Nolan asks, his voice low.

"They're coming."

The forest explodes.

Trees split, branches fly in splinters as the fiend lumbers towards us, cutting a path of devastation through the woods. It's too fast for me to do anything but jump back, feet catching in a net of brambles. They tangle around my ankles, and blood beads on my hands when I pull myself free, wasting valuable seconds.

Nolan swears loudly, drawing his weapon. "They followed you?"

"They weren't fooled by our ruse." Cas barely seems fazed.

The fiend jumps, but Cas's already fighting, knife blazing red as sunset. The fiend howls as a long cut slices its body. Cas slashes with the blade, his face a brutal mask. My heart pounds in my ears. I want to run, but somehow I can't look away. What I'm seeing defies all logic. Cas and the fiend move so fast my eyes shouldn't be able to comprehend it, but every strike lodges itself in my brain. I want to jump forward and join the fray, but the fiend howls like a dog that's been shot. Blood soaks into the forest floor as it falls to its knees. I look around for a place to run—but two more monsters leap onto the path in front of us.

"Climb a tree!" Nolan shouts over his shoulder, running to place himself between me and the enemy.

For a second, the image of me punching that fiend earlier flashes through my mind, and I almost ignore his idea and rush forward. But common sense prevails. I pick out the sturdiest-looking lower branch and step onto it, grasping the branch above for balance. It creaks and sways beneath my weight, but I reach up and pull myself higher, higher, curtains of dark leaves brushing against me. I glance down and see Cas and Nolan fighting back-to-back, their blades—Nolan fights with a knife, too—glowing red in the gloom around them. I almost fall when I disturb a nesting blackbird, which takes off with a shriek. Heart hammering, I straighten up, pulling myself one branch higher, until the red sky peeks through at me.

Something is flying towards me. Bigger than any bird I've seen. Dread clutches my throat. It's one of the fiends. I've never seen one that can *fly* before, but the shape grows larger by the second and I know I'm in real trouble.

Raw panic washes over me. I duck down, drop to a lower branch, but my sweaty hands slip and my feet go out from underneath me. A hoarse scream escapes as I fall. I grasp for solid branches but handfuls of leaves slip through my fingers. I hit the ground with a shudder. Pain shrinks my world to a small bubble. My back's on fire. My chest burns, as though

I've broken something inside. I cough, and feel wetness at the back of my throat. Blood.

The fiend crashes through the canopy. Rather than meaty fists, like the others', its hands are curved claws, like a deformed bird's.

The fiend attacks.

I can't move fast enough. Pain stabs my chest all over, but at the same time, the world goes into slow-motion just like at the house. My fist rises to meet it, skin blazing like a torch.

Fiery light explodes around me, and the fiend cringes away.

I'm on fire. But it doesn't hurt, not at all. As the fiend recovers, preparing to slice through me with its claws, I aim a punch at its flattened face. Red light flares from my fist

But the fiend ducks. Faster than before. My hand connects with nothing, and the claws slice my skin. I scream, the world speeding up in a dizzying haze. Blood spurts from my chest.

It didn't work. The thought floats through my head, disconnected. I'm bleeding, dying.

I lost. *No.*

The claws come down again. I raise my hands, feebly, and wait to die.

Dots cover my vision. The world drifts around me, gnarled trees twisting into hideous fiends. Voices sound, but I can't hear anything for the buzzing in my ears. Yet before me, I see Cas's sword fly out, knocking the fiend back.

I can't move, but I'm still alive. Helpless. Slipping away by the second. *I can't die now.*

Cas pushes the fiend back, out of my sight, and then everything goes black.

Voices reach me, somewhere in the darkness.

"*You* carry her."

"Selfish asshole—" I'm assuming that's Nolan, talking to Cas.

Next thing I know, I'm in Nolan's arms, and we're running through the forest. Almost as soon as I become aware of that, the pain crashes over me again. Branches whip at me as we cut a path through the darkness.

"Hang in there!" Nolan says.

I want to ask where we're going, but my mouth isn't working properly, and my head hangs limp. Pain. Numbness. More pain, and screeching that causes more convulsions up my spine. During one of the bursts of pain, a howl cuts through the buzzing in my ears, telling me the fiends are on our trail again.

That should strike me as important. But I'm too tired, too numb. I drift off again.

Next time I wake, Nolan is yelling at Cas. I can't make out the words, but I catch a blurred glimpse of Cas's face and he looks angry. The trees have thinned out, and the sky above blazes, as though reflecting my pain, the moon a mocking eye staring down at me. The world is painted in angry red-and-black stripes. My companions' argument forms a background noise.

A screech jolts me to full awareness again. Somehow, I'm in Cas's arms, not Nolan's. I blink up at him, confused, as he hisses at me through clenched teeth. I catch the words, "Don't ever tell anyone about this."

I think I nod. I can't feel my head at this point. My world is a haze of pain. I can't breathe.

Next thing I'm aware of is that Cas is holding a knife over me.

CHAPTER FOUR

I can't move. Cas says something else I don't catch, then holds his other hand. The blade flashes as he slices open his own palm. Blood drips onto my body. I notice in a detached way that my shirt's ridden up, exposing my torso. There's a lot of blood. I've cracked ribs, maybe worse. Scratches cover my stomach from the fiend's claws.

Cas's blood mingles with mine.

A burning sensation spreads through my body. I gasp, my spine arching, as my skin flares. Pain ignites every inch of me. My veins are on fire. I can't breathe, I can't even scream. The world disappears as I'm swallowed by pure, searing agony.

Shaking. Someone's shaking me. Violently. A voice breaks through the haze.

"C'mon, Leah, get up—Cas, you don't need to do that."

A rustling sound. The burning stops. The world comes into focus with a clarity that stuns me. The pain recedes as quickly as it came, leaving only sweet, blessed peace.

"Don't you dare fall asleep!" Cas shakes me again. This time, my eyes stay open, focus on the angry slant of his mouth. "We have to leave. Get on your feet. You'll be able to move now."

"How?" is the first word to come out. I swallow, tasting blood, but I no longer feel broken inside. Not even the slightest ache. I'm healed.

Cas's blood healed me.

I look down at myself, moving my hands over my ribs. Dark blood streaks my shirt and jacket, but nothing hurts. Cas stands, and I catch a glimpse of the hand he cut to heal me. But there's no cut.

"Questions later," says Nolan—I'd not seen him until now. He's noticeably paler than before, and he stands at a distance from me and Cas. "We've got to go. Now."

I stand. Cas's not looking at me anymore; he's already started walking again, then running. Nolan watches me warily. My legs feel steady, so I take a step. Another. Energy fills me, and I start to run, to catch up with Cas.

"Can't you bother Nolan?" he says, before I can speak.

"I was just going to thank you for saving my life," I say. "Good manners cost nothing."

"But they're inconvenient," he says, tonelessly. *Well, that's friendly.*

I'm starting to get out of breath already. "How do you run so fast?"

"Are you going to ask annoying questions all the way to camp?"

"Just curious." I catch a glimpse of his hand again. No cut, not even a scar. "You can heal."

"I can," he says, not elaborating.

"Does that mean I can do the same? I mean, I'm one of you… right?"

His eyes turn cold. "I said, no questions."

Right. I caught on fire, almost died, and then walked away after he healed me with his blood. Do most people brush those things aside?

"Okay, whatever. It's just that it doesn't make any sense you saving me considering what an inconvenience I am. Am I one of you, or what? How can you know that?"

"Because if you weren't, my healing you wouldn't have worked," says Cas, simply. Then, in tones that cut right through me, "I never wanted to save you."

"Thanks a bunch, then." I look around for Nolan and see he's running, too, but a noticeable distance from Cas. The two weren't exactly friendly to each other before—well, not on Cas's part—but they stood back-to-back when they faced the monsters. Now Nolan runs at the verge of the path where the trees lean over it, as though reluctant to get close to him.

What Cas did to me scares him.

Strange. I thought Nolan himself pushed Cas into healing me. I puzzle over this to distract myself from the sting of Cas's words, and the occasional faint cry that tells us the fiends are still in pursuit. They must be tiring by now—we're moving far quicker than ordinary humans can. I used to be fairly quick on my feet and had a decent score in cross-country running at school, but not on this level.

Now I'd give anything to have those days back, when running was just a sport, not survival.

I still have difficulty keeping up with Cas, but the ache in my legs is from exertion, not injury; the pain in my side is a stitch forming, not broken ribs. My heart hammers, my feet pounding the ground. Just to be alive is a miracle. A miracle I can't explain. Whatever Cas did to me, that fire-coloured light appeared again before the fiend attacked me. Whatever I am, it's more than human.

I see Cas watching me out of the corner of his eye. As our gazes meet, he looks away, his pace quickening. I'm starting to get out of breath, so I let myself fall slightly behind until I'm alongside Nolan.

"Are you okay?" he asks, seeming to have recovered from his earlier wariness. "I should have asked before."

"I'm fine," I say, glancing over my shoulder. "Are the fiends… are they definitely following us?"

I haven't heard any loud noises of pursuit in a while, but I'm aware that I have no weapon and I'll be defenceless if we're attacked again. Whatever power I might have, the fiend still as good as killed me. I don't expect Cas to save me again.

"They've fallen behind," says Nolan, and relief seeps through me. "But they'll have our scent. I've never known them this persistent before."

Neither have I. Each encounter I've had with the monsters is etched on my memory in vivid colours, brief but brutal. They find their target, kill them, then take off. The fiends don't kill to feed, but for the sake of killing. That's always been clear.

"Guess we'll have to keep running," he says. "It's not too much farther to our camp."

"Camp?" I echo. "There are more of you?"

Stupid question. Maybe they really do belong to some kind of cult.

"Yeah, we split up to hunt the fiends. I never expected to go so far out, but those fiends seemed fixated on something. They go where the energy blasts are, usually."

He falls silent. Perhaps he thinks I don't want to talk about the explosion. With everything that's happened since, my survival from that seems less like a dream. It's my life before that seems dream-like. Running and hiding and running again. Barely speaking to anyone. I don't think I've said this many words in a row since Lissa died. I've certainly never felt curious. But now, new questions spark to life in my head with every passing moment. I keep my mouth shut, reluctant to put myself further in debt to these people. But there's one thing I can ask.

I check he's out of earshot before I speak. "Why did Cas save me? He as good as said he hates my guts."

Nolan hesitates for a long time before answering. "Because I asked him to," he says. "And because he could."

That makes no sense. I want to say so, but Nolan's subtly quickened his pace, leaving me in the dust.

I'll have to get answers later.

Light blooms over the horizon as we finally exit the forest. The sun rises in the fiery sky, rays reaching out over the barren earth. We're heading for another Burned Spot, and I can see a group of tents clustered on the scorched ground.

Nolan walks faster, but Cas hangs back, as though reluctant. We cut across a field of dry grass which sharply ends where the energy wave must have reached, destroying anything living nearby. I can still smell the burning, though I might be imagining it.

I start to see people amongst the tents. Three or four red-cloaked individuals sit on tree stumps in a circle, mirroring the discussions that used to take place every night in our group. At first, people wanted to talk about the world before, like it was a decade ago, not mere weeks. Then Randy stopped them, said it was upsetting the children. Like we hadn't seen enough for a lifetime of psychological scarring already.

Two more red-cloaked figures pace the outskirts of the tents, obviously keeping guard. Nolan calls to one of them.

"Hey! Val!"

As we get closer I see it's a tall woman with long, dark hair swept back in a ponytail and piercing grey eyes. Her gaze instantly focuses on me, the stranger.

"This is Leah," Nolan tells her. "She's—well, she's a natural. One of us."

"Is she?" Val looks me up and down.

"She survived an energy blast," says Nolan. "We found her cornered by two fiends."

"Whereabouts?" She doesn't seem surprised by his words.

"A mile or two from here. She was camping with a larger group. The blast took everything out in the area."

Her face softens in sympathy. "I'm sorry," she says to me. To Nolan, she says, "That's all of us now. We were going to send a couple of people after you if you didn't come back soon."

"We got side-tracked," he says. "The fiends were really pursuing us. They even followed us into the forest. I've never heard of that happening before."

"Me neither." She purses her lips. "Tell the others. And Leah, welcome to the group."

"Thank you," I say, though I don't know what this means, yet. Like I said to Cas, good manners cost nothing. It's the one of my parents' lessons I can still hang onto in this crazy world.

Cas himself has already strode off alone, towards the back of camp. Nolan nods to Val and beckons me to follow.

I have to walk right into the middle of camp? I tense even more at the idea of being the centre of attention. Do I really want this? Val seems sincere, but then again, so can anyone. I've met people willing to pretend to be or do anything for their own survival. Not that this group looks like it's on the verge of death, but you never know.

Questions war inside me with the growing urge to get out while I can.

Nolan looks back, realises I'm not following. He walks over to me again. Another young man—boy, really, sitting on a rock nearby—glances to see where he's walking, and our eyes meet. His narrow. He's suspicious of me.

Maybe Val's kindness was an act. Maybe they don't trust me any more than I trust them.

"Leah," says Nolan, in a low voice, "it's okay."

I shake my head. "Tell me," I say. "Can I trust everyone here?"

"Can you… of course." Nolan bends down so he's more on my level, which is a tad condescending, but I know he's attempting to comfort me. Like a kid.

"Right," I say. "Then, is there a way out? If I decide I don't want to join?" I say this loud enough for the other boy to hear. He doesn't react.

Nolan speaks in a low voice. "It's tricky, because our base is isolated and we don't want to draw the fiends near. But if you decide you don't want to—" He glances around, like he's checking no one's listening. "If it's really what you want, I can help you get to the nearest town."

He sounds like he means it. Not that I can trust that, but it's the best I'm going to get. I breathe out, nodding.

"That okay? You can ask any questions if you aren't sure."

"Will you teach me how to fight them?" The words come out in a rush.

"The fiends?"

I nod, again.

"Of course." He steps back. "That's what we're here for."

I follow him to the group sitting in a circle in the centre. A sharp-featured man sits beside a dark-skinned woman and an older man with streaks of grey in his hair. The last of the group is a girl who looks younger than me, who has a book open in her lap. Her heart-shaped face is framed by curtains of fair hair. The way it's fluffed up reminds me of Lissa.

By now, all eyes are on me. I tense up again, but keep my eyes ahead, not on my feet.

"This is Leah," Nolan tells the group.

Four pairs of eyes assess me. I half-expect someone to comment on the lack of hair on my head, which is ridiculous. People with missing limbs are a common sight these days, as are corpse-like, starved beggars on the road, unlucky survivors. But this group look pristine compared to the few ragged strangers we ran into on the road over the past two years. Their skin's unblemished despite the intense radiation and the dust storms. Where in the world do they come from? How did they escape?

The younger girl's the first to speak. "Hi, Leah." She smiles, and it's a genuine smile, too. "Welcome to the group." She looks at the older man, with the grey in his hair. "Can I give her the tour?"

"Elle, we're leaving soon," he says. "Leah, welcome. I'm Murray. Do you want some water?" He offers me his flask.

At once, it hits me how thirsty I am. I nod gratefully and accept the flask. I try not to drink all of it, but once the cool water hits my parched throat it's an effort to pull away.

"We have plenty, take it all," says Murray.

"Thank you," I say.

I'm disarmed by his kindness. It's not something you come across every day, especially amongst strangers. The memory of a half-starved man on the road chasing after my sister, trying to snatch her water-flask, flickers to the surface. Why do I keep thinking of Lissa now? It's like meeting the strangers has lifted the lid on everything I tried to suppress.

As I drink, the others stand up, and people start pulling down the tents and packing them away into hiking-style backpacks. For a minute, it's like being back at camp. The girl closes her book and slides it into her bag. She smiles as she sees me watching her.

"I'm Elle," she says. "Murray is my dad. He's the man in charge."

She's not as young as I first thought—fifteen, maybe. Her soft features are a sharp contrast to the bleak landscape. She's not a natural survivor. The others look older—but some are younger than me. These people can't have all come searching for the fiends. Something doesn't add up.

Nolan hasn't told me everything.

"Why did you come here?" I ask Elle. She strikes me as someone willing to talk.

She glances back at Murray. "I'm not sure my dad wants me to talk about it. But I can tell you anything else." Her bright eyes remind me more of Lissa by the second, if she'd lived and grown up.

"Okay," I say. "What's a natural?"

"Ah. Um, well, you probably know that we aren't like normal people. We don't get hurt easily for one thing. But Nolan said you didn't know about it?"

"I survived an energy blast," I tell her. "And I was attacked by fiends. I should be dead…three times over, now." If Cas hadn't healed me. But from what Nolan said, that's not normal even for these guys. Whoever—or whatever—they are.

Her eyes widen. "Wow."

"So, what's this group about?" I'm not used to asking so many questions. "Stupid question. I just want to know what I'm getting myself in for."

"Don't worry." She smiles at me. "You'll be safe with us."

"So where you live—it's safe from the fiends? Is that even possible?"

"Yeah, we're well-hidden. We live…" She glances around, as though checking no one's listening in. "In the mountains. Hidden."

"The mountains?" I say. "Where?"

"Um. I'm not supposed to say. It's going to be a trek, though. Are you hungry?"

I nod. I haven't even thought about food, but my insides feel hollow and I won't be able to walk for long if I don't eat something soon.

"I'll ask Dad to get you something. And he'll have some spare hiking boots somewhere, don't worry."

This just gets more and more surreal. I watch as she runs over to her father and says something to him. He rummages in the bag he's packing and pulls out a loaf of bread. Elle scurries back over and hands it to me with an apologetic expression on her face.

"Sorry it's a bit stale. We've been here a few days."

It's been forever since I've even *seen* bread that wasn't mouldy. I inhale deeply, and almost laugh at Elle's confused expression.

"We didn't exactly get fresh food on the road," I say. *More like road kill.* I inwardly shudder as I remember Randy's attempts to disguise cooked rat and rabbit as regular meat.

"Really?"

I nod, taking a grateful bite. It tastes like heaven, and I have to tell myself to slow down and not inhale it in one go. When I'm done, I remember I'm supposed to be getting answers.

"So you were hiding when the energy blasts started?" I ask.

"Yeah," she says, but doesn't meet my eyes.

I try to think of a question that won't lead to evasions.

"Elle!" someone calls. "Come and give me a hand with this, won't you?"

"Coming!" says Elle. "I have to go. We'll talk more later."

How can someone smile like that, with the world the way it is? It's starting to feel more and more like I've stumbled into some bizarre alternative universe.

But I nod at Elle, and she scurries away. I look around, wondering where Nolan and Cas have gone. Nolan's helping pack tent pegs away, while Cas is in conversation with Murray.

They're looking at me, but when they see me watching, they return to their conversation. It doesn't take a genius to figure out that they're discussing me.

CHAPTER FIVE

We walk through fields and forests, past abandoned farms and villages ravaged by the fiends. Occasionally we pass another Burned Spot. I've given up trying to identify where we are and instead concentrate on staying awake. Tiredness drags at my limbs, but I know logically that I should be more than just tired. I shouldn't be able to walk at all.

Nolan's talking to someone further back, while Cas has stalked off ahead of the group. I walk apart from the others, who are talking too loudly for my liking. Can't they see how conspicuous a group of red-coated, noisy people are? We'd be easy pickings for the fiends, and not everyone can fight. But I hold my tongue. I'm not normally one for judging people, and it would hardly endear me to the group if I started lecturing them.

The new hiking boots Nolan gave me fit almost perfectly, once I've put on two pairs of thick socks someone dug out from the packs. The woollen material cushions my feet, and someone was even kind enough to give me a cap to protect my head from the bright sun—I lost mine a while ago, in the forest.

I just wish I had a weapon. What good will I be if the fiends attack again?

Elle bounces up to me. "Sorry about that," she says. "I had to tell my dad about something and then… what's up? You look sad."

I shrug. I wasn't aware of my facial expression. "Nothing," I say. "I'm fine."

"You lost someone, didn't you?" She lowers her voice, eyes darting about like it's a taboo subject.

I swallow. I'm too tired, too overwhelmed, to think about the others now. *They'd want you to get answers from these people. They'd want you to live.*

I nod. "Everyone. I was the only survivor."

"I'm so sorry." Are those tears in her eyes? Who cries on behalf of strangers?

"I'm okay," I say, lamely. "So, um, Nolan told me that your group fights the fiends. Could you tell me more about that?"

"Sure! Well, we don't *all* fight—only you Pyros can do that, because the fiends don't get knocked down easily."

"Yeah… about that," I say. "It makes no sense. I mean, I think I'd have noticed that I can survive getting kicked into a wall before now. When I was seven I fell off a bench and broke my ankle, but that fiend hit me into a brick wall and it barely did any damage. Even when I fell out the tree. I broke a couple of ribs, but it should have been worse."

"Um, that's probably because you were awakening," she says. "That's the one thing outsiders—naturals—have in common. My dad's studying it, and he says that the energy blasts are what's triggering it. Before there were only a few of us, but there are a new bunch of people waking up alive from energy blasts. Only you Pyros can survive them. But you know that already, right?"

"Yeah," I say, though my mind's swirling. One question at a time. "But the part I don't understand is how I fought the fiends. I was injured, but it was like my hand—my whole body, really—caught fire."

"That's because you're different," she says, with a laugh. The sound is foreign to my ears.

"I know *that*," I say, and inexplicably, my own mouth curls up at the side. "I'd just like to know what—what I am."

"Pyro," she says. "Well, that's just a nickname we've adopted. I've thought of a nickname for you, anyway."

I blink. "You have?"

"Yeah. Leah the Phoenix. You rose out of the ashes, right?"

"Um. I guess."

A mythical bird that burns in fire at the end of its life and is reborn out of the flames? My chest tightens. I'll never forget the others. Randy… Opal… they kept me alive for the past two years. I don't know that I'd have lived through Lissa's death without them. But for the sake of surviving, I have to look forward, not back. Randy told me that himself, like he told everyone in the group. Not all of us listened. Some sank into grief so deep, they stopped eating or sleeping and either died from sickness or were killed during night raids from scavengers desperate enough to attack a group of other humans. Those of us who stopped looking back and started looking out for our own survival were the ones who lived.

"Are you okay? I won't call you that if it upsets you."

"It's fine. I like it." I don't manage a smile, but that doesn't matter. "Have you found other people… like me, then?"

"Not really." She bites her lip. "It's not common. Like a genetic mutation. It's dormant until the energy blast triggers it."

Dormant. But could it have happened before?

I think of Cas's blood, mixing with mine, healing.

Could I have saved my sister?

It doesn't matter, a voice in my head tells me. *That's over now. It's done.*

I turn back to Elle. "How does it work?" I ask. "Using my… abilities, I mean? It happened by itself, but can I control it?"

"Of course." She smiles. Her confidence takes me by surprise. "You'll learn how."

"But they're… they're impossibly strong. They came out of the earth, and why? To kill us? Why can we fight back, but no one else can?" In my class, I wasn't the fastest runner, or the strongest, or the most intelligent. I was average. Only luck, and finding Randy when I did, kept me alive this long.

"Dad's researching," she says. "Trying to work out why the Pyros are different."

"You don't know?" The impression that this group had answers starts to slip away.

"Not exactly." She bites her lip. It's that expression again. She's hiding something.

"Well, how did you know to hide when they came? When the energy blasts…"

The image of a city crumbling, live on our HD screen, comes to mind. The horrible images playing like something out of a sci-fi movie. Before the connection cut off.

"It's kind of complicated. You'll have to ask my dad. We live away from regular people. I'm not like the others, but my dad's the leader, so I grew up with the Pyros."

"You did?" That explains her lack of knowledge of the outside world. Not that I'm one to talk. I've no idea whereabouts we are or where we're going, either.

"Yeah. Where did you grow up?"

"Gloucestershire. I lived in a small town, until… two years ago."

Time has no real meaning, but for whatever reason, Randy wanted to keep track of the months. Two years ago, I was days away from my sixteenth birthday, studying for exams which supposedly decided my future. London fell when I was in the middle of a drama rehearsal in preparation for my GSCE practical exam.

I'd seen the first energy blast broadcast on the news. Somewhere in the Middle East. People thought it was a nuclear explosion, and no survivors got close enough to confirm if it actually was. The world was more preoccupied with the freaky weather. A blizzard hit in the middle of May, blanketing the whole of the UK in snow. Coastal areas flooded. Earthquakes became global.

Then, within two days of each other, the two big disasters struck.

First came the earthquake, a movement so vast it tore apart the surface of the Earth. The ground split open along a fault line no one had known existed, a massive jagged line cutting through the Earth's surface. Earthquakes devastated too many countries to count. And then the fiends came out.

But few people saw the news report about the fiends, because the second disaster had already taken out the national grid before they could broadcast.

Blasts of energy burst out of nowhere in the middle of major cities. They gave no warning. Everything within a mile of each blast was obliterated, even buildings and landmarks. People stood no chance.

There have probably been even more since then. The world's changed beyond recognition. I spent the first fifteen years of my life secure in the knowledge that Britain was safe from almost all kinds of natural disasters. But now, all the people in charge who used to reassure us how safe we were have gone. No army, I presume. No government. No contact overseas, if there's even anyone to contact anymore.

"We have to take care of ourselves now," Randy always said, while polishing his service revolver. No need for anti-gun laws now. Nor the stringent laws against carrying knives. If I'd had any kind of weapon on me, at least I wouldn't have been utterly defenceless when the fiends attacked. Or maybe I just shouldn't have gone to school that day in the first place. Mum and Dad wanted our lives to have a semblance of normality, which was laughable given that London had disappeared off the map a couple of days before. But other than the lack of power, our town kept it together. Most of the teachers and pupils showed up to school.

Of course, the survivors regretted it.

Elle's eyes grow huge as I describe the fiends' attack. I should probably stop speaking, but I've never told anyone this—never been allowed to. By the time I get to Lissa's death, she's crying.

"That's so horrible," she says, sniffing.

The world we're walking through now is bleak and cold, but beautiful all the same. Green fields and rolling hills, with a row of mountains ghosting the horizon. No Burned Spots here, but no towns or villages, either. No signs humans lived here at all. The world would be reverting to its natural state—

were it not for the energy blasts. They're as unnatural as the red sky.

"Do the energy blasts just target people?" The question slips out before I can hold it back.

Elle's posture stiffens. "I don't really know about the energy blasts."

I add the question to the lengthening list of things to ask when we reach wherever we're going. The blast was the start of it all.

"What's with the uniform?" This seems like a safe question to ask. "I mean, I like it, but isn't it a bit conspicuous?"

The whole group's conspicuous. I do a head count. There are twelve of us, and everyone but me wears one of those dark-red coats.

"You like them? I make most of them myself," she says. "That's what I'll be doing when we get back."

"You make them?" I blink, confused. That wasn't the answer I expected.

"Yeah. They're fire-proof and super-durable."

"Fire-proof. Does that include… energy blasts?"

She nods. "They're conspicuous for a reason. Dad asked for it specifically. We have to let people know who we are. And it draws the fiends' attention, too."

"That's deliberate?"

"Yeah. If they've gone after a group of normal people, then it's a challenge to them. They can't resist."

"I guess that makes sense," I say, "but what about those of you who don't fight? You don't want to draw their attention, right?"

"We don't leave the base often," she says.

"Why…?" I bite the question back, sensing from her tightening expression that this is yet something else I'm not supposed to ask. "When I was with Nolan and Cas, we tried to get into this town, but the gatekeepers refused to let us in because of the uniform. They don't trust you—us."

"They don't?" Disappointment clouds her face.

"I've been on the road for ages," I say, "and I didn't know anything about you until last night. But I know my old group's leader knew something about you. I saw some of you once, in a town."

Elle frowns. "I don't understand why people don't trust us."

"No one trusts anyone these days," I say, knowing my words have upset her. "It's probably nothing personal."

I manage to coax a few small details about where we're going as I ask Elle about her childhood. This occupies us for a while. The terrain under our feet becomes rougher as we get closer to the hills, and I'm glad for the hiking boots. Elle lets slip that we've been heading north, further into Scotland. We could be in another world for all I know.

Until two years ago I'd no idea this much open space even still existed. Mum and Dad took us on holiday to exotic overseas places. Spain, the south of France, Tenerife. Lissa and I wanted to go to beaches and theme parks, not close to nature. If we stayed in England for the holidays, we went to tourist spots on the coast—Blackpool, Cornwall. I've never even *been* this far north. But all the holidays are part of a distant, disconnected past. The memory of sitting in a giant metal bird and flying seems more unreal than the fiends. More impossible than the past twenty-four hours.

Humans could once fly. Now all we can do is run.

But I'm done running.

Sunset lights the sky on fire before we reach our destination. The mountains loom over us, austere and snow-capped, bright against the blazing sky. We follow a long, winding trail that cuts through fields and forests, even passing a small town where lights suggest some inhabitants remain. But Murray—or whoever's leading—doesn't stop, and our path soon veers away. There's a strip of something just visible between the hills, reflecting the sky. Possibly a lake. A loch? I make it my focus point as we walk, to avoid thinking about the ache in my legs. I know I should be keeling over with tiredness by now, but I file it away with the other impossible things I've survived already. The bread I ate earlier barely took the edge off my hunger. My feet burn in the warm shoes, and the skin on my face starts to sting. I've caught the sun.

Just when I think my legs can't take any more, people start to slow down. The lake comes into view—only it's not a lake. It's the sea.

"That's our place." Elle points to the range of mountains I'd thought lay just ahead of us. Now, a mile of glittering blue separates us from it.

I just gape at it. How are we ever going to get across?

"There's a path," says Elle, guessing my thoughts. "This didn't used to be an island. The land changed."

"Where's this path?"

"You'll see it in a minute."

We move further along the road, past a sweeping wave of green forest. The sea remains a glittering mass, but a tip of land extends into it, and as we draw closer, I can see that it connects us to the island.

"So it's not technically an island," says Nolan. I jump, not having noticed him beside me. "You getting along all right, Leah?"

I nod. "Yeah, I'm good."

"We're calling her Phoenix now," says Elle.

"Really? I like it," says Nolan. "Elle gives everyone pet names. I'm supposedly Owl."

Elle laughs, teasing him. "Well, it's true, you do look like an owl when you bother wearing your glasses…"

They're like family, really.

I'd like to feel like part of a family again.

CHAPTER SIX

As it turns out, the path to the island is more of a bridge, which turns into a series of stepping stones. I follow Elle onto the first stone before my brain remembers how much I hate the water.

Something about the salty, eye-stinging wetness makes me cringe. I stop, feet wobbling, while Elle deftly jumps from one stone to another as though it's as easy as walking on solid ground.

Cut it out. You walked away from the fiends, for God's sake. It's ridiculous. I don't have any other phobias. Heights don't bother me, and neither does the dark. But water? When I was younger, I fought against the school's compulsory swimming lessons with everything I had. I avoided rivers where possible. And in this new world of fire and explosions, a fear of open water doesn't even come into conversation.

Drawing in a deep breath, I jump, and my feet hit the rock. At least these hiking boots have a good grip, but visions of slipping on the wet moss and falling into the sea slow me down. I can't let the people behind me see my fear, so I fix my gaze on the mountain ahead and not on the sea either side of me. I already died three times. I can walk across a bunch of stepping stones.

And then we're on a beach of jagged rocks and grass, the mountain looming over us. I catch up to Elle and the others.

My heart sinks as I see Cas looking at me. The disgust in his expression makes me flinch. *He* saw my fear. What have I done to make him despise me so much?

"What's Cas's problem?" I ask, as we wait for the rest of the group to catch up.

"Huh?"

"Cas," I say. "He's hated me without reason since the minute we met."

"Oh, God," she says. "Casimir gives the worst first impression! And second impression. He scares the living crap out of me and I've known him all my life."

"He's always lived here too?"

"Yeah, I think. He's four years older than me. Nineteen."

Strange. Cas doesn't act like a teenager. But then again, I don't feel seventeen.

"He's the resident grump. I'm amazed he said more than a few words to you, to be honest."

"He saved my life," I say. "That's why I'm confused. But I guess Nolan made him do it."

"Nolan." She sighs. "You got to lie in his arms, right? You know how many people would kill for that opportunity?"

I blink. "Um, no?"

She sighs. "Lovely Nolan."

"Do you have a crush on him?"

"No!" But a flush spreads up her neck and onto her cheeks.

It's been years since I've even been able to *think* about crushes. Not when running for my life. The extent of my experience is an awkward make-out session in a cupboard on my fifteenth birthday with my then-crush, Shane something. The hours discussing it with my old friends seem trivial now.

I look for Nolan, wondering where he's gone, and see Cas, standing at the edge of the path we've just crossed, looking out over the water. A flame coils from the sea's surface and leaps into the sky. Fire and water intermingle, setting off a mesmerising wall of flames. My breath catches at the sight. It's more impressive even than the sunset.

"That's our defence," Elle explains. "It keeps the fiends away from the entrance."

"Do the fiends even come out here?"

She bites her lip. "We're lucky we didn't run into any on the way. They follow us whenever we leave."

I stare at her. "I thought Nolan and Cas were hunting *them* down."

"Yeah, they were. But they hunt us down, too. They know where we live, and they can't get in."

"Well, that's something," I say, rubbing the goose bumps on my arms. It was naïve of me to assume I could ever really be safe, but the idea of those monsters always just outside the door unsettles me. I'm used to moving around, not stopping, always one step ahead of the fiends. I haven't even thought about the possibility of staying in one place for longer than a night.

I stare at the wall of fire. The angle of the sun projects Cas's shadow onto it as he turns his back.

Murray is already leading the way. A path meanders through the valley and gently slopes upwards, curving around the hillside. It's like a photograph—green fields and foaming rivers and autumn-coloured hills dressed in heather.

Compared to the agonising minutes of crossing the sea, this takes no time at all. Elle gives a running commentary about how when the Earth split open, mountains became islands and sank into the sea, and Scotland has probably drifted halfway to Iceland. It should be twenty degrees colder than it is, but since the world changed, the Earth's so much hotter than it was two years ago.

I knew that already, but I listen, wondering how she can know so much if she's barely been outside.

"Dad taught me," she says, when I ask. "Back when we were connected to the Internet, he watched it live. He has the only working computers in the country, I think. We have our own power supply here."

"Electricity?" My voice rises in surprise. I've seen houses with solar panels and the occasional wind farm—not that there's enough wind to power it anymore—but things like working lights, computers, and mobile phones disappeared with the rest of the technological age. I think I always assumed *someone* had to be prepared. I knew a couple of computer geniuses at school who could build computers from scratch, after all. But after going so long without seeing the brightness of an artificial light or hearing the hum of a computer, they disappeared into the distant past along with all my other memories.

"Yeah, hydroelectric power. We have to be careful with it and not overuse it."

"Wow," I say.

As we get higher up, the temperature drops. I start to shiver, wishing I had a thick coat like they do. The path grows narrower until we have to walk sideways, pressed against a rock face, the wind whipping at us. My hands and face go numb. *People used to hike here for* fun?

We stop briefly to make sure everyone's caught up. "Whereabouts is your home?" I ask Elle, looking around. I can't see any signs of human habitation.

"Inside the mountain," she says. "It used to be an extinct volcano, but not many people know that."

"Seriously?"

She nods.

I look up at the mountain's distant, snow-capped peak, and shake my head in amazement.

The last part of the journey passes quickly. I'm expecting Murray to lead us right to the top, but instead, he disappears from sight. I inch along the path, thinking he's gone around a corner, but as the others gradually disappear, too, I see that there's an opening in the rock, and they're going *inside* the hill.

Elle beckons me to follow. I have to duck my head under the rock shelf as I enter a narrow tunnel. It's so well-hidden, no one could find it unless they were looking for it. I walk at a crouch until the ceiling gets higher and the passage widens into a corridor. The air is filled with the sound of footsteps, echoes bouncing off the walls.

Then the tunnel opens out into a cavern, lit by a panel of light on the ceiling. It's so bright, it dazzles my eyes and I stumble forwards, my vision blurred white.

More corridors branch off, and I can see steps and paths carved into the rock itself. The centre is an enormous crater, fenced off with a metal railing. Lava pools below, smoke curling off the surface.

"I thought you said the volcano was extinct?" I say to Elle.

She flashes me a smile. "That's what people think."

This couldn't possibly get anymore surreal.

Everyone splits up and starts going to different rooms. I hover around by the rail, Elle by my side, eagerly telling me where all the important places are. Training hall, dormitories, recreation room. I can't take it in.

Some of the others pass by me, but I feel too awkward to say hello. It's been too long since I really had a conversation. Opal liked to talk, but she knew Randy disliked it so she kept quiet a lot of the time. The rest of the group only discussed everyday necessities, unless they were reminiscing around the campfire, and even then the subjects of discussion were limited. Anything up until before the first energy blasts was allowed. We couldn't talk about the fiends, the Burned Spots, even how we'd ended up joining the camp. Randy had found my sister and me crouching inside an abandoned cottage out in the middle of nowhere. It had been the nearest shelter we could find. A stray fiend had attacked her as we were fleeing, but we could both run fast and we managed to escape it.

Two weeks later, she'd died of her injuries.

I push the lid on the memories. After she died, I had no choice but to decide whether it was worth living on. Some of the others were hostile, seeing both my sister and me as stupid kids, a hindrance. So I worked hard to make myself useful. I thought I'd have to do the same here, but no one seems to expect me to. It's so strange.

Others are starting to emerge from the corridors branching off, and there are suddenly a lot more people around. A couple of them glance at me. Suspicious.

Cas passes by, and I look back at Elle, determined not to see that hatred in his eyes again.

"Leah?" Nolan interrupts Elle's chattering.

She goes brick red; I'm almost tempted to laugh, but that would be mean.

"Yeah?"

"Murray wants to talk to you about what happened. I told him my version, but he wants to hear it from you before he inducts you into the group, all right?"

"Er, sure," I say. "Induction?"

"Nothing to worry about," says Nolan. "Just standard. We haven't had a new member in a while, and certainly not from outside."

I catch sight of Murray beckoning me into an alcove. With a nod to Nolan, I follow, ignoring my quickening heartbeat. Electric lights aside, this place feels too enclosed for my liking after camping under the stars for so long. I already miss the sensation of the breeze on my skin. It's not as warm as I'd expect given the pool of molten lava—do they have air con?—but it's still almost stuffy in here.

To my astonishment, there's a metal door set into the wall, like that's normal on the inside of a volcano. Murray opens it and leads me into what looks like a cross between a workshop and a laboratory.

I'm pretty sure my jaw hits the floor. A leather chair sits behind a desk with an honest-to-God, working computer. The electric hum hits my ears like sweet music. My fingers twitch compulsively. I used to be glued to my iPad before the power cut out and I couldn't charge it anymore.

"I'm sure you have a lot of questions," says Murray, sitting at the desk and motioning me to sit in another metal seat in front of it. I perch on the edge, my eyes darting about the room, taking in the incomprehensible mess of wires and machinery on the work benches behind the front desk. If it wasn't for that, I'd almost have the illusion of being back in the head teacher's office at school, minus the rock walls. Not that I spent a lot of time there. Bar a couple of fights, my record was practically spotless.

"Yeah," I say, in answer. "I do. For one thing, how can this place even exist? Elle told me you have your own power supply, but I never imagined…"

"We've been isolated for years," he says. "Most of the younger generation grew up here, and some never leave. It's not normal for such a large party to go out, but the strange behaviour of the fiends makes more sense now we know they were after you."

"After me?" My heart drops.

"They target Pyros," he says. "They attack and kill humans, too, but something draws them to us."

"Us," I repeat. "Nolan said you were around before the fiends."

"Did he now?" Murray sighs, resting his chin on his steepled hands. "We made a lot of mistakes. This is a war that's been going on for centuries. Our group has fought against the fiends for a thousand years, or more, but until two years ago, they never made an open attack on humanity. There were too few of them. But their leaders were shapeshifters, and used to blend in amongst humans."

My mind spins with what he's implying. *Amongst humans? They were here all along?*

"They destroyed the world." My throat's dry, my heart pounding. Now I'm on the brink of getting answers, some small part of me doesn't want to know any more.

Murray nods. "Well, you know something about what happened. The Fiordans—that's the name of their leaders—led an army of fiends to invade Earth. We were too late to prevent it, and the aftermath ravaged our world. The fiends were trapped here."

"Trapped?" I say. "Don't they live inside the Earth? Isn't that where they came from?"

"Not originally. The fiends inhabit a world that's as barren as they're trying to make this one. The two sides were on a tipping point two years ago, although only we, the Pyros, knew about it. The fiends' world was dying, and they wanted ours. And in the process of invading, they destroyed it."

He reaches and takes my palm, and I stiffen.

"Do you have any kind of a birth mark, or a strange marking on your skin?"

I shake my head. Even if I've seen enough with my own eyes to know at least some of what he told me is true, rationality still tells me it's a trick. A louder voice tells me to stay put, that these are the answers I asked for—even if they're far from what I want to hear.

"Or… on your head?"

He wants permission to remove the cap. I clench my fists to stop them shaking and give him a curt nod. *Just get it over with.*

A sharp intake of breath. "Behind your left ear," he says.

"What's there?"

He rummages in a desk drawer until he pulls out a mirror. He holds it up in front of me, and I choke on a scream at my appearance. I look like a stranger. Angry red sunburn has blistered my face, and I look even worse without a hair on my head.

"Oh," I say, tonelessly, "that. I thought it was a scar from something I don't remember."

It's a round mark about the size of a penny, with a smaller, unburnt shape in the centre. Strange for a scar, but it's not really in a place I look at often.

"No, it's our mark." He draws it on a scrap of paper. I'd assumed the shape was round, but now it looks more like… a flame.

"So my parents were—?"

"Not necessarily. The genes can skip a few generations. Or sometimes it happens after an accident—a blood transfusion. It's in our blood. We never paid attention to it, until…"

"Until what?"

"Until it became relevant. Elle may have told you, it's my mission to research the fiends, to find any way of beating them. When they invaded, the way back was cut off. They're trapped in our world, and they aren't happy about it. So they keep attacking us, no matter how many we kill."

"So is that why you were outside?" I try to read his expression, but it's inscrutable.

"Not exactly." He leans forward. "What you have to understand is that this group is relatively young, and few people remember what the old way of life was like. Our ancestors used to move from place to place, as a group, but we've been settled here for nearly a hundred years—enough time to forget how hard it is to find new recruits, let alone bring them to safety. There are potentially other people like you, survivors who don't know how they survived. Our mission is to find them and give them a choice, as I'm going to give you. You have the mark. What you do now is up to you, but if you join, there's no going back."

"Really?" I say, suspicion flaring. "Like a cult?"

"We're definitely not a cult," he says. "I realise this isn't what you're used to."

A wry smile sneaks onto my face. "What's normal?"

"Fair point." He smiles back at me. "As one of us, you'll have a few options to choose from. You can train to go out in the field, or join the research division. That's what Elle chose to do. But I can tell you're a fighter."

"Out in the field," I say. "Like the military?"

"Believe it or not, we used to live inside a hill next to an army training estate. That's how we remained hidden from the public. But we've had to move here, into hiding. It's the only place the fiends can't get to."

"So…" I try to wrap my head around it. "So they're not from this world at all, but they live here now?"

He nods. "They created a bridge when the divide opened. We managed to close it, but too late.

There must be a hundred thousand of them still roaming the earth, and the aftershocks from the first energy blast are still happening now."

"But that's what makes people… different, right? The energy blasts?"

Another nod. "Yes. On the fiends' world, the blasts have destroyed all life apart from the fiends. They're immune. The energy blasts we experience here are an aftereffect of the bridge forming, and there doesn't seem to be a way to stop them. But they also awaken genes in people who have the potential to become Pyros. The…"

"…survivors," I finish. "Right?"

His expression turns sad, pensive. "I wish it didn't have to be that way, but yes. We try to find them before the fiends do."

"You weren't looking for me, were you?" I'm still wondering why there was such a big group out there, even the non-fighters, when you'd think it would attract the fiends.

"No, but we're glad we found you."

"And I'm… a Pyro." The word tastes foreign, like it belongs to someone else. Someone who can do the impossible.

Someone who can kill the fiends. Save people.

"It's a little melodramatic," says Murray. "I confess I can't remember who came up with the term, but it stuck."

"Because of the fire?" Here, in the heart of a volcano, I can believe it really happened. I really fought the fiends.

He nods. "You'll learn more about adapting to other weapons in training, but the ability to call the fire is the reason for our name."

And the reason I'm alive. "Training?"

"We have a system," he says. "If you want to join missions, there are levels of training you'll have to complete first. Val's in charge of training new recruits at the moment, but I'll ask Nolan to help out if it'll make you more comfortable having someone you know."

"I don't mind either way," I say. "Honestly. But I guess you're assuming I'll say yes?"

"Was that a bit presumptuous? I apologise. Like I said, it's up to you."

"You say there's no going back?"

"I think…" He pauses. "If you wanted to leave, we could take you to the nearest town. But joining will give you a purpose other than survival. We can fight them. Whether it's genetic or evolutionary survival, we're designed to kill the fiends. I could hazard a guess that it's what you want, right?"

I can leave. Go to that town, with the barbed-wire fences, and live. Like Lissa would want me to. Like Randy and the others would.

The image of that fire bursting from my hand nudges its way back into my head. Who am I kidding? I can't walk away now. Not now I have the chance to fight the creatures that killed my sister, that destroyed my world.

I find myself nodding. "Yes," I say. "I'm joining."

CHAPTER SEVEN

I'm expecting to have to take a vow to lay down my life for Queen and country or something like that, but instead Murray shows me to a room where several other teenagers—three boys, four girls—sit or lie on narrow beds, talking or reading. All of them gawk at me when I come in, the conversation dying down. *Crap.* I can almost hear their thoughts as they take in my appearance, except Elle, who smiles at me.

So they have mixed dorms here. I wish I had my own room, because I know I'll be reliving the energy blast in my dreams. I don't want to wake them up with my screaming.

"This is Leah," says Murray. "She's new here. Be nice, okay?" To me, he says, "There's a bathroom through that door at the back. The laundry cupboard there should have a change of clothes. We'll need to measure you for uniform tomorrow."

And he disappears, leaving me alone with seven curious-eyed teenagers. I haven't been around people my own age in so long, my throat dries up, and I haven't a clue what to say.

I settle for, "Hi, I'm Leah."

The others rattle off their names so fast I can't take them in.

A dark-skinned girl of around my age, possibly named Poppy, asks, "What's happened to your hair?"

Well, that was fast.

"Close encounter with an energy blast," I say.

Cue impressed faces.

"You serious?" says a guy with dreadlocks in a Scottish accent. I *think* he said his name was Tyler.

I nod, walking to the laundry cupboard. It's filled with identical white shirts and grey tracksuit bottoms. The pyjamas are grey, too. In fact, that's what everyone in the room is wearing. I grab a pair, aware of seven pairs of eyes on my back the whole while. I ignore the prickling self-consciousness and go into the bathroom.

A real bathroom, with real running water. I can't help myself. I make for the shower, after checking the door is bolted behind me. It's nothing as fancy as the shower in the house, but I don't care. I start the water running and sigh as it soothes my sunburnt skin.

I want to stay there, under the water, the sound cutting off the outside world, but underneath, I can hear conversation coming from the room, and I'm conscious that there's only one bathroom for eight of us. I turn off the shower and dry myself quickly, pulling on the pyjamas. They've even been ironed and folded. I shake my head at the thought that civilisation disappeared so quickly in the outside world, along with personal hygiene. The clean smell is both familiar and discomfiting. I don't linger by the mirror, but hope fervently that my hair grows back soon. In my old life, I was never the self-conscious type, but being thrown back into something resembling my old school is disconcerting to say the least.

All heads turn in my direction when I come out the room. I sigh, figuring I'd better get used to it until the next newbie comes along.

I'm here for a reason, anyway. To learn to kill the fiends.

There's one free bed. It has a small wooden chest of drawers beside it, but I don't have any possessions to unpack. I sit, drawing my knees up to my chest, waiting for someone to break the silence. I'm not about to start a conversation with everyone looking at me like I returned from the dead.

"Is it true you killed two fiends?" The boy with dreadlocks again.

I shake my head. "No." Then I wonder why I'm being honest. Do I want to make friends here? These people are supposed to be fighters, training to battle the fiends. I don't know about the mortality rate, but it can't be good. We might be super-powered, but we're not invincible.

Not that humans fare any better.

"Ah. It's just I heard you talking to Elle. But is it true you fought them off?"

"Yeah," I say. I don't mention the part where they almost knocked me through a wall. Really, I haven't done anything heroic other than get kicked around and almost die. "Have any of you guys fought one for real?"

"No," says a girl with blond curls and a sullen expression. "They won't let us go out in the field until we're qualified. Sucks to be us."

"You just want to be paired with Cas," says the dreadlocked boy.

"I do *not,*" the girl protests, flushing. "He bit my head off when I accidentally got in his way during training that one time."

"And she totally swooned," says the first girl who spoke to me. Poppy.

"Don't be stupid." The girl looks at me. "Never mind that, how'd you burn your face?"

I gape at her. "Uh… I walked outside?" Have these people never left?

"Leave the poor girl alone," says another guy, about Elle's age. "We can get the story tomorrow, she looks like she's about to pass out."

I *am* tired, but I don't want to sleep, knowing what nightmares lie in wait. It's weird being inside, not out in the open under the blood-red sky.

"I'm fine," I say, stifling a yawn.

"Okay." The blond girl launches into a long tirade about something, and just like that, I'm forgotten. I lie back in bed, intending to rest my eyes, but almost as soon as my head hits the pillow, I sink into oblivion.

***

The sound of chatter wakes me up. I'm so used to waking up in total silence that for a heartbeat, I think I'm still asleep. Mercifully, I didn't dream about the fiends or the explosion. Hushed silences and whispers have been my life for so long that the shouts and laughs from the others make my heartbeat kick up like it did when there was danger nearby, and I have to make myself sit up calmly in bed, as though it's something I do every day.

"Did you sleep well?" Elle asks me, unwittingly drawing everyone's attention to me again. I sigh inwardly. Better get used to it.

Elle insists on walking me to the mess hall, where meals are served. It makes me look less like a loser for not knowing where things are, but her constant chatter ensures that everyone stares.

"Sorry you're stuck in the mixed dorm," she says. "Once we pass the training, we get our own rooms."

That makes sense. The level of noise constantly takes me by surprise. It hits me like a hammer to the skull when we enter the hall, which is full of tables. Shouts and chatter drum relentlessly in my ears as I walk beside Elle, head held high as though I'm oblivious to the stares.

Really, I'm the one who can't stop staring. There are so *many* of them—at least a hundred people of all ages, from younger teens to adults.

Then I think of the fiends, and suddenly a hundred seems a tiny number. I entertain a brief fantasy of there being more places like this, but from what I've heard so far, it's unlikely.

The food distracts me. Fresh-baked bread sits in baskets on the tables like it's not a forgotten commodity in the outside world. Fresh fruit, too.

"Where do you get all this?" I ask Elle.

"We've been self-sufficient for years," she says. "The water comes from reservoirs in the hills, and my dad's farm takes care of the rest. We have greenhouses on the other side of the hill where we grow fresh fruit and veg."

"Wow," I say, simply, as an enticing smell hits my nostrils.

God, there's even coffee. I follow the smell over to a table at the front of the room set up like a hotel buffet. In the old world, I'd never have thought the sight of bacon and toast and coffee would ever be as out-of-reach as first-class holidays and winning the lottery. This place, totally self-sufficient, has managed to preserve things that died out in a heartbeat in the outside world.

I try not to let my reaction show, but Elle's sharp eyes glitter with amusement as I pile my plate high.

"Hungry, right?"

"Yeah, starving."

"'You'll probably be on kitchen duty at some point," she says. "We have a rota. Louie's head chef."

We sit with the rest of our dorm-mates at the table. I don't join in the conversation, but listen and try to memorise people's names. Just when I think I have them down, another group of teenagers joins us, and the table becomes unbearably crowded. I give up my attempt to pay attention and let the noise fade into a buzz.

After, Elle gives me a tour. She shows me where the various higher-up Pyros live. I've only met Murray so far. There's a training hall, where I'm supposed to report to Nolan in an hour—apparently, they even have clocks here—and a weapons room.

"But I thought weapons couldn't harm the fiends."

"Most can't," Elle says, "but ours are special."

Like Cas's knife. I haven't seen him at all, but since there are so many people here, I don't know why that surprises me. Nolan's been put in charge of making sure I'm physically able before I get put in training classes with the other novices. They even have school-type classes like Maths and History here, but only for the kids under sixteen. I don't feel like I'm missing out. Nothing I learned in my four-and-a-half years at secondary school has done me any good in the wilderness.

I'd rather learn to fight.

I took basic self-defence classes when I was younger, but it's been a while. Life after the world ended has always been about running away, not fighting back. As for weapons, I've never handled one. Despite eight-year-old me's pleading, my parents never caved in and let me take lessons in swordplay. That one was during my anime phase, when it was my lifetime ambition to own a katana.

First, I have to be declared fit to enter training. I'm not keen on being poked and prodded, but Sandra, the doctor, reassures me that my hair will grow back soon, and that I'm in better form than I should be, considering what I've been through. Only light bruising on my body hints that I might have been mildly injured, certainly not almost-fatally. But she still insists on taking a blood sample. I stare as my blood flows down a tube into a glass container, thick and dark red. When she's done, Sandra holds the container up to the light, frowning. Then she takes it into a back room.

Something about the medical bay makes me fidgety and uneasy. Perhaps it's the clinical smell associated with hospitals. I'm relieved to be given the cue to leave for the training hall.

As it turns out, Nolan has no intention of letting me near the weaponry on my first go. Instead, I get beaten up.

In fairness, he does take it easy on me. But the Pyros have a different definition of 'easy'. After yesterday, I figured I must be stronger and faster than regular people. But head-to-head with someone like me, I'm suddenly average again.

I'm supposed to duck and dodge punches, but I'm too slow, and fall for the first feint. Nolan sweeps my legs out from underneath me.

"Whoa! Are you all right?" Nolan looks startled. Even he didn't expect me to go down that fast.

"Yep." I stand, wincing slightly. I only grazed my elbow, but I have a feeling that if he'd hit a regular person like that, it'd have been far worse for them.

Pull yourself together, I tell myself as Nolan, satisfied I'm unhurt, aims a jab at me. *You took a hit from a fiend, for crying out loud.*

This time, I manage to block, just. *Hell, he's fast.* But didn't I move just as fast when the fiends attacked me? How do I tap into that crazy adrenaline? It was like the whole world slowed down. Only, moving slowly does me no favours right now.

I last a few seconds before another swipe at my legs takes me off my feet.

I stand. My heart drops when I see Cas on the other side of the hall. I duck my head, flushing at what an idiot I must look like.

But I can't help watching out of the corner of my eye as he heads for the far wall, where the target practise is. I know before he throws the dagger that it'll strike the target directly in the centre.

Smack. Again, my back hits the ground.

"Sorry," says Nolan. "You ought to pay attention, you know." He holds out a hand to help me up. I don't take it, jumping to my feet, even though both my elbows feel bruised.

"I'm just not used to getting hit this much."

He smiles at me. "Bet you'd rather get beaten up by me than by one of those fiends."

"Yeah…" I trail off. Thinking about it, I really ought to be in more pain than I am. Unless Cas healed every injury I had, even the ordinary bumps and bruises I got on the road.

"Just try to relax. It's in your blood. Let your body respond. Don't hold back."

I nod, thinking of the way I struck back at the fiend when I hadn't had a clue what I was doing. Then I think of the blood sample in the lab, and what Murray said. It's in my blood.

"Ready to try again?"

I nod.

Concentrate. I keep my eyes on him, trying to put myself in the same mind-set as when I faced the fiend. Never mind what happened the second time. I *can* do this.

Nolan's fist flies at me, from the right, and I raise my hand to catch his. I stop his punch inches before it can connect with my face, and he stares at me, surprise etched on his features. It happened so fast, it's a blur in my mind.

But I did it.

"Great!" His face breaks into a smile. I knew you were a natural. Okay. We'll move onto striking next."

Now, it's all business. He teaches me the best places to hit a fiend and actually do some damage. I'm paying full attention now. This is why I'm here. This is what I need to know.

We break after half an hour. Cas's left the room by now, leaving a row of dummies with daggers sticking out of them behind. Possibly, he has some pent-up anger issues. That would explain a lot. Nolan says I can practise on the dummies if I want, but I'm not to touch any of the weapons until I've passed the first level of training.

"Not that I don't think you can handle it," he adds. "It's Murray's idea, not mine. He's overprotective for someone who oversees a bunch of half-indestructible soldiers."

"Is that what we are?" I ask. "An army?"

"Sorry, bad choice of phrasing," he says. "You've not signed your life away."

"Good to know." I step back, looking around. More people have come into the room. The other novices pair off to practise combat skills, same as Nolan and I are doing. My heart sinks when I see Elle knocked down by a guy built like a pillar. She's not a fighter. What's she doing in here?

"Oh, no," says Nolan. "Garry never listens when people tell him to go easy."

"Is that even allowed?"

"I don't make the rules. Val's in charge of combat. Everyone has to take part, even the non-fighters. We never know if the base is going to be attacked."

Base. More army talk. But that hardly matters now. My old instinct to stand up for the underdog makes me step forward, just as Elle goes flying, missing the mat and landing hard on the wooden floor. Nolan winces.

The big guy, Garry, shakes his head. "Jesus, where the hell's the challenge? Get up," he snaps at Elle.

"Why isn't anyone stopping him?" I demand.

Nolan holds out an arm to stop me. "Wait," he says. "Leah…"

Elle sits up, groaning, propping herself up onto her elbows, but Garry knocks her back with a swipe of his hand.

It's too much. "Hey!" I shout, not caring who hears, "Why don't you pick on someone your own size?"

Garry turns on me. I saw it coming, but it's too late to stop my legs from moving, my body planting itself in front of Elle before he can hit her again.

His fist catches me full in the face, and I black out.

CHAPTER EIGHT

Images flash through my mind—a room full of strange apparatus, like a laboratory—an outstretched arm, but not mine—and then, an image, a symbol like the outline of a flame.

A second later, I come to, a ringing in my ears. Once again, I'm flat on my back on the floor of the training hall.

"Leah! Leah! Thank goodness." Elle bends over me.

I stifle a moan of pain as I move my head. "Hey. You okay?"

"You're the one who—" She hugs me. "Sorry if I'm hurting you."

"I'm fine." My gaze focuses. I glare at Garry. "Ever hear about not hitting girls?"

"There are no rules here," he spits at me, looking disgusted, and he turns to go.

"Wait." Like I'm going to let him get away with *knocking me out*. I sit up, feeling an egg-sized lump on the back of my head. Great.

I stride over to him, ignoring my throbbing head, and swing my fist. There's a satisfying *crunch* as it connects with his jaw.

"What the hell?"

Garry turns on me, furious. I dodge another punch, duck down, quick as a flash, and ram my other fist into his cheek.

This time, he staggers back. A rush of satisfaction fills me.

Someone actually *applauds*. Tyler. He's so busy grinning at me he doesn't see his partner's strike coming until it knocks him to the floor.

The whole hall dissolves into chaos as people start turning in my direction, abandoning their own sparring to see where the action is.

"*What* is going on here?" a voice demands.

It's Val, the woman I met guarding the camp yesterday.

Elle tries to explain. Garry keeps interrupting. I'm tempted to lie down. My head's really hurting now.

In the end, Garry gets a scolding from Val while Elle and Nolan haul me off to the infirmary again. Despite my insistence, I'm subjected to another examination by Sandra.

This time I try to peek into the room at the back. When she opens the door I get a glimpse of a room filled with medical equipment, which might be why I saw that odd vision. But that didn't look like *here*—and whose arm was that? While I'm pondering, I rub the back of my head and find the lump has… gone. The pain has, too. Like I imagined it.

When Sandra proclaims me fit to leave, I hesitate.

"I wanted to ask you something," I say. "About—about Cas."

Her shoulders stiffen. "What about him?"

"He healed me before I came here. That's why I wasn't injured. Is that… normal for us?"

A fraction of a pause. "I can't divulge other patients' secrets."

I blink. "Okay. I just wondered. I think Nolan told him to do it, but…"

"Cas isn't the easiest person to get along with, but he's one of us."

Okay. I leave the room none the wiser, but growing slightly irritated with the lack of answers. But I'm here for a reason. To learn to fight.

The second day is better. My old self-defence lessons come back to me and I'm able to hold off Nolan for longer. Plus, I get to join in with some of the other exercises with the other novices. I'm one step closer to being accepted. Or so I tell myself.

Elle's beyond grateful for my defending her yesterday. She's told everyone about it. Garry glares daggers at me when we pass each other, but I'm accustomed to ignoring idiots. One thing I picked up from school, I guess.

But I can't help noticing some of the younger novices edge away when I come near, as though expecting me to attack them, too. Someone's been spreading rumours—yet another echo of school. It doesn't bother me, but my heart sinks when we're paired off that afternoon for more combat exercises and I catch a couple of people looking at me uneasily.

I'm paired with Poppy. Thankfully, she doesn't ask me about my hair again, nor does she look at me as though expecting me to hit her like I hit Garry.

"Want me to go easy?" Her tone's uncertain, as though half-expecting me to snap at her.

I relax my face muscles into a smile. "Nah. Hit me with the best you've got."

She smiles back at me. "You might regret that."

She's good. Not as refined as Nolan, but I suppose he's had years of practise. She's so delicate-looking, I bet people underestimate her like they did me.

Even I do for a minute until a jab to my ribs takes the breath out of me. At least I manage to stay upright. My back's well-acquainted with the floor by this time.

"You all right?" she asks.

"Yeah, sure."

We're pretty evenly matched. We end up jokily goading each other as we swipe and jab, until I finally manage to sweep her feet out from underneath her.

"Hey!" she yelps, swatting at me. "No fair!"

I find myself laughing. It catches me off-guard for a moment. The first time I've really laughed since Lissa died. The first time I've joked with someone.

The thought of Lissa makes my chest feel tight. Would she have fit in here? Was she like me? I'll never know. *Don't think about what might have been, Leah.*

Poppy delivers a jab to my side and unbalances me. I stagger, cursing myself for getting distracted so easily.

"Earth to Leah? You all right?" she asks.

"Yeah," I say, pushing myself up from the floor again. A flush rises as I see Cas pass by, our eyes almost meeting. I didn't even notice he was in the hall, but a pile of dummies with knives stuck in their vital spots is testimony to his presence.

Idiot. Stop staring at him.

"You know, you're not what I expected," says Poppy, as we head back to the dorm to change. "Coming from out there, I mean. I've heard awful stories about what life's like. Enough to drive someone to insanity."

"Guess I got lucky," I say.

She lets me take a shower first. I've the rest of the day free, while most of the other novices are in lessons, but when I come out of the bathroom, I find Tyler, the guy with dreadlocks, lying on his bed reading a book.

"Hey," I say, figuring starting a conversation with everyone will be the quickest way to stop them looking at me like I fell out of the sky.

"Hi." He looks up from his book. I peek at the cover. It's a classic, Dickens by the look of it. "Elle was looking for you."

"She was? I thought she was in class."

"Elle's like a child genius. She doesn't go to half her classes. Not that I can talk. I dropped out before I turned sixteen, so…"

"I'm glad I don't have to go to school anymore," I say, though if I could have my old life back, I'd even take algebra lessons. "What did Elle want?"

"To take you to the lookout spot." He puts the book down and stands.

"Lookout spot?"

"Yeah, there's another way out of here, through a cave. It leads right down into the valley, but you can see for miles."

"I haven't anywhere else I need to go, right?" I say. "Murray didn't see… well, I haven't seen him."

"Oh, he's always in the lab when he's not on missions."

"Missions," I say. "Speaking of…" Now could be my chance to get some answers. "Do you know what Murray and the others were doing when they found me?"

Tyler gives me a puzzled look. "I thought they were looking for you. I mean, they just left, and when they came back with you I assumed… Well, that's what everyone says, anyway."

I stare. "Nolan and Cas found me by accident. They were chasing the fiends."

"That's what their missions usually are," says Tyler. "They use a radio to reach out to local towns—don't ask, Murray's in charge of that—and send out teams when the fiends get close. They also check out energy blasts, see if there are any survivors. But they wouldn't need such a big group for something like that."

"Exactly." I frown. "But Elle didn't tell me. She said her dad wouldn't let her. Pretty much everything I asked got the same answer."

"That's odd. I'd say ask her dad, but Murray's not known for divulging secrets either."

"It's strange," I say. "I mean, he's the leader. What if he'd died out there?"

"He can take care of himself," says Tyler, "but you're right. The guy's been here longer than any of us."

"Were you born here?"

"Nah. I'm from Edinburgh originally. We moved around a lot. The guys in red came recruiting around the time the energy blasts started taking out the big cities.

"Really?" I say, surprised. "I thought everyone grew up here."

"No, not at all. I'd say most of us novices came in around two, three years ago at most. The others had been here a little longer, but I guess people would have talked if they'd seen groups of strangely-dressed warriors going around randomly testing people to see if they had the gene."

He breaks off. "Ah, crap. Shouldn't've said that."

I'd assumed as much from what Murray had said—or not said.

"So it's genetic, then? Definitely?"

"Honestly, I've no idea. I kind of listened in on a conversation I shouldn't have. Murray and some of the junior doctors were talking genetics and it sounded like they were discussing whether it's random or inherited, being like us." He shrugs. "I mean, I think I'd have noticed if my parents were crazy-strong, but then again, they died when I was five."

"I'm sorry," I say automatically.

He shrugs again. "I don't really remember them that well. Probably for the best. My whole town got wiped out in an energy blast, along with everyone else I ever knew."

"Same with mine," I say. My chest tightens as images of the second energy blast flash through my mind. What would Randy and the others think of me now, practically living in luxury? Fighting for fun?

The dormitory door opens and Elle walks in. "Hey, Phoenix," she says.

I blink, having forgotten the nickname.

"Phoenix?" says Tyler, nonplussed.

"Apparently, it's my nickname," I say.

"I think it sounds neat," says Elle. "Anyway. Want to come to the lookout?"

"Told you so," says Tyler. "Yes, we do."

"For what?" I ask, confused by the smirk now on his face. "The view?"

"You should probably wear a coat," says Tyler, getting up and crossing to the laundry cupboard. "You have one yet?"

I start, distracted. "The red ones? No…"

"There'll be a spare." Tyler's already rummaging through clothes. "Reckon this might be a bit too long…"

I hesitate a second, but for all the secretive looks between them, Tyler and Elle just look like they're sharing something amusing, not sinister. I try to relax and take the coat from him, wrapping myself in it. It sweeps down to my feet, crimson and majestic. I feel half like a kid playing dress-up, half like I'm part of some strange, secret group.

"Nice," says Elle. "It suits you."

It's certainly warm and snug, but as I'm smaller than average, the long sleeves would be a hindrance during a fight.

"Shall we go?" says Tyler.

Elle leads the way as we skirt around the crater. I look down into the pit, and see someone down there, standing on a rock in the middle of the pool of lava.

I stop dead, staring. I can feel the heat curling off the lava's surface even from here. Who the hell would even consider going that close?

"Who's down there?"

I squint. My heart jolts. It's Cas. He stands on the rock, eyes on the swirling lava.

"Attention-seeker," says Tyler, dismissively.

"What the hell is he doing?"

"God knows." Tyler shrugs. "I know we can survive crazy temperatures, but I don't fancy swimming in lava. Too many rocks."

I turn to Elle and find that she's already disappeared into a tunnel. With one last glance behind me, I follow her, Tyler on my heels.

A chill breeze sweeps into the tunnel from outside, raising my coat's hood. I have to hold it a couple of inches off the ground to stop it from dragging, but I'm glad for the warmth. The tunnel's tight and claustrophobic, but I can smell the fresh, cool air from outside.

"I've missed this," says Tyler. "I swear it's been weeks since I've been outside."

"Really?" I look at him, surprised.

"I'm not qualified for missions yet," he says.

"How do we qualify?" I ask. "I mean, is it an age thing?"

"No, we have to pass tests. The whole routine's been thrown off because half our group disappeared for the past week. Normally there'd be endurance-training, but there aren't enough free supervisors at the moment. I miss wall-punching."

"Wall-punching? Is that…?"

"You know we're freakishly strong," says Tyler. "Nothing like pummelling a rock wall to work off some frustration." He grins at Elle.

It sounds bizarre… but then again, I survived almost being thrown through a brick wall when the fiends attacked me. Maybe I could punch through stone. I've never tried.

"You had to tell her, didn't you?" Elle shakes her head. "It was supposed to be a surprise."

"Huh?"

"I love it when a newbie takes their first punch," says Tyler. "I think Poppy's facial expression was the best, she looked like she'd found a cache of gold hidden in the wall." He grins. "It's like a rite of passage. Don't let us down, Leah."

So this is their plan? I think of sports team inductions at school, camaraderie. Friendship.

We come to an opening and the light from the setting sun is almost blinding. After two days under artificial light, the *wrongness* of the burning red sky is even more striking. Below, the valley spreads out, dressed in heather and bisected by a river.

"Pretty, huh?" says Elle. "I love it out here."

"Yeah, sure." Tyler's teeth are chattering. "Now, let's watch Leah punch a wall."

"You were serious about that?"

"Hell, yeah. Come on, entertain us."

They're both looking at me. The idea's so ridiculous, I feel a grin break out on my face.

"Go on, then," I say. "Whereabouts is a safe place? I don't want to bring the whole mountain crashing down."

"Ooh, get you," says Tyler. "Not even us Pyros can do that. We do have a limit, believe it or not."

"Here," says Elle, who looks just as eager as Tyler. "Up here." Lithely, she begins to climb. There are indentations in the rock wall which act as steps, and I start scrambling upwards behind her. Elle pulls herself over a ledge, and soon my hands find the path and, almost effortlessly, pull me up alongside her.

We're at a higher point on the path. I look up and see grey clouds swirling. If the sky was dark, they'd be invisible, but they stand out like bruises.

Elle grins at me, pointing at a bare stretch of rock wall. "There will do. Hit it."

"You look positively evil," I tell her, earning a grin.

She steps back to give me space.

"If the walls fall down, it's on you two," I say, balling my hand into a fist. The rock wall looks as solid as it gets. I hesitate and turn a suspicious glance on both of them. "Are you having me on?" I ask. "If I break my hand, I won't be any good to your cause."

"Nope, not a joke," says Tyler. "Get it over with, I'm freezing here."

I pull in a breath and draw back my fist. Before I lose my nerve, I imagine I'm hitting a punching bag and swing my fist forward…

Crack.

The rock splinters beneath my hand, fragments crumbling around the fist-sized hole in the wall. I let my arm fall to my side, stunned.

"Epic!" says Tyler, laughing. "Your face!"

"Thanks," I say, but find myself smiling anyway. In that moment, stupid as it might seem, I feel like I can do anything. I can punch through freaking *rock*. I could take one of those monsters.

I punch the wall again. No pain, only exhilaration. I laugh at the absurd pleasure it gives me. Like feeling in control of something in this crazy world.

A sound hits my ears, echoing up from the valley. The high-pitched screech raises the hairs on my arms and sends my heart slamming into my ears.

Tyler's eyes widen, and Elle clutches my arm, horror etched on her face.

"How—they *never* come this close."

But the noise is unmistakeable. The sound of nightmares. I look wildly around and spot them, two hunched shapes moving across the valley.

Another follows. Then another. A line of human-like shapes, creeping between the stunted trees below. Though we're too high to see any of their features, the image of the monstrosities is clear in my mind.

I imagine running downhill to meet them, testing my new combat skills. Taking the monsters head-on. Indestructible.

Don't be stupid. I might be able to punch a hole in a rock wall, but those creatures almost killed me twice. It would be downright suicidal to engage them now.

"Shit," says Tyler. "We've gotta get down from here."

"We have to tell my dad," says Elle, her face chalk-white.

But first, we have to lower ourselves over the verge. I offer to go first but regret it almost immediately. Now my hands are shaking, it becomes much harder to grip the ledge, and above me, Elle's even worse. As I take another step down, her foot slips and her hands fumble the ledge. She lets out a scream.

"Calm down!" says Tyler, who's still standing on the path above. "You're okay. Just go slow."

"My hands are slipping," she says, faintly. Her grip loosens again, and her left hand fumbles and lets go.

Panic sends my pulse racing. I speed up my pace, in case I need to catch her. If I fall, I wouldn't suffer nearly as much damage—hell, it probably wouldn't even hurt. But Elle isn't like me.

Her legs are shaking too much to step into the footholds. Gritting my teeth, I let go and drop the last two feet. I slam into the ground, but it doesn't hurt. Holding my arms out, I call to her, "I'll catch you! Let go!"

She's already slipping. I hear another screech behind me, but I can't turn around. Elle falls into my outstretched arms, and buries her head in my shoulder, sobbing.

"Hey… you're fine."

Tyler doesn't look too pleased about climbing down either, but like me, he lowers himself a few feet and jumps. The impact jolts the path, and I set Elle down beside me, twisting around to see where the fiends have got to.

They're closer, moving far faster than any other animal can. Seven or more shapes move in a line towards us. I think of the wall of fire in front of the mountain—how did they get past that?

"Come on!" says Tyler.

We slip back into the chamber and, by silent agreement, sprint back into the main cave. My mind whirls, and I can't stop looking over my shoulder, even though I know the fiends won't have come close yet.

Finally, we emerge into the crater. Red-robed Pyros stare at us as we run past. Elle takes charge, aiming right for her dad's office.

"Dad!" she shouts.

Murray's head appears in the doorway. His hair's standing on end and he wears a pair of thick-framed glasses.

"Elle! Don't run in the corridor. It's dangerous."

"There are fiends out there!"

"What?" He blinks at her, lifting his steamed-up glasses.

"It's true," I say. "There are fiends down in the valley coming this way."

"Impossible. The shield's up, no one can get in."

"We saw them from the back walkway," says Tyler.

Murray's shaking his head in disbelief. "Elle, I've told you not to go up there."

"I know, but I wanted to—"

"What's going on?" Cas appears behind Murray, an irritable expression on his face. "What are you lot babbling about?"

"Fiends," I say. "Down in the valley. They're coming this way."

Cas narrows his eyes at me. "A likely story."

"I don't lie," I say, riled. "I'll show you if you don't believe me."

"Cas!" says Murray. "We should at least send a team to check this out. You can round up a few people, can't you?"

"What a waste of time," he mutters, but at a warning glance from Murray—or possibly because I'm still glaring at him—he walks off.

"I'll go," I find myself saying.

"But you don't have a weapon," says Elle.

"They might be the same fiends that came after me before."

It's flimsy logic, but she drops it. I don't admit, not even to myself, that part of me *wants* to get into a fight with a fiend. Make them suffer like they did to me. Now I know how to hit them where it hurts.

"Leah, you haven't learned enough yet," says Murray. "I can't let you do go out there."

"I can fight." I look around, seeing other Pyros coming into the corridor. Cas backs out of a room, arguing with someone.

"You fought off those other fiends with instinct alone, but you haven't fought one with a real weapon yet. You haven't learned how to combine it with the fire."

"So? Nolan taught me how to hit them."

"Leah." Murray's face sets, stubborn. "I know you must be frustrated, but I can't have you risking your neck."

I'm not going to back down. "Look, I *saw* the fiends. I know where they are."

"Murray!" Cas shouts, turning his back on the three other red-robed people he's arguing with. "Where the hell are these fiends?"

Murray looks at me. Indecision masks his face. He knows only Elle, Tyler and I saw where the fiends were.

"I'll show them," I say quickly. "Look, I'll stay out of the fighting if that's what you're worried about. There are more of us than there are of them."

At least, I think so. I'm not staying in here while the others run dangers. With Randy's group, there was an understanding that I'd be the one to suss out whether a place was safe or not. It took a while to get to that point, admittedly, but now I've got to start all over again. I'm not about to stay behind.

"I'm going, too," says Tyler.

"Elle, don't you even think about it," says Murray, as his daughter opens her mouth to speak. "Come and help me tidy away in here."

"Are we going or not?" Cas says, eyes narrowed at me. Like he doesn't believe me.

Screw him. "Yeah, seeing as I'm apparently in charge," I say.

"Be careful!" says Murray, as Tyler and I lead the small group away, towards the fiends.

CHAPTER NINE

"Where the hell are you going?" Cas demands as Tyler and I approach the tunnel.

"We saw them from the walkway," I say.

"What were you doing out there?" asks Val, who walks behind us with several other older Pyros. From the mutters amongst the group, I'm thinking at least half of them don't believe us.

"Just admiring the view," says Tyler.

"Or running away?" Cas suggests. Apparently he's in major asshat mode.

"Don't argue," says Val, sharply. "If this is a real attack, we have to take it seriously."

"*If* we're under attack," adds another guy.

"Why is everyone having trouble believing me?" I say. "I'd never lie about something like this. Never. Besides, Elle and Tyler can back me up."

"I believe you saw *something,*" says Val. "But bear in mind no fiends have ever got past our defences before."

"Unless they got in when everyone was gone?"

"They couldn't have known about that," says Val. "In any case, they don't plan ahead, and they don't work together, either."

"Yeah," says Tyler, "But I saw them, too. If they weren't fiends, then I don't know *what* they were."

As the tunnel's end nears, I start to feel a prickle of unease, remembering the fight in the forest. Falling, falling from the tree with a hideous winged fiend slashing at me.

I clench my fists, nails biting into my palms.

Out of the tunnel. Tyler and I stop, almost in unison, as the first cry echoes around us.

Val curses. "Get ready," she tells the others.

It's too late to think leading the way might have been a mistake. The fiends are on us before I can register the danger. Several pairs of hands grasp the edges of the platform, while three brutes have already climbed up. They bare their long, curved teeth at us.

How the hell did they climb so fast?—the thought flashes through my mind before common sense and the old panic take over. I push the fear aside and move into an attacking stance, while Tyler lets out a half-whimper, half-groan.

"Shit," he whispers.

Cas shoves him aside and strides to the front of the group, knife suddenly in hand. A flash of fire ignites the air, and he buries his knife in a fiend's neck. It falls to its knees with a *thud* that shakes the whole platform.

Hell breaks loose. Cloaks rustle and weapons are drawn as more fiends climb onto the narrow ledge. The floor shakes, and the edge of the platform crumbles under the weight of a giant hand. It swipes at my feet, inches away, and I jump back.

Heat rushes through me, and I lash out, kicking at the creature's head. With a screech, the fiend launches itself onto the ledge and lands beside me, arms reaching out to crush me. I dodge, and feel the heat rising from my skin, like I'm living fire. I get in a punch to its arm before it falls under Cas's blade.

But there's little room to manoeuver here, and one wrong move could send any one of us falling to their death. Cas stands perilously close to the edge, slashing out with his knife. Blood spurts into the air like liquid fire. I try to move forward and join him, but Tyler grabs my arm as a rock bounces down from above, crashing into the platform.

"Sweet hells, they're above us!" someone yells—just as a hideous form drops in front of the cave entrance, clinging to the rocky wall with its ugly face twisted in a snarl.

"Keep it away from the cave!" someone shouts, as we form a line. I'm caged in next to Tyler, trapped by a wall of rock on my other side, but we have to stop them getting into headquarters. Only the three at the front of the tunnel—led by Cas—can get close enough to the fiends to strike.

A large rock falls past, bouncing down the cliff, and the ground shakes again. Something hits me on the head, sharply, and stars wink before my eyes. Another fist-sized rock strikes Tyler on the shoulder, and he grabs my arm, eyes wide with fear.

"They're going to bring down the tunnel," he whispers.

I glance up at the ceiling and another rock falls amongst the group. More pushing ensues as panic spreads. The walls either side of us tremble as the fiends strike the rocky ceiling overhead. *They can't be planning to collapse the tunnel!*

Rocks and dirt fall with every strike. As people around me begin to panic, stumbling in the semi-darkness, I find myself pushed towards the cave opening, right into the path of an oncoming fiend.

I don't get time to hesitate. My body reacts on instinct, and I feel the onrush of power as light erupts from my palm. Before the fiend can strike me, I duck, hitting the fiend on its vulnerable jaw. I feel bone splinter beneath the blow. The fiend staggers back, pulling me with it into the open air again. I yank myself free and kick it in the side. Fiery light surrounds us, the fiend's rocky skin blazing all over with each blow as I drive it back towards the edge. With one final kick, I send the creature stumbling over the verge.

I did it. But I can't celebrate yet. Wheeling around, I see Cas climbing the rock, stabbing at the fiends clinging to the cliff above. One of them catches my eye and lets out a screech. Before I can do more than raise my hands—still blazing—it launches itself at me.

Holy hell, it can fly.

Ugly, jagged wings sprout from its back, and its hands are curved claws—like the one that attacked me in the forest. It lands in front of me, claws slashing, but I dodge and punch it in the face. Smoke rises from its skin where I made contact, and it falls back slightly, allowing me to get into a defensive position.

"Behind you, idiot girl!" shouts Cas.

Something rock-hard crashes into the back of my head, and I stumble forwards, right into the path of the first fiend. A brief moment of panic—*I should have grabbed a weapon!*—stalls me, but then Nolan's lesson kicks in. Strike and block. Aim for the face. The ears or eyes. Blood roars through my veins and I'm caught in the rhythm of the fight. One hit. Then another. Its arms are too muscular to do much damage, but I'm more powerful than a human could ever be. I block a strike with my forearm, recalling training, sending the fire to that part of my arm—the fiend yelps and stumbles away from the light, down the path.

Triumph flaring, I jump forward, again, faster and further than a human can. The fiend hovers lower than the cave, but still within reaching distance of the others. I won't let it come near them. I have to drive it away.

The creature's wings beat and it kicks with a clawed foot, trying to get around me. Even though it should know it's beaten, it wants to get back to the cave. *Get away from them.*

I can jump higher than a person, so I launch myself off the ground, tackling it. The momentum knocks it out of the air and we tumble down the cliff in a whirl of dust. Coughing, my eyes stinging, I come upright, on top of the fiend's heavy body. It lifts its head and I strike its face with my elbow, and a burst of fire for good measure. The fiend's jaw hangs slack. I've stunned it.

Moving off the fiend, I ready myself and kick as hard as I can. The fiend's claws scrabble at the cliff but fail to grip, and it tumbles down into the valley.

I look around for Cas and the others and see nothing but rocks and dust. *When did that happen?* The cave's just about visible above, but I can't see the others, nor any other fiends. Maybe Cas killed them. But I'm alone and exposed, and I've no idea how many of those things are still out there.

"Get away from there!" Cas jumps down to land beside me.

"Where are the others?"

"Back there. What the hell are you doing? Do you have a death wish?"

I glare at him. Now the adrenaline's wearing off, I ache everywhere and my head throbs. When I check for injuries, though, I can't feel a lump on my head where the rock struck me, nor any kind of marks from when the fiend and I tumbled down the cliff. Silently, I follow him back up the path. Fallen rocks lie everywhere, and I can't even see the tunnel. How far did I fall?

"Is it safe to go back in there?"

He meets my glare with one of his own. "Of course not, but safer than what you were doing. We'd be building a blockade up there if *someone* hadn't gone wandering off."

"I didn't go wandering off, I was attacked," I snap. "That fiend with wings—did you see it?"

"Wings?" His eyes narrow in disbelief. It's becoming a familiar expression.

"Yes, wings. Like the one that attacked me in the forest."

"I didn't see that," he mutters, eyes narrowing further. He still holds his knife, which is blood-soaked up to the hilt. Wait—the blade itself is deep red in colour.

But not all the blood's on the blade. It drips down his wrist, staining his hand.

"You're bleeding."

"I know that," he says, through clenched teeth. "Get up there. I'm going to check for…" He trails off.

My eyes follow his stare. There's something further down the path, a mass of fallen rocks, and just beside it, the opening to a cave.

Are more of them lurking inside?

I clamber down, hugging the rock face, wary of the still-falling dirt and stones. Cas lets out an irritated noise, but I hear him start to follow me.

I reach the rocks. It looks like part of the wall's collapsed, and I can see inside the cave. It's pitch-black, of course, but the fire still radiating from my skin allows me to see part of the way in.

Then I see the body.

It's more of a skeleton, really, lying just inside the entrance. I clamber over rocks to get a closer look. The way the rocks fell looks like they weren't originally part of the cliff wall—like someone moved them there. To hide something... like a secret cave.

"Get back, idiot," says Cas.

I ignore him, searching for a way around the rocks. Then common sense kicks in, and I raise my fist. I hit the rock with everything I have, watching it crumble with detached satisfaction.

"Get. Back." Cas pulls me back by the sleeve.

I whirl to face him. "Could you not do that?"

"I asked if you had a death wish," he snarls. "Apparently, you do."

"Look at that," I say. "Someone lived in here."

I glance at him. His expression betrays nothing.

"Did you know about this?"

I shove my way through the path I created, into the cave proper. Now I can see better, I make out other shapes. Like… cages.

Metal bars, crisscrossing from floor to ceiling. Two, side by side. I can see the back wall now. Nothing here but a couple of cages. The skeleton's inside one of them.

Prisoners?

But now I see the skeleton up close, something doesn't look right about it. The basic shape of the bones is all wrong, and it's long, stretched out, with odd protuberances from its shoulder blades.

Is it even human? I've never seen a fiend's skeleton…

Something else catches my eye. Carved into the back wall, above the skeleton, is a symbol of some kind. I tilt my head, trying to make out the words scratched beneath it. It looks like a flame, though I only recognise it because it mirrors my own birthmark. The mark of a Pyro.

Cas's hand lands on my shoulder again. "Get out of here," he snarls.

"Why?" I say. "Don't you think Murray needs to know about this? Or does he already?"

Did they capture a fiend? Keep it imprisoned, maybe to study it? That can't be right... or can it? How long's this place been hidden?

"Go and tell him," says Cas. "I'll stay and keep an eye out here, make sure none of them come back."

I hesitate. But there doesn't seem to be anything else in here, living or otherwise. "What, leave you alone?"

He gives me a hard stare. "What did I just tell you to do?"

In that moment, I can't decide who scares me more, him or the creepy skeleton. But I don't dare argue. I scoot back up the path, feet slipping in the dirt, until I reach the walkway. The cave entrance is half-buried by rocks, and I look around, convinced I hear something falling, but the air's still. No fiends, no falling rocks. A screaming sense of *wrongness* zings through my veins. I run through the tunnel, almost colliding with someone.

"Leah!" Tyler grabs my arm. "Jesus, don't run off like that again. You could have fallen to your death. Even we couldn't survive the drop."

"I have to get Murray," I say. "There's something... Cas and I found something weird." My voice shakes too much to continue. I have to get moving before my legs collapse under me. *Why's this happening?* Why do I feel so lightheaded? My vision swims, and a strange image, the outline of a flame, flashes before my eyes again.

That same symbol…

We catch up to the others halfway down the tunnel. I spot Val, tending to someone's wound. She catches my eye and mouths something, but I don't catch it. I push past, ignoring people's questions, and don't stop running until I reach headquarters.

Murray's already there, hovering outside his office. I skid to a halt, panting for breath.

"What's happening?" he asks, urgently.

"There's someone out there. Dead." I cough, my throat dry from inhaling so much dust. "The fiends attacked us, but they've gone now. Cas and I found this cave, there's a skeleton…" My vision's flickering again, a strange feeling washing through me. Like the echo of remembered pain. *What's happening to me?* "You have to go there. Now."

"I'm going." He glances back into his office. "Elle, stay in there. Could you keep an eye on her, Leah?"

I want to argue, but I can't let Elle go after him either, not if there might be more fiends about. I nod, and Murray sweeps off into the tunnel.

Elle comes out of the office and throws her arms around me. "I was so scared for you! I heard the noise from the tunnel. I thought the roof was going to come down!"

"Let's hope it doesn't," I say, grimly. "We killed the fiends, or drove them off, anyway."

"I'm sorry that happened."

The way she says this strikes me as odd, or maybe I'm still on edge.

"Do you know anything about it?" I ask.

She shakes her head, trembling. "I don't know. It's scary. They might be coming back."

I'm assuming she means the fiends. I can't reassure her, because I'm not sure we killed all the fiends, either. I only drove them away; I never made any kills. And what if they find another way in?

I ask Elle as much.

"No, there aren't any other passages. The front entrance is sealed to anyone but us. Now the defences are back up, you have to spill your own blood on the rock to get in."

"Blood?"

"Only the Pyros can get past. Not fiends, or anything else. It's fool-proof. I never thought they'd be able to get in the back, I've been going out there for years."

"You couldn't have known," I say, moving back towards the tunnel entrance, wondering what's taking the others so long to return. Visions of fiends tearing their way through the walls hover at the edge of my mind, and I get the momentary feeling of being trapped, like in my old town when the fiends attacked it from outside. A town under siege. We can't get out if they block the caves.

Stop that, I tell myself. Panicking will get me nowhere, and I'm more than accustomed to being cornered. We have a room stocked with enough weapons for a thousand people, and we're practically weapons *ourselves*. I don't have to worry about being alone anymore. Maybe part of me still hasn't accepted that.

Tyler runs out of the tunnel and almost crashes into me.

"What happened?" I tense instantly as he stumbles back, rubbing his elbow. "Are they getting in?"

"Gone. We think. Val's set up a boundary."

Elle appears behind me, sees Tyler, and squeals, throwing her arms around him. "Are you okay?"

"I'm fine," he says. "Really. The others are coming now."

"What about Cas and Murray?" I say, thinking of the twisted skeleton, the strange, yet familiar, symbol.

"I dunno. I didn't see them, but it's dark in there. Val says the tunnel's not going to collapse but you never know." He shivers. "That was some scary shit."

"I know," I say. My mind whirls, wondering what it all means. How the fiends got this close—and more to the point, *why*. I hang back by the tunnel entrance, as the others start to appear.

Val comes up to us. "We owe our thanks to you three for warning us. If you hadn't, things could have been far worse."

"Is the tunnel safe?" asks Elle. "It's my fault for not telling anyone about it."

"It's not your fault, Elle. The fiends shouldn't be able to get this close to us. The water should have scared them away. In any case, the cave is now secured against entry."

The image of being trapped pushes to the front of my mind again. I rub my hands over the goose bumps on my arms. It was an illusion to think I was safe here. The enemy was outside all along.

"What about Cas?" I ask. "Are he and Murray still out there?"

"I didn't see them," she says, "But I'm sure they're fine. They're more than capable of looking after themselves. You two should come to the hall with me. I need to spread the word of the attack to the rest of the group."

"But my dad," says Elle, biting her lip. "I want to see him."

"I'll wait here with you," I say, and she looks up at me gratefully. But it's not the two men's safety I'm worried about. I want to know about that cave. I want to know what it all means. And I have a feeling there's something happening here that people don't want me to know about.

CHAPTER TEN

After an hour, the waiting bores me. I suggest to Elle that we go back to Murray's office, but she shakes her head.

"I don't want to miss him," she says.

But I'm restless. I pace around, walking across to the railing over the lava pit and back again. Tyler's gone to tell Poppy and the others in our dorm what happened. He didn't understand why I wanted to stay so badly. But every time tiredness tugs at me, demanding that I chill out, I think of that strange symbol, and everything else I've observed comes bubbling to the surface. The way people avoid certain topics. Like Cas healing me. And now this.

Finally, the sound of two voices raised in conversation reaches my ears and I tense. Cas and Murray emerge from the tunnel, and seem to be having an argument.

"…just covered it up. What was he thinking?" That's Cas's voice.

"He wasn't," says Murray. "It was too much for him. You must know something about what that's like."

"Shut up," says Cas. "I'm going looking for them later. They might still be out there—hell, of course they will be."

"Are you implying they're working together? I told you, we can't assume—"

"No, I'm implying they're going to try and kill us again, because that's what they do," Cas says. "And you, old man, need to face facts."

He turns the corner and sees Elle and me standing there.

"Dad!" Elle shrieks, and throws herself at Murray.

"What happened to the—?"

Cas cuts me off before I can finish my question. "Gone," he says, curtly, and stalks away without another word.

"Hey—what?" I turn to Murray. He hugs Elle back, saying something I don't catch, and goes after Cas.

I look at Elle. "What was that about?"

"I don't know," she says. "I think we should go back to the dorm."

No way am I doing that after waiting so long. I let her go ahead, then double back. Murray and Cas will probably have gone into his office. I walk that way swiftly, relieved that there's no one else about.

The office is empty, though. Just dust and stacks of papers on the desk, and a closed door at the back I didn't notice before. Curiosity gets the better of me and I try the handle, but it's locked.

Have they gone back outside, through the tunnel? Surely not, after our close call earlier. Still, that's the only other place I can think of. So I take off in that direction.

Sure enough, I hear voices. They're not too far inside the cave, so I press myself to the wall just by the opening. That way, I can see if anyone's coming.

"I shouldn't have let her go outside," Murray says.

I stop, hands pressed to the wall. Is he talking about me?

"She'd have found a way even if you'd stopped her. She's annoying like that."

"Really? I haven't heard you actually talk to any of the novices… ever," says Murray. "Yet you saved her."

"Don't remind me."

My heart drops sickeningly at his tone. Why does it bother me? He's nothing to me.

"I've asked Nolan to keep an eye on her," says Murray. "But she seems to be fine. Nothing unusual."

"You can't know that." A pause. "You think you've found your Transcendent, don't you?"

Your what? I edge closer, as much as I can without making myself conspicuous.

"We can't know for certain," says Murray. "But... well, you saw her fight, not me."

Another pause. "She's undisciplined," says Cas. "Besides, she asks too many questions."

"An enquiring mind isn't a sin," says Murray. "But I admit I haven't quite figured out how much to tell her."

"What, you'll just say it outright?" Scepticism tinges his voice. "She'll run."

"I don't think she will. She needs us as much as we need her."

"You'd risk it?" Cas makes a derisive noise. "You're putting an awful lot of faith in her."

My mind's whirling. I want to burst in there and demand to know what they're talking about, but I know that's not the best approach. Murray seems sure whatever it is won't make me run away.

Not that that's a comforting thought. I inch around the wall, ready to ambush Murray when he comes out the cave.

A hand touches my shoulder. "Leah," someone whispers, and I turn so suddenly, our heads almost collide.

It's Val.

I stare at her. No way to disguise the fact that I was eavesdropping.

"Come on," she whispers, beckoning me.

She's not going to tell Murray? I hesitate, surprised. But Cas and Murray have gone quiet. If they're on the way out, they'll find me instantly. I take my chances and follow Val.

She walks with me into another corridor, just beside Murray's office door. I'm not sure where this one leads. I haven't memorised the way around yet, but it seems deserted.

"That was a close one," she says, with a relieved laugh.

I blink. "You're not going to give me a lecture?"

"Of course not." She smiles mischievously. "I spent my first six months here snooping around. Murray won't be mad, it's Cas you have to watch out for. But I suppose you knew that already."

How much did she hear? She's looking at me like she expects me to speak. Can I trust her? Murray's words spin around my head. I thought I could trust *him*. What could be so important that they had to discuss me behind my back? I'm just a child, in their eyes. Do they really think I'll lie down and accept the grown-ups' secrets are beyond me? It's ridiculous. Cas is only two years older than me, after all.

"Leah, you don't have to look at me like I'm the enemy."

"I'm not. Did you hear any of that?" I decide to bite the bullet. "They were talking about me in there."

Val shakes her head. "I didn't, but I can hazard a guess. Did you hear the word Transcendent?"

I nod, wary. So *she* knows, too.

"It was only a matter of time." She sighs. "Honestly... I was all in favour of telling you right away, but, well, I was outvoted. There are some Pyros who are different, who have certain abilities that others don't. Stronger ones. We call them Transcendents."

"Transcendent?" I say. Even more than *Pyro,* it sounds foreign. "And Murray thinks I might be that?"

"It's too early to tell," Val says. "But yes, that's what Murray was hoping. The way you fought today made it pretty clear your instincts are better than some of the seasoned warriors'. But we have yet to find a Transcendent. Every case has been a false alarm."

I fold my arms, my heart racing. *Am I even different from people here?* "And what does it mean, being Transcendent?"

"Well, I don't know. I wasn't in Murray's inner circle when the last one was here. It's been years," she adds hastily. "Murray's been searching for so long. Of course he keeps an eye on new recruits seeing as there are so few of you. It doesn't mean you *are* Transcendent, only that there's a chance."

"Right." That's entirely too little information for my liking. The *last* one? What happened to him, or her?

"I'll talk to him," says Val. "See if I can get him to disclose more information. I don't like how he keeps people in the dark any more than you do."

"Okay," I say. "I'm not keen on the idea that Nolan's apparently been sent to keep an eye on me. I thought he was just training me."

"Nolan?" She shakes her head. "That guy's slippery as an eel."

"Huh?" That doesn't sound like Nolan. But then again, do I really know anyone here? No one trusts me enough to tell me the truth. Even about my powers.

"Tell you what," she says. "I'll see if I can take over as your teacher. Get you started on weapons training. The quicker you get through that, the more likely it is Murray will trust you. Even get you on a mission."

Her expression is open. Not hiding anything. I feel the coil of tension in my chest unknot slightly. Maybe I have found someone I can confide in.

"Thanks," I say, and I mean it.

***

I dream of fire.

I *am* fire. My hands blaze, my body's haloed in light. The world around is tinged red, from sky down to earth. The ground soaked in blood. A battlefield. It looks unreal, like a child's painting, all block colours and sharp lines. A scene half-familiar, half-not. Because I recognise the line cutting the world in two, even though I've never seen it up close.

The divide.

And Cas stands next to it. Hand held out, palm first, like a warning. Somehow, though I'm at a distance, I can see a pattern carved into the underside of his wrist, dripping blood.

"Don't come near me."

"It's too late." The voice isn't mine, though it's female. "He got both of us." The words come out of my mouth with no connection to my thoughts. It's like I'm watching a film play out before me.

I hold out my own arm. With a thrill of horror, I see my own arm's been carved up to the elbow, with red, tattoo-like lines that seem to pulse before my eyes.

He's still there, but I can't look directly at him any longer. The fire's too bright.

I chance it anyway. The image burns onto my eyelids. Cas, edged with fire. He starts to speak again but everything blurs, and I'm awake.

***

Despite the worry about fiends lurking just outside the doors, I quickly settle into a routine. Every day brings new training exercises and challenges. I already know the principles of self-defence—I took lessons in taekwondo and karate until I was fourteen—but Val goes over the basics again, explaining that she's still convincing Murray to train me with weapons. I also have theory lessons with an older guy called George, and meditation. Apparently the focus will help me access the fire, though I'm ahead with that already. In the first fight with the fiends, my hands went ablaze by themselves, like my body acted on its own. But the last time, I moved in tune with my newly developed reflexes. In control. Apparently the unexpected field training gave me an edge. I just wish it meant people took me seriously and didn't treat me like a five-year-old.

I'm not stupid. I know rules are there for a reason. But if there's something odd about my powers, I deserve to know what it is.

One morning, Elle tips me off that Murray's teaching a class on genetics that day. Even though I've not been to any non-combat-related classes since I came, there's nothing preventing me from listening in on one. Elle's glad to have someone to sit next to at the back of the room; she finds it embarrassing that her father's teaching the class and hopes he won't pick her to answer questions.

It's the first time I've seen him all week, and I barely concentrate on the first half of his lecture, not that I have any paper to make notes on, anyway. Elle offers to lend me some, but I end up doodling on it.

I snap back to attention when I realise he's just said my name.

"…and as Leah knows, the fire can activate in an urgent situation, even though she was unaware that she was one of us."

A few people turn and look at me.

"There could be many more people like her out there. We certainly can't rule it out. So to answer your question, there may very well be other missions further afield."

I guess someone must have asked if we're going to get to leave any time soon. I've been wondering the same thing. Not that I'd trade this relative safety for a night in the open with the fiends prowling around, but the lack of news has made me antsy, given me an urge to fight that hitting a punch bag can't satisfy. I want to feel like I did when I kicked that fiend off the cliff. Powerful. In control. If I can save just one person from the fiends…

"What about us?" I ask Murray. "Will we get to take part in missions?"

"Were you listening, Leah?" He shakes his head slightly. "You will, if you pass next week's tests. But you haven't been here that long, so we might need to leave it a little longer."

"But I want to—"

"You can't throw your life away, Leah," he says. "I know you're used to acting first, thinking later, but we've learned the hard way that risks can get us killed. If it wasn't for the attack last week, we wouldn't even be considering it. But you'll get your chance."

Everyone's staring at me again. A flush creeps up my neck.

Murray returns to talking about genetics. I try to pay attention this time, since I know it's relevant to figuring out why I am like this. I'm glad to be alive, of course, but part of me can't help but wonder. Why me? Why was I saved? Because of *genetics?*

Stop it, I tell myself. Randy calls this survivor's guilt—been there, done that.

If I really want to fight back and protect the other humans still out there, I need to find a way to get myself on a mission.

***

I carry on with training exercises, waiting for my chance. Val's tight-lipped about whether she managed to get through to Murray or not, but I enjoy training with her all the same. She's only a few years older than me, but I feel like I have more in common with her than I do with the people my age. Perhaps because she led most of the first missions after the world ended, so she saw first-hand what it was like out there just after the fiends came.

"I don't know how you survived, Leah," she says to me one day. "Mentally, I mean. You saw things that would have broken most people, and Pyros are no more emotionally capable than ordinary humans are."

Yeah, Cas proves that much.

I just shrug. What is there to say? I survived at first because I had Lissa, and then, well, it was easier pretending there was a reason to live than giving in. Every day I lived was a kick back against the fiends.

"Hey, I'm not knocking humans," she says, misinterpreting my silence as being insulted on behalf of non-Pyros. "If anything, I'm kind of glad we have feelings like normal people do. It makes us less like the fiends."

I appreciate it when she says things like that. So, slowly, I start to open up to her. Share anecdotes, even. After one training session, I have her in hysterics relating some of the things that happened at school. Val left school at fourteen after her parents died and came to train with the Pyros, so she's interested to hear about it.

"I guess it was kind of like a boarding school, our old headquarters," she says. "Except there weren't really any classes based on age, more on ability. I was one of the strongest Pyros, so I was pushed through to training when I was sixteen. Well, I chose to. I didn't like school much. I preferred hitting things." She smiles.

"Old headquarters?"

"There used to be two," Val explains. "I started out at the other one. Still pretty isolated, but it was closer to a normal town so we used to get to visit there sometimes."

"Who ran that place then?" I ask. "Were there a lot of you?"

"More than there are now." Her face falls, and I feel bad for asking. "So many died two years ago. Including most of the other senior staff—there were originally three leaders, including Murray. Others were wounded. Some died afterwards, when we transferred to this headquarters."

"So Pyros can get injured?" Stupid question. The fiend in the woods would have killed me if not for Cas. "I mean, if energy blasts don't affect us like they do ordinary people, then why can other things hurt us?"

"Honestly? I don't know," says Val. "It's part of Murray's research actually. Something in our blood, in our genes, protects us from energy blasts and from the worst of the fiends' attacks, but we're not invulnerable to anything else. We can still get shot, stabbed, even fall over and break bones. I wish we knew more."

So do I.

The missions start up the next week, and I watch the others leave the caves and come back a few days later. None of the novices. Cas's on almost every mission, the first to volunteer according to Elle.

I'm still trying to puzzle him out, mostly because he seems to be at the centre of the weird things I've observed. For one thing, whenever he *is* actually here, he's always hanging about

Murray's office, looking like he doesn't particularly want to be there. Maybe it's because I spent so long with Randy's group that I felt I knew everything about each of us, but I still can't get used to being around a bunch of total strangers, despite all their efforts to welcome me. Most of them came to live here almost immediately after the first attacks. They were recruited in stages from around the country. They saw the horrors, but didn't have to spend two years surviving alone in the wilderness. Or, like Elle, they've barely been outside. This certainly applies to the older members of the group. There's a complicated family tree linking Murray's family to some of the others, apparently. Elle's mother died giving birth to her, which explains why she's so close to her dad. And why she didn't inherit the Pyro gene: her mother wasn't one of them.

"I never knew her, so I don't miss her," she says, one day as we're walking to the training hall "But I used wonder what it would be like growing up in a normal family. But that was before…"

Before normal became terror, I guess.

"So was it just you here, growing up? Who lived here before?"

"Me, my dad, a bunch of other scientists. Most of the older Pyros, and Cas."

"So he grew up here, too?"

"Kinda." She doesn't meet my eyes for some reason. We're almost at the training hall by now, and I lose my chance to carry on questioning her when Cas himself walks past.

"Murray wants you," he says to Elle, curtly. He doesn't acknowledge me. *Lovely to see you, too.*

"Okay," says Elle. "I'll see you later?"

"Sure," I reply, and enter the training hall by myself.

No sooner do I enter than Val waves me over. "I think you're ready for weapons training," she says.

My heart leaps. At last. "Really?" I say, trying to keep a straight face.

"Yep. So… you have a choice to make. There's no shortage of swords, knives and the like, or you can go for something more unusual. Or just use your fists, if you prefer.

"Quick question," I say. "Shouldn't the fire melt the weapons? And how do they not break when they hit a fiend? Those things are pretty solid."

"I was getting to that," says Val, amusement flickering in her eyes. Maybe I was a bit over-enthusiastic at the prospect of getting to use the weapons. But the image of Cas slashing at the fiends with his knife jumps to the forefront of my mind. I want to be able to fight like that.

Val takes me into a small room where they keep the weapons. They're more… elaborate than I imagined, though I suppose I never got a close look at Cas's blade. The rows of daggers remind me of a museum display I once saw, of ceremonial daggers from a forgotten time. The carved hilts are all slightly different. Some are small enough to be pocket-knives, the type street gangs in urban areas might have carried.

I look at them all, trying to imagine what each would feel like in my hand, whirling through the air, slicing through the fiends' rock-hard skin.

"Take your pick. I'll be training you in all of them. You'll be having one-to-one training sessions twice a week. It's proven to be the best way to teach it, so we can give each individual the best training we can."

She stands back to let me choose. I reach out hesitantly, run my fingers over blade handles, and eventually pick a dagger with a gold Celtic design on the hilt.

"You want to try out the athame? Okay. We'll alternate over different sessions so you can try everything out. You have a sharp eye, so I think you'd be suited to throwing knives—not that it's usually a good idea in a one-on-one fight, but it'd be good for you to practise with targets before you start hitting things."

To my annoyance, she takes the dagger away from me and gives me a handful of small throwing-knives instead.

But she's right. I get the knack quickly. A chalk-drawn diagram of a fiend on the wall is my target, and every knife hits it in a fatal spot. Buzzing with energy, I turn to Val to find that she's wandered away to check on someone else.

I didn't ask her how these knives are so much stronger than normal ones, but now I start to notice a strange quality in the metal. Some of the older knives are slightly scratched and beneath the metallic exterior, they're rust-red in colour.

I waylay Val as she walks past to ask her about it.

"Well," she says. "You know we're stronger and faster than regular people, and our enemies are also unnaturally strong. No weapons can harm them, not even bullets. But it's natural that we want to use something other than our own fists to defend ourselves, and the Pyros have a long tradition of weapon-making, using our own ashes as the basis."

"*What?*" My eyes travel from the dagger in my hand, to Val. "As in… dead people?"

"The bodies of our fallen warriors. Pyros are strong, and the same goes for our blood and our bones. If we fall, we can still help one another this way. It probably seems odd to you."

Yeah. Definitely odd. And a reminder that I don't feel completely in place here. The younger Pyros seem so ordinary, almost a relic of the world we lost, but at times like this I get a glimpse of a much older world, steeped in strange traditions and unfamiliar ideas.

I sense someone watching from behind, and turn to see Nolan crossing the room towards me.

"Hey, Leah," he says.

"Hi," I say.

"Are you done here? Murray wants to see you."

"Sure," I say, as Val nods, and winks at me, for some reason.

I walk alongside Nolan, wondering what that was about.

"How're you getting on?" he asks me.

"Pretty good," I say.

"Looks like you were having fun with those daggers." He grins at me.

"I guess," I say. "At least until I learned what they were made of."

"Ah." He grimaces. "I know, it's not pleasant. But it's just something we do. Well, Murray does."

"Is that what he wants to see me about?" I grin.

"No, of course not—" He realises I'm joking. "No, he actually needs your help with a mission."

My heart leaps. "Really?"

"Really." He smiles. "Usually we get one practise mission. You'll be with three or four more experienced fighters, to get a taste of what it's like outside. I'm not sure what he's playing at; he knows you've had more than enough experience of the world out there."

Val, I think. Did she persuade him, like she said she would?

I still can't quite believe I've been here almost a month. In the caves, time's organised into hours, days and weeks, like part of the world we left behind. But before I came here, I wouldn't have known two years had passed if Randy hadn't kept track. Time blurred without routine, and I couldn't remember individual days.

I can't decide how I feel about going outside again. I imagine the open, star-dotted sky—but also the danger. The cries of fiends, never far away.

Murray's waiting outside his office with Cas and Elle. The former looks bored, the latter worried, bouncing on her heels.

"There you are," says Murray. "Sorry for the short-notice. I take it Nolan told you what this is about?"

"Yeah. What's the mission, exactly?"

Cas makes a disparaging noise. *What? It's not a stupid question.*

"What?" I say.

"Nothing. I just don't see why we have to bring someone who has no experience in combat."

"No experience?" I half-laugh. "Two years surviving in the wilderness isn't enough?"

"You don't know anything," he says.

Well, that's friendly. "Enlighten me. I've been here a month, I reckon I've picked up a thing or two."

Cas rolls his eyes. "We're going to the divide. I don't reckon you've seen anything like *that* before."

"The divide? That's nowhere near here, is it?"

"The world has changed," says Murray. "Look here." He unfolds a hand-drawn map. It shows a collection of islands, bisected by a thick line from north-east to south-west, where it cuts off the top part of the map just below a circle drawn in black marker.

Goose bumps spring up on my arms. I know what it is. The United Kingdom. The line is the divide, and the circle is where we are.

If I close my eyes, I can still see the form of the UK as it used to be, imprinted in my memory by all the maps I saw when I was younger, on classroom walls and worksheets and even our own living room. This hand-drawn map is proof of the irrecoverable nature of change. *Stupid. Did you really think it could ever be the same?*

I blink, averting my eyes from Cas to hide the flicker of a tear.

"So we're going to the divide... why?"

"We need information," says Murray. "There is an old research station to the south of the divide, and with everything happening, I haven't had the chance to send in a team. It was once one of our research bases. It's only a few hours' travel, and I assumed it had been destroyed, but we've recently learned that part of it survived."

Cas says, "If it's so simple, I could go alone. Why do there have to be three of us?"

"You know why." Murray gives him a stern look. "You'll be safer with three of you, and you've worked together before. You'll leave first thing tomorrow. Is that understood?"

CHAPTER ELEVEN

We set out early the following morning, and the sunlight is jarring after so many days living under artificial lights. I'm glad for my hat, which keeps the worst of the heat off my face. Cas is as stoic and uncommunicative as ever, but Nolan and I talk during the less steep parts of the climb down the mountain. He wants to know how I'm finding life these days. We discuss fighting strategies for a bit, but something's bothering me until the question slips out.

"Don't the fiends live in the divide?" I ask him. "What if they attack us?"

The image from the news the day London fell comes to mind. The monsters pulling themselves out of the earth in spurts of fire, tearing roads apart and sending cars and people flying, crashing through buildings with their stone-like fists.

"Not this close to the sea," says Nolan.

Still, something about this situation is unnerving. To me, the outside world means the fiends. Mostly I want to know where we're going, and what we hope to find there. But that question goes out of my head when we reach the foot of the hill and the stepping stones are waiting, mossy and slippery. Cas strides ahead, casually, and I follow, trying to ignore my fast-beating heart.

Nolan steps up behind me and says, quietly, "I won't let you fall in, okay?"

I nod my gratitude and take my first step.

It's over quicker this time, and despite only one heart-stopping moment where I almost slip, I'm relieved to make it to the other side. At least I'm wearing my sturdy hiking boots. It's the first time I've gone outside in my new uniform, too. I catch a blurred glimpse of my reflection in the water—the long dark-red coat, the short dark hair just starting to grow back—and nothing looks like me. Maybe I still haven't let go of the image of myself at fifteen, before everything went to hell.

But I'm someone else now. I just wish I knew who.

Once on flat ground, Cas leads the way through fields, in the opposite direction to the way we came. Our path follows the coastline, where cliffs hang over dark waters. I understand how people in a pre-technological age must have felt, starting out at the vast unknown world of the ocean. It seems like anything could be waiting out there, and there's no way of knowing. Images of dark shapes swimming beneath the surface taunt me, and I keep my eyes firmly on the path ahead.

Then, sooner than I expect, we see the divide.

At first, I think it's a row of rolling hills, stretching across the horizon. But the line doesn't stop where the cliff meets the sea. The water moves strangely around that area, and though it's been years since I went near the coast, I don't remember the water only flowing in one direction.

As the hill draws closer, I start to see that there's something not right about it. The yellow grass of the field is cut away, coming to an abrupt halt where the ground is scorched red, like the beginning of a Burned Spot. But the divide lies across the surface like a jagged, ropy scar, as far as the eye can see. It's barely two metres across, but how deep, I have no idea.

"There it is," Nolan murmurs, pointing. My eyes move from the divide to a small, ramshackle building near the gap. Its blank windows glare back.

"What are we looking for in there?"

"Information, like Murray said. Some of our group once used it as a research base, it's only just been confirmed safe enough for us to go back."

Still, being so close to the place the fiends came from makes me uneasy, and the feeling grows as we approach. Cas is so far ahead he's already inside the building by the time we reach it.

The door hangs from its hinges, the entryway in shadow. Ominous creaking sounds suggest the building's on the verge of collapse, but that's the least of my worries right now. The creeping feeling of being watched hangs over me like the loose ceiling tiles, and my hand rests on the hilt of the knife in my belt. I picked the weapon I got on best with in practise, but any would do to take on the fiends.

I'd rather avoid a fight, but I can't help thinking there's something else I should be doing when I spend hours in training exercises. All the old building seems to contain are rooms full of what look like hospital beds, and a sterile smell that even the burning stench from the divide hasn't erased.

Then we enter the laboratory. That's the word that springs to mind, anyway, and the hairs on my arms stand up. It's cold in here, as well as dark and dusty. Cas shines a torch around, revealing a collection of empty glass tanks and the once-white walls, now stained rust-red. My insides lurch. *Is that blood?*

Nolan grimaces. "Oh no. Not—it wasn't here?"

"What?" I ask, instinct telling me to get the hell out of here. But morbid curiosity prevails. As I look around, I see stacks of papers on a desk, also stained red. Cas picks one up with no inhibition, his eyes scanning it.

"This one."

Nolan takes it from him. Though the paper faces away from me, I see the symbol through the transparent sheet.

It's that symbol again. Like a flame.

"Is no one going to tell me what's going on?" I step forwards to look at the paper, but he moves it out of my line of sight. "What's the problem?"

"I told you." Cas glances over his shoulder. "Murray should have just sent the two of us alone."

"You know the rules," says Nolan, with a guilty expression that irks me even more.

"So I just came here as an extra?" I glare at both of them. "Thanks a lot. You know, I'm not completely useless. I'd be happy to help if you give me a clue as to what the hell all this is about."

"Murray doesn't like us discussing his research," says Cas. "Personally, I don't give a rat's ass. If you really want to know, this station was originally to research the process by which one of the Pyros might become Transcendent."

Transcendent. That's what Val said I might be. Something more than a Pyro, but what?

"What exactly *is* a Transcendent?" I ask. "No evading the question. You owe me an answer."

"I'm sorry," says Nolan. "I didn't want to keep you in the dark, but—"

"We're wasting time," says Cas, picking up a stack of papers. "This is what we're looking for. Unless…" He approaches another door at the end of the room. A broken, cobwebbed window shows another room similar to this one, filled with empty glass tanks. It gives me a sinister feeling. A faint dripping sound reaches my ears.

I push the door open to find Cas in the act of stabbing his knife through the locks on a cabinet. In the eerie half-light, the metal of his blade gleams red, like blood shaped into a weapon.

The locks crumple like they're made of fabric. That's one impressive weapon.

"Nothing," he mutters. "Damn. I thought they might have left something behind, seeing as they obviously left in a hurry."

"Who even lived here?" I ask.

"Scientists," says Nolan from behind me.

"What, from our group?"

"Kind of. It's complicated. Murray's family weren't all Pyros, but they helped with research. This base was one of many, but it was abandoned when the fiends came."

Cas swings his knife. The blade begins to glow, like the flicker of a flame. My eyes follow its path.

"What's with that?" I ask him directly.

"A knife."

"Hilarious," I say. "I meant, why's it glowing?"

"Because it's made of our alien blood."

"Are you going to stop taking the piss out of me and give me a straight answer?"

Nolan clears his throat, looking embarrassed. "He's telling the truth, Leah."

"What, someone's blood went into this?" Of course, the weapons we carry are formed of the ashes of fallen warriors, but *blood?*

"The power's in our blood," Nolan explains. "The scientists were experimenting for ways to transfer that energy into weapons."

Cas interrupts by swinging the blade into the wall. It cuts through the plaster and brick like paper.

"What?" he says. "This place is falling apart anyway."

"You two, we need to hurry if we want to make it back before sunset," says Nolan.

"Hold on," I say. "What did you need me here for if you're not going to tell me what's happening?"

"We needed a three-person team," says Cas. "God knows why. You're not even qualified. You're just a child."

I've had about enough. "This again?" I fold my arms. "Look, the both of you are acting like children. Not me. So quit being patronising."

"Whatever." Cas casts one lasts, dismissive glance around the room. "I'm done here." There's an undercurrent to his voice, some emotion I can't place.

Nolan's already gone. Frustration buzzes beneath my skin. If Cas won't answer my questions, I'm going to corner Nolan instead. But he's not in any of the other rooms. Leaving the building, I find him standing a few feet away, watching the divide.

I walk over to him. As I approach, I see the walls of rock, falling down into darkness. I picture a drop leading into the core of the Earth itself, through layers of rock and lava…

I stop dead. A shape clings to the rocky edge of the divide, a winged, humanoid monstrosity. My heart starts drumming in my ears and my hand leaps to the dagger at my waist.

"Shit." Nolan sees what I'm looking at and draws his own dagger. "Cas!" he shouts at our partner's retreating back.

Cas reacts instantly; his hands blur as he draws the sword from beneath his cloak. He runs forward and clears the divide in one bound, before I can so much as blink. My heart slams into my chest as I take off after him, Nolan shouting my name. The dagger's in my hand, which is shaking with both adrenaline and fear. The divide suddenly seems wider, a gaping void I have to jump over, but I don't stop. The breeze rushes through my hair and my coat streams out behind me as I fly over the gap, to where Cas is already climbing down to the fiend.

My heart leaps into my throat as he clings to the edge one-handedly, slashing at the fiend with the other hand.

"Are you mental?" Nolan yells from behind, jumping the gorge.

The exact same thought just crossed my mind. I hover near the edge, but the fiend's out of sight, and jumping down to meet it would be asking to fall. Cas positions himself so that his feet barely brush the cliff's sides as he stabs at the monster. Then the fiend lets go.

I step back as it rises on jagged wings, and lunges at me. My knife comes out but I'm too slow, and miss. Talons dig into my shoulders as the monster skims overhead, then wheels around and faces me.

It's like an even uglier version of the winged fiend from the forest. The skin of its face is stretched over elongated, rotting teeth, its eyes wide, bulbous and grey. The wings look like they belong to another creature entirely, like a pterodactyl. Clawed hands move towards me and I step back, my feet catching on the cliff's edge.

That was close.

Nolan's already there with his weapon drawn. He strikes at the fiend, which retreats into the air, letting out a guttural sound. Then it dives again, fast as a blink. My hand moves automatically, heat travelling down my arm to the knife. As I watch, like a half-stunned observer, the blade lights up, fire-coloured and deadly. One swipe cuts the fiend's face. It screams, and slashes with its claws. But Nolan jumps in front of me, deflecting it. Cas catches it from behind with a vicious stab. The blade protrudes from the fiend's chest.

I slash again. Again. The fiend's trapped between the three of us, and I can see its eyes darting about, like it's aware of its situation. Blood pours from cuts all over its body and the gaping wound from Cas's knife.

Nolan lifts a hand before Cas can deliver the killing blow.

"What—?"

"Hold it," says Nolan. "Can you speak?" he addresses the fiend.

I blink at him. *He's lost it.*

But the fiend swivels its eyes in his direction, like it can understand him.

"What're you—?" My question's cut off when the fiend opens its mouth, a half-scream, half-groan almost shattering my eardrums.

"You… are nothing." The words come out half-broken, but recognisable as English. Incredible as it seems, the fiend actually spoke to us. *No way. Impossible.* The fiends don't *talk*. They're not human.

"What are you doing here, fiend?" Nolan asks, as though this doesn't surprise him at all. Cas looks unfazed, too. Once again, I've been left out of the loop. Ordinarily, I'd demand answers from him right now, but I can't stop watching the fiend's face as its mouth works, forming words again.

"Not your concern."

"I think you'll find it is." Nolan jabs the fiend with the point of his blade. "You knew we were coming here."

The fiend doesn't answer. A growl slips between its teeth, tinged with pain.

"I'm warning you," says Nolan. "Your kind are supposed to be extinct. Where did you come from?"

"You… know the answer to that."

"The way was shut," says Nolan.

"Did you think you drove us away forever? We can kill you any time, human." The words come out faster. My heartbeat is loud in my ears. I can't look away.

"You know what will happen if you attack headquarters."

"Would you risk human life to destroy us? Of course not." The fiend lets out a coughing sound. The hairs on my arms rise as I realise it's laughing. "You're hypocrites. You and Murray both."

"How do you know about Murray?"

"People tell me things, human. More than you tell your new recruits, I don't doubt." Another coughing laugh. "We'll take your world, humans, one way or another. You might get a visit from someone familiar very soon."

"Your kind already attacked us at our base," Cas intervenes. "You sent one. Was that a message for Murray, or for me?"

"You? What's so special about…?" The fiend's eyes bulge as it twists to face Cas. "You're *him,* aren't you? How very convenient. To die at your hands would be an honour."

Cas's blade's at his throat, quick as a flash. *What did that mean?* I don't dare speak, and I'm not sure I can.

"You're asking to die?"

"Death comes to everyone, but you know that better than most, right?" The fiend coughs. Blood spatters the ground.

"Just answer me one question," says Cas. "Is Jared alive?"

"You know." The fiend's teeth are bared in a pained grin.

My mind spins. Cas's talking to the fiend like someone he *knows*. What the hell is going on?

Another laugh. More blood spatters. "Maybe you should look to your own before you appoint blame. I know what you're doing. She's part of it, isn't she?"

And it raises an arm, twisting to show us the wrist. Harsh lines cover it up to the elbow, etched into the skin like a tattoo shaped like a flame.

Two gasps. Nolan and Cas wear almost-identical expressions of horror.

While they're standing frozen, it reaches and grabs my arm.

I freeze, panicking. My arm lights up like a beacon, a blaze of light reaching into the sky. But something's different this time—more like the first time my powers activated, when I felt disconnected from my body. A vibration grows beneath my skin and the air around my arm shimmers. Heat rushes up my arms, and the ground trembles under my feet. A sound echoes in my ears, like the distant beat of a drum.

The air ripples. The fiend's eyes dim, its body swaying as Cas's and Nolan's blades pierce its skin. But before it can hit the ground... its body falls apart before my eyes.

Or, that's what it looks like. The vibration in the air reaches the monster and distorts it, like a reflection in tinted glass. Skin flakes away, particle by particle, until its entire body is enveloped in white flames. The drumbeat grows louder in my ears, and I drop to my knees as trembles overtake the ground. Tremors in land and air.

An energy blast.

It spreads out in waves, a force of its own, beyond anything natural. A crumbling sound tells me the research building is no more. Even the edges of the divide buckle as rock falls away...

"Leah! Leah!"

Voices. Someone shaking me. A tremor so strong my teeth rattle against each other. The earth's not shaking anymore.

It's me.

I caused it.

The noise stops. I register the impression of a hand holding mine. Nolan—no, Cas. *What?*

My absolute confusion is enough to send the last tremors away. I drop his hand, stand up quickly. Nolan crouches at a distance, braced against the ground. The concern in Cas's eyes—such a foreign expression on his face—fades in a flash. He glares at me.

"Way to nearly get us all killed," he snaps.

I nearly... *what?* My mind tumbles over itself and it takes a good minute to form the first question.

"How?"

"Let's go," he says, curtly. "Come on, Nolan."

He strides away, leaping over the divide again. That alone is unchanged by the blast.

"Wait!" I yell—like *hell* I'm letting him run off without answering my questions after saying something like that.

I run after him. My legs are still shaking, and I almost trip at the edge of the fall, but Nolan grabs my arms and steadies me. I ready myself and jump, and then run again to catch up to Cas.

"Wait." I step in front of him, dagger pointing directly at his chest. "I'm not moving until I get some answers. Now."

CHAPTER TWELVE

Cas rolls his eyes. "You do know the fiends will be here soon? And we need to make it back before sunset."

"What, so you can disappear again?" I narrow my eyes back at him. "Nice try. What if I want to say I'm not coming back?"

An eyebrow arches. "You are coming back."

"That's funny, I thought you didn't want me there. I distinctly remember you wanting to leave me to die in the wilderness."

Cas's eyes narrow, but he says nothing. I have him there. Savouring the brief moment of triumph, I say, "Told you. Now, answers. Did I just use some kind of energy blast?"

"In a manner of speaking." Cas moves out of range of my knife. Not that I'd actually stab him with it—well, maybe. If he doesn't tell me what I just did. Nolan catches up, visibly pale and shocked.

I direct my questions at both of them. "What I did isn't normal, is it? And the fiends—you knew that monster, or someone who knew him. How?"

"Pick one question."

"Pedant," I mutter. "Fine. What the hell did I just do?"

"Ask Murray."

"Murray's told me even less than you have." I cross my arms. "Look. I know you don't like me, and I'm not overly fond of you either. But I just caused a freaking explosion. If there was a person, a normal human, standing nearby, then—" I can't go on. I can't think of what happened the last time I got too close to an energy blast. Randy's face comes to mind, and an onrush of images of the other people I spent two years in the wilderness with. Tears tremble at the edges of my eyes. I squeeze them shut and look away, renewed anger making my body shake.

"Yeah, they'd be toast," says Cas.

"Cas!" says Nolan, shoving him. Hard.

"Don't touch me," says Cas. "She wants the truth, she gets it. Without Murray's sugar-coating. You'd think we weren't fighting a war."

"You're not fighting a war," I point out. "You're screwing with me. Are you not telling me the truth because *you* don't know?"

"You insolent—"

"She has a point," says Nolan. "Leah, we really don't know. I haven't seen a power like yours since…" He trails off as Cas gives him a murderous stare.

"And no one thought to tell me I could cause a freaking *explosion?*" I stare at the two of them, unable to believe it.

"We didn't know," said Nolan. "I thought…" Again, he trails off. Cas's eyes are narrowed to slits, and he looks about ready to stab someone.

"Let me get this straight," I say. "You didn't know. But that fiend knew something. Right? It knew Murray, and it knew *you.*"

I struggle not to flinch as Cas's stare pins me to the spot.

"It's true," says Nolan. "Must be one of the older fiends. I didn't think they had long memories."

"Long memories," I say. "So it's been here since…"

"The invasion," says Nolan. "The fiends are leftovers from the original war, trapped in our world. Most aren't intelligent enough to remember it."

"Most of them don't *speak*," I point out. "It doesn't have to do with the Transcendent, does it?"

If Cas's expression was like a laser before, now it's a freaking nuclear strike.

"You're the one who brought it up," I snap at him. "At the lab. I'm not stupid."

"She isn't," says Nolan. "And Leah… I guess it sort of does. The Transcendent was our secret weapon during the invasion. But we still lost the war, and we thought we'd lost most of the research, too."

"Right," I say. *Weapon?* "And what I just did… could the Transcendent do *that?*"

"Enough," Cas snaps. "We need to get back before Murray sends a rescue team after us, or more of those *things* show up."

"Don't you try to divert me," I say. "Fine. We'll talk on the way back, and you'd better hope Murray gives me some answers."

"He was right," says Nolan. "We can't keep her in the dark."

"*You* shouldn't even know about it," says Cas. "Spying on us, were you?"

"You asked me to keep an eye on her!"

"Me?" I interrupt. "So you don't think I'm mature enough to hear the truth? Next time I'll be sure to stand right behind you if I get another freakish power-boost and blow everything up."

"You can't kill a Pyro," says Cas. "And if you get yourself under control, you won't be harming any humans, either."

"What the *hell* does that mean?" I bar his way as he makes to walk forward. "You can't say that and expect me to put my head down and accept it. Am I a danger to everyone?"

"No," says Nolan. "But you'll need to talk to Murray. He'll explain about your powers. Neither of us know enough to be able to help you."

"Like I'd take *your* help." I direct this more at Cas, but it's Nolan who flinches. Wow. I actually scared him. But I feel faintly sick instead of triumphant. My head throbs, and I just want a straight answer. "I can cause... energy blasts. The fiend knew I could. How?"

"I have no idea," says Cas flatly, but I'm sure he's lying.

Nolan frowns at him, but shakes his head. "No clue."

I let out a breath. "So. Did the fiends cause the end of the world, or…?" I can't end the sentence. *The Pyros didn't cause it. Did they?*

"They invaded," says Cas, whose entire body is tense, mouth drawn into a line. "We survivors moved back into the mountain, losing most of Murray's research in the process."

"Transcendents?"

Cas's glare means *yes*, I guess. He turns to Nolan, his eyes cold. "You tell Murray to keep her out of future missions. We can't afford to let her damage our reputation. If the humans turn on us, then we've no hope of beating the fiends."

"Excuse me? Damage your reputation? In case you've forgotten, that town refused to let us in before because they didn't trust your type. The group I lived with were the same."

"Sorry," says Nolan. His hand brushes my arm, and I step away. The desire to run seizes me. To run away from the lies and deception. I can survive alone, and even the fiends can barely touch me… but that would mean abandoning everyone here. Abandoning the war.

"Cas," says Nolan, "If anything, *you're* the one who's done the most damage."

A swishing sounds as Cas drawing his knife and points it at Nolan.

"Don't even go there," he says through clenched teeth. "I'm sick of the sight of both of you. And the sun's going down."

Crap. He has a point. The sun's almost on a level with the distant hills we came from, and we still have to walk all the way back. I glance behind at the divide, and though I see no movement, the hairs rise on my arms at the thought of more of those fiends down there.

"Right." Nolan puts away his weapon. "Let's move."

Cas's already several metres away, his cloak streaming behind him, knife still in his hands.

I walk, questions whirling around my head. The silence between us grows unbearable. Finally, I say, "That fiend that attacked us was different. How did you know it could speak?"

"I've seen it before," says Nolan. "It's a genetically enhanced fighting machine, one they taught to speak English. I thought they were all dead, but apparently not."

"I never saw one like that until we were attacked in the forest," I say.

"They're getting bolder."

"Genetically enhanced," I say. "So do the *fiends* have, like, scientists?" I always thought of the fiends as brutish, thick-skulled fighting machines. The idea that they might possess near-human intelligence doesn't exactly fill me with confidence.

"Humans they captured, presumably," says Nolan, but it sounds like a lie. Perhaps it's the look on his face. I can't read it.

"What was that symbol?"

The guarded look flickers. "Symbol?"

"The one tattooed on its arm. It's the same as our symbol. It looks exactly the same."

Nolan's lips press together. "I have no idea."

Another lie. Anger buzzes under my skin, like residue from the energy blast I caused.

"Right," I say. "Thanks for clearing that up."

Nolan sighs. "Leah, what you have to understand is that Murray keeps secrets for a reason. So does Cas, so do all of us. Certain information's dangerous to spread around. The more people know things, the more leverage the fiends have against us if they attack. If they were to take any of us, we've lost the war. We have knowledge which could tip the balance either way…"

"Why, did they take people captive before?"

Is that how they gained the intelligence to create genetic enhancements? More, even worse monsters? Don't they have the advantage already?

Was someone Murray knew taken already?

"We were betrayed," he says, rubbing his arm convulsively, like it hurts.

"Last time," I say, trying a last-ditch tactic to get some information. "The Transcendent died, right?"

He inclines his head.

"The fiends killed him? Her?"

Nolan sighs. "She died after closing the divide—the breach. That's why they haven't been able to come back."

That's what happened? My mind spins. Is that what I am—a sacrifice, if the fiends break through to our world again? Is *that* what being Transcendent means?

The words hover in the front of my mind before I open my mouth. "Am I Transcendent?"
The sentence remains hanging in the air, like it's weighted.

"Don't lie to me," I say, quietly. "Val said Murray thought I was, and now I caused that energy blast. I've never seen another Pyro do that. So. Am I?"

Nolan inclines his head, looking at me pityingly. The anger buzzes again.

"I am," I say, answering the question for him. "If that's the case... does Murray expect me to die for you, like the last one?"

A long pause.

"No, Leah," Nolan says, softly. "It was an accident, and it won't happen again. But I wouldn't talk about it in front of Cas. He was on the front line last time as the Transcendent's shield. He couldn't protect her."

I suck in a breath. "Is that why he's such an asshat? He thinks I'm live bait?"

"I'm fairly sure he was an asshat since birth," says Nolan, his expression relaxing.

That almost gets a smile out of me.

"But this whole thing's worrying." Nolan sighs. "I was surprised Murray even sent us out that far. I expected him to keep us inside, or at least look for the fiends that got away first."

"Some of them got away?"

"Apparently. The ones that attacked us sneaked into the area when we were gone, around the back. Murray must have left a gap in security. Nothing can get in now."

"But some might still be in the area?"

"If they are, they're keeping their distance. But no one knows what they hoped to achieve by sneaking in. There were too few of them to inflict any serious damage, unless they didn't know the rest of us had come back. It makes me think they were attempting a stealth mission."

"What for?"

"To steal something. That's what Murray says. I know I'm not supposed to talk about it, but I don't know what he hoped to achieve by keeping things from you. You've seen the world outside. You aren't like Elle." A shake of the head. "He means well, but he shelters us too much, and her most of all."

"You can't blame him for that," I say. "All they have is each other, right?"

"True. But he thinks pretending the past doesn't exist is the only way to move forward. I have a bad feeling the fiends don't agree. If they're experimenting again, it's only a matter of time before they make another offensive attack. We have to be ready."

A rustle beneath his cloak reveals the papers he picked up from the research building. He skims through them, frowning. In the dimming light, it's impossible for me to read them.

"What exactly are those?"

"Notes on Transcendent experiments. I know Murray wouldn't want to leave them where the enemy could get at them. I'm surprised they were still there. The enemy would never have let anything useful lie around, especially if they're performing similar experiments themselves."

"Wait, what? The fiends are creating a Transcendent? So they do have human intelligence?"

"That was the biggest mistake we made," says Nolan. "We assumed our own experiments would be of no interest to the enemy. The fiends are unintelligent creatures with no interest in science. But when we were betrayed…" He lifts his head to look in Cas's direction. "There were unforeseen consequences."

"Betrayed?" I echo. "How?"

"Another senior Pyro saw that we were losing, tried to make an alliance with the enemy. We think he must have shared some information. And… and if they're doing *this,* then they might have been one step ahead of us for longer than we thought."

I don't know what to say. I've not been with the Pyros for long, yet it's the closest to normality that I've experienced in this new world, the closest to order and purpose. I can't imagine anyone I've met so far turning traitor. Who'd help the enemy after what they did to Earth?

"Sorry for freaking you out," says Nolan. "When that thing appeared, Cas damn near threw himself into the divide. If we lose our lives carelessly, then who will be left to fight? I vouched for you when Val was trying to persuade Murray to let you come outside, but I never expected this."

"You asked him to let me come?"

"I told you, he's worried. But you've proven yourself. A bit more weapon training and you'll be ready for the big missions. I just hope I'm wrong and the enemy doesn't have hold of our technology. The last thing we need is them to find a Transcendent of their own."

"How *can* they tell?" That part, I don't understand.

Nolan shakes his head. "If we knew more about how the fiends operated... they track humans by scent, so perhaps that has something to do with it. They can always tell Pyros from ordinary humans."

"Is there a specific criteria for being Transcendent?" I ask. "Because Cas isn't—is he?" Nolan knows about his healing power. But if that doesn't make him Transcendent, what *is* Cas?

"Cas is... a special case." He looks ahead, and my eyes follow his gaze towards the hills. Cas has disappeared.

"Where did he go?"

It's dark now, or as dark as it gets in a world where the sky's eternally red. The sun has slipped out of sight, and a cool breeze sweeps the dry grass flat and ripples over the surface of the water below the cliff. The sea moves continually, pulled towards the edge of the divide.

"Idiot," Nolan mutters.

"Have you both always lived with the Pyros?" I ask.

"Cas has been there since forever. I joined when I was fourteen. I was orphaned and my uncle was Murray's assistant. He was the one who found me." He shrugs. "It was the only option. Luckily they signed me up before I could accidentally give myself away."

I watch him as he kicks up dust with his boots, wondering if that easy confidence hides something else. Everyone at headquarters has secrets. I think of the novices and wonder how little they know of what's really going on. Would they be as keen to go out in the field if they knew the enemy might have a weapon we could never hope to beat?

A screech sounds behind us, high and insistent.

"Crap," says Nolan.

Another fiend. Several, judging by the cries. *Did using that power attract them?*

With a nod of understanding, I start to run.

We make it. Just. Crossing the stepping-stones is even worse than the first time, with the knowledge that the fiends are right on our heels, but with Nolan's help, I make it across. Cas has already disappeared, his cloak a red blot on the hillside as he climbs alone, not on the path but recklessly pulling himself up the rock face with his bare hands.

"And he says I have a death wish," I mutter.

"Cas hasn't got a normal sense of what constitutes danger," says Nolan. "Murray says he's a born Pyro soldier, but sometimes I get the feeling he doesn't know how to be a normal *person*."

I've been getting the same impression. Except those few times I detected a joke hidden in one of his barbed comments, I felt like I talked to someone with a one-track mind focused only on killing. But I can't help being curious as to how Cas ended up like that. Everyone suffered through the same tragedy, after all, and Nolan's still friendly, Murray's still welcoming, and Elle is the most innocent of anyone I've met in this new world. But maybe I'm overthinking it. If Cas has no intention of letting anyone in, is there any point in me wondering?

We finally reach the cave entrance into the mountain. Murray stands waiting for us, his face creased in worry.

"Where's Cas?" is the first thing he asks.

"Didn't he come in? He was just ahead of us," says Nolan.

Murray shakes his head. "What happened?"

"I'll explain," I say, shooting Nolan a silencing look. If there's anything else he and Cas didn't tell me, now's my chance to get answers. I quickly tell Murray what we saw, including the fiend. Before I can get to the part about what I did, we reach his office. Elle runs out, sees me, and throws herself at me. It takes me by surprise, so I stumble back.

"Are you okay?" Her voice is high with worry. "You were gone *ages*. I thought you wouldn't make it by sunset."

"We just beat it," I say. Nolan's warning about not spreading information comes back, and I decide to ask Murray about Transcendence when we're alone. Maybe then he'll be straight with me.

"What happened?" Elle repeats Murray's question.

"Found the lab, Nolan and Cas picked up some papers. And a fiend attacked us from the divide. We killed it." I don't know how much I'm allowed to tell her. Nolan, meanwhile, hands over the papers. The one with the flame symbol isn't there—Cas must have it.

Murray's face is grave. "It's happening," he says. "They've got an advantage over us now. I'll send out some more patrols tomorrow to make sure none survived the attack the other week. We can't afford to risk any being near the base. Not now we have this information."

"What, you think they're going to steal it?" I ask. "What if they already saw it? That lab was right next to the divide, right?"

Those fiends were close by. If they're really close to human intelligence, surely they'd searched the place.

All eyes turn to me.

"She has a point," Nolan says. "I admit, I thought it would be gone."

"And yet there were no signs of the enemy, aside from the one fiend?"

"None."

"That's perplexing," says Murray. "Fine. I'll spread the information and organise tomorrow's patrols. But we need to be careful."

"Some of us need to be more careful than others." Nolan glances at me.

"What?" I say. "I didn't take anywhere near as many risks as Cas did."

"Cas is a special case," says Murray.

"So everyone keeps telling me." An inexplicable feeling of anger clenches my muscles. "He said I'd damage your reputation if I go outside again."

"He said what?" Murray blinks at me, shocked.

"Oh, quit your whining," says a voice. Cas appears behind us, his face a hard mask.

"Cas," says Murray, in relief. "There you are."

"Yes, and I have something you may find useful." He hands over the piece of paper with that flame-like symbol on the back. Perhaps it's my imagination, but it seems to flicker in the light. Like fire.

Murray hisses out a breath. Elle blinks, looking confused.

"That's all we got," says Cas. "But I can go back and look for more tomorrow."

"Not if there are more of those fiends around," says Nolan.

Cas glares at him.

Murray sighs. "You're not invincible. Even you."

"I beg to differ." Cas absently runs his hand over the edge of the blade at his waist. *Pyro ashes and blood.*

Heat rushes up my arms and fire dances to the surface of my skin. The distant sound of a drumbeat echoes in my ears, and I feel the hint of a vibration beneath my feet. My hand's on my own weapon before I even realise it's moved.

What the hell is happening?

"Stop that," I say.

Cas turns on me, hand dropping to his side. "What's your problem?"

"Didn't you feel that?"

"Feel what?" He sheathes the blade.

"That," I whisper, holding a trembling hand out. The curl of a flame still hovers near the surface of my palm.

"You need to learn to control yourself," he says, curtly, and walks away.

I turn back to Murray. "Did you see that?"

His face is ghostly pale. He saw, all right. His head jerks in a nod.

"It happened when the fiend touched me," I say, watching his expression carefully. "There was this... vibration, in the air, and a light, and the fiend—it fell to pieces. I did that." My voice lowers with every sentence, and the anger drains out of me at the memory. What if it *did* happen again?

"It's a defence mechanism," says Murray. Is it just me, or is his voice shaking? "You're—well, awakening."

"What?" I blink. "As a Pyro? Or—or a Transcendent?" I'm conscious of Elle and Nolan watching, but desperate enough not to care.

"Maybe both." Apparently, it doesn't come as a surprise to him that I know what a Transcendent is. "Can you leave us?" Murray asks Nolan and Elle. "I want to talk to Leah alone."

Nolan gives me a concerned look and Elle hangs back, biting her lip, but they leave the office.

I turn back to Murray. "Please tell me you meant what you said about it being a defence mechanism. I don't want to *kill* Cas."

Or maybe some part of me did. But that's no laughing matter at all.

"It shouldn't activate around other Pyros," says Murray, a frown spreading across his face.

"Did the other Transcendent tell you that? How much do you know? I'm the only one, right?"

He nods tightly. "I suspected your case was an odd one, but I didn't want to speak to you until I was sure. The last Transcendent died—I don't know if Nolan told you that."

"He did," I say. "He said she died on the front lines during the invasion."

"She did," Murray says, heavily. "The important thing is establishing how extensive your powers are, but we can't test the energy blast in an enclosed place like this."

I guess he's warning me not to go practising on my own. As if I would. First Pyro, now super-Pyro? It's a little much for me to wrap my head around.

"The fiend knew," I say. "Could I always do it?" Horror shoots up my spine. *Did I cause the energy blast that killed Randy and the others? I can't have... I can't!*

"Leah, you haven't hurt anyone," says Murray, as though he's guessed what I'm thinking. "You only awakened as a Pyro after you survived the first energy blast. Your Transcendent powers must have come along later..." He trails off, frowning.

I relax. Slightly. "So I awoke as a Pyro back then, and I awoke as Transcendent... today? But that can't be right. The fiends have touched me before." Well, punched me. And there was that one that almost tore me to pieces. Before...

Murray's eyes widen. "Cas healed you, didn't he?"

"Yes," I say slowly, "But I don't see what that has to do with anything."

"You were close to death, but he brought you back. I've been a fool." He stands, running his hands through his hair. "I need to speak to Cas, now."

"What, you think that fiend gave me some kind of superpower? Or *Cas?*"

"I don't know what to think. But Leah, you are no danger to anyone. Don't worry."

Don't worry? After he just dropped that bombshell on me?

"And the last Transcendent?" I ask. "Did *she* hurt anyone?"

"Not intentionally."

"Not *intentionally?*" I can't believe we're even having this conversation. "Murray, if there's a chance I might be a danger to anyone here, I'm leaving. No question."

Murray's shoulders slump. "I'm sorry, Leah. The Transcendents disappeared generations ago, and we didn't expect to find another one. When we did, a few months before the fiends' invasion, it seemed too good to be true. We expanded the search for others, but when the Fiordans—the fiends' leaders—invaded Earth, we were forced to send the Transcendent into battle before we could fully assess her abilities."

"Nolan said she died closing the breach," I say. "Is that what stopped the invasion?"

Murray nods tightly. "It wasn't supposed to end in her death. But the fiends never should have amassed that much energy in the first place. We had little information to go by, because it had been so long since any Transcendents existed. All we had were old records, destroyed now, which said the

Transcendent was capable of harnessing the energy between the two worlds. We thought that meant she could close the bridge, and we turned out to be right... at the expense of her life."

My breath catches. "And if they invade again?"

Our eyes meet. I read the truth there: if I really *am* Transcendent, he'd give me the choice. Just like he let me choose whether to stay with the Pyros or walk away.

Except this time, the choice might be between the rest of humanity... and my own life.

CHAPTER THIRTEEN

I don't sleep that night.

Part of it's adrenaline from the last few hours. I'm *Transcendent,* whatever the hell that really means. Even though Murray reassured me I can't do any harm, my brain decides to replay the last energy blast whenever I close my eyes, so I give up on sleep. The idea of being a sacrifice doesn't appeal much either. Sure, the fiends haven't invaded in two years, but the one we ran into yesterday knew *something.*

The fiends are intelligent. They're not just random killers. And that makes them doubly dangerous.

Early the next morning, I speed-walk to Murray's lab, and collide with someone just leaving the office. Cas wears his customary scowl, but doesn't speak to me this time before marching off like I've mortally insulted him.

My head swims with new questions, despite the sleepless fog behind my eyes. Murray sees me standing outside and beckons me to come in.

"Is everything all right?"

"Are you joking?" I say. "I just found out I'm freaking artillery."

"That isn't true," Murray says. Papers are strewn all over his desk. "We fully intend to defeat the fiends before it ever comes to the point of another mass attack on humanity. As it is, Leah, you've earned the right to come to meetings with the senior Pyros, if you like. You'll have access to the same information we do."

Mollified, I nod.

"For now, you're in training. The quicker you advance, the quicker we can determine what your abilities are."

Guess I can't argue with that.

"Go to the training hall. I already told Val what happened; she can set you up with some training exercises. We'll help you control this, Leah. Don't worry."

At least training takes my mind off things. I nearly jump out of my skin when I take hold of the same knife I used to fight yesterday and it reacts to my touch, flaring bright red.

"That's new," says Val, frowning. "I've never seen someone bond to a weapon so quickly."

"Bond to it?" I say, staring as the silver coating peels away from the blade before my eyes, revealing the reddish colour beneath.

"You can channel your power through a weapon of your choice. Normally we'd trial you with all of them first, but you seem to have adapted to that knife."

I turn the knife over in my hand. It looks more like a piece of sharpened rock now. The hilt fits to my hand perfectly, like it was made for me. *Stupid thought. You've only used it twice.*

"So I can't use any other weapon?"

"You can, but it makes sense to play to your strengths. Besides, try letting go of it now."

I blink at her, quizzically. "How d'you mean?"

"Trust me. Let go of the hilt."

I'm sceptical, but I do as she says and unfold my fingers from the hilt. The knife stays stuck to my palm.

"Oh, wow." I turn over my hand, palm upwards, and the knife stays there. Experimentally, I use my left hand to take it, and the spell's broken. But when I unfold the fingers on my left hand, the knife remains stuck.

"Neat, isn't it?"

"This is crazy." But a smile steals onto my face, the first since everything that happened yesterday. The feel of the knife in my hand gives me a sense of control. *I can control this. I will control this.*

Val spends the rest of the morning teaching me more fighting techniques, before caving in and moving onto the use of my fire-calling power. She teaches me how to focus, like in the meditation exercises, and to move the fire from my skin to the blade, though we keep well away from anything flammable. It's all I can do not to get distracted by the mesmerising patterns of flame as the knife swings and arches through the air.

"Don't use it unless you're under attack," Val says. "But you're allowed to keep the knife with you at all times now. Even in the dormitory."

"What, does Murray think we're likely to be attacked?"

"There are still fiends unaccounted for around the base," she says. "It's better to be careful. Just don't go threatening Garry with it." She grins.

"Like I would," I say, grinning back.

But when I return to the dorm to change, everyone falls silent as I enter the room. Whispers follow me around all day, making me wonder how much people know about what happened.

Bored with the stares, I seek out Elle. I have the afternoon free while she has classes, so I hang about outside the classroom, practising swinging the knife into an imaginary fiend. When the novices stand and start to file out of the room, I stop, returning the blade to the handy belt at my waist. I can't get over how easy it is to move in this uniform, despite its bulky appearance.

"Elle," I say, catching her arm. "Can we talk?"

"Sure."

Several of the other novices dodge around me, and I see ducked heads and frowns as they converge together into groups. I'm not imagining it—they *are* avoiding me. Even Poppy doesn't meet my eyes as she walks past.

Elle's as chatty as ever, babbling about whatever she learned about in class while we try to find a place to talk alone. Now the walkway at the back is closed off, we're stuck inside the mountain. We find an alcove in the wall.

"Why's everyone avoiding me?" I say. "What do they think happened yesterday?"

Elle's face falls. "I thought you'd ask that. I don't know how, but a rumour got out about you and Cas."

Whatever I expected to hear, that wasn't it. My mouth falls open. "W*hat?*"

"Because he healed you, and that made you Transcen—"

She cuts herself off before she can finish, but I know what she was going to say.

"Transcendent," I say. "So, that's how it is. They think *Cas* did it."

Her gaze is fixed on the floor, small hands clenched into fists. "I'm so sorry. Murray didn't want me to say, but—"

"Stop," I say. "Let's backtrack a bit. I thought Transcendents were born that way. Not made."

Except Murray *said* he didn't know.

"It's kind of complicated," says Elle. "My dad was looking at the research again yesterday and his new theory's that when Cas healed you, it caused a transfer of energy that gave you the same abilities he has."

"But I thought he wasn't Transcendent."

Elle fidgets. "No, but he has these other powers, and we think the energy combined. Transcendents are only advanced Pyros, not a whole new species."

"He can heal. Why?"

More fidgeting. "I don't—you'll have to ask my dad."

I feel bad for interrogating her—but not bad enough to stop.

"Okay. I just wondered. So do people think I'm dangerous?"

"No one really understands Transcendence, not even my dad," says Elle. She's still fidgeting, which means she's hiding something. "But you're not dangerous. They're being stupid. It's because Cas—you know. He's not friendly."

"Great, so they think we're BFFs now?"

A smile touches her mouth. "Well, you're both kinda scary."

"Seriously?" I shake my head. "I'll have to put them right on that one. I just freaked out a bit. People keep telling me I can't hurt anyone, but what if I'm around, you know, normal people again?"

"You'll be fine. It's just about control."

That's not very reassuring, considering that in all likelihood, the next time I encounter normal people—I can't think of them as *humans*, distinct from Pyros—will be when I'm protecting them from the fiends. Not exactly a controlled situation.

"Leah, it's a good thing." I stiffen as Elle puts her arms around me. "It means you can help us. It means you might be our hope."

"I can't—I can't." I step back, away from her. The alcove suddenly feels too confining. "I can't have people depending on me."

Fighting for humanity is one thing, but the last thing I need is people looking to me to save them. Not when I already let down everyone who mattered to me. Not when people died and I lived.

Don't these people matter to you? a voice in my head asks. And I can't answer. Despite my promise not to become attached to strangers again, this past month has been like living a life I thought I'd lost. Joking with Elle and Tyler, messing around with Poppy in training, talking to Nolan and Val. Even fighting alongside Cas. These experiences are a part of me now, and I can't cut them away.

But neither can I be their saviour.

"I can't do it," I say.

"You can," says Elle. "Leah, you should just ignore what people like Cas say."

"It's not that." It's the idea of responsibility for others' lives. When I first joined Randy's group, people whispered that there must be some supernatural reason I survived the blast that destroyed my town, and seemed disappointed when

I turned out to be ordinary, and my sister died in my arms without me being able to save her.

But what did I expect when I signed up? That I'd somehow be able to make up for everything, just by fighting the fiends? I shake my head, disgusted with myself.

"Elle? Leah?" Nolan, who was walking past, stops to stare at us. "What are you doing in there?"

"Just talking," I say. I can't have everyone knowing I doubt myself, not if people really do think I can be some kind of saviour. I'm reminded of the people who insisted there was some purpose to the insanity when the energy blasts and natural disasters started, people who had faith that someone might appear and save us. No one did. And now we're the only hope humanity has.

I can't deal with that thought right now.

"Well, you're coming on the first scouting mission tomorrow, Leah."

"I am?"

"Murray said. Are you sure you're okay?"

I just nod, not meeting his eyes.

***

A body lies at my feet. Though it's burned almost beyond recognition, somehow I recognise… her? She reaches out, and I extend my hand, but as our fingertips touch, hers begin to crumble. Skin and bone become ash which floats away on the wind, like sand slipping through my fingers. A sob rises in my throat, but I don't know who I'm crying for.

I wake in darkness, sharply alert. When sleep refuses to come back, I go for a walk, fully dressed. Something itches beneath my skin, like I'm about to burst into flame again. Walking the empty corridors helps. I pace close to the railing, looking down at the lava stream below.

I stop. Someone's down there, perched on a rock. Cas.

Oh, crap.

I back away, but trip on a rock. The clattering sound echoes, and Cas raises his head. "What?"

"Nothing." I swallow, backing further away—but stop as I realise his outstretched hand is *underneath* the flow of lava pouring over the rocks in a miniature waterfall.

"Doesn't that hurt?" I ask, staring.

"What do you think?" He gives me that derisive look. "We don't burn. You can put your head under if you like."

"You're mad."

He moves towards the waterfall, ducks his head—and immerses it, like in water.

A gasp escapes me. "Cas!" Before I can think about what I'm doing, I vault over the railing and drop to the lava pool below. My feet catch on the edge of a rock, the shoes on my feet sizzling.

"I'm fine," he says, pulling his head out of the lava. "See?"

His face gleams with liquid rock, and he wipes the lava away with a hand. It looks so ridiculous, I have to laugh.

"You like to stick your head in lava for *fun?*" I ask.

He just shrugs. I study his face. It's difficult to see from here, but it's one of the rare times he isn't wearing a frown or a flat-eyed stare. An improvement.

Except... damn. I have to find out if what Elle said was true. If Cas's the reason I'm supposedly Transcendent, why does he hate me so much? Does he really regret saving my life... or what?

I fidget, shifting closer to the lava stream. Cas has something in his other hand. His knife.

"What're you doing with that?" I ask, indicating the gleaming sword.

Cas glares. Great. Now things are back to normal.

"Come on. You can't expect me not to be curious."

"No, I expect you to keep your nose out of my business."

I cross my arms. "I'm a little tired of you people keeping secrets from me. Did they say the same to you when you joined up?"

Too late, I remember he didn't join. He was born into it. So are his parents dead?

"I don't see why I should waste my time answering your questions. You keep playing with fire, you'll get burned."

"Says the guy who stuck his head in lava." Now I'm pissed off enough to stick around and poke him until he gives me answers. He's enough of an asshole I don't feel bad about it. "Seriously. If I'm supposedly so dangerous, why the hell would Murray even let me stay? I doubt he likes me enough to risk killing all of you."

"He's an idealistic moron," says Cas. "He's letting you stay for the precise reason he's let *me* stay here so long. Any hint that you might be a danger to everyone and he'll have you locked in one of those cages."

I stare at him. He's breathing heavily, one hand resting on the blade.

"So that's it," I say. "You and I aren't the same as the others. Elle told me," I add as he gives me a sharp look. "There's no point in hiding it. What the hell did you do to me?"

"Saved your worthless life." Cas spits the words out. "Nolan pushed me into it, the idiot. He has no clue."

"Then tell me," I say.

"You want to know that you're cursed."

I blink, not following his words.

"Does that mean 'Transcendent'?" I ask. "I thought you weren't—"

"I'm not," he says, bluntly. "There are other so-called gifts besides yours, you know."

"Like what?"

He narrows his eyes and doesn't answer.

"If anyone gets killed because of me, I'm blaming you," I snarl, having had enough. "I can't read minds, Cas. I don't give a crap about your reasons."

"This is war," he says.

"I'm aware of that," I say, "but it seems a pretty big disadvantage if one of your warriors kills people on *our* side. You said you're as dangerous as I am. What did the fiend do to me?"

No answer.

"Tell me," I say softly. "Tell me what I am. Give me a straight answer."

"There *is* no straight answer," he says. "I am not Transcendent, but I'm no Pyro in the ordinary sense." His mouth twists in a mockery of a smile. "You want to know the truth, Transcendent? The Pyros created me. But their scientists learned the hard way that Transcendents can't be engineered. Most died. You saw that body in the cave? That was one of them. They were still doing the same experiments when I was a kid, because I didn't meet their expectations. I didn't pick up any of the Transcendent abilities except healing. I never intended to transfer my power to you, but Nolan *insisted* I save your life. Apparently, I did more than that. Looks like you're the missing link."

The world tilts beneath my feet, the breath catches in my lungs. He's still speaking, but what he says is impossible. *Impossible.*

Engineered Transcendent. Energy transferred.

"You... knew?"

"I suspected," he says. "We already knew Transcendents can't be engineered through unnatural means. But blood transfer... apparently that's the key. It's not as though I make a habit of using it."

No. I guess not. My heart sinks, settling somewhere at the base of my spine. "I can heal," I say quietly. "I can create... energy blasts. But can't I die? I'm not—immortal, am I?"

"Oh, we can die." His sharp gaze pins me to the spot. "It's just very difficult to kill us. Even for the fiends."

"Because we heal," I whisper. Already images are filling my head. I look away, swallowing hard. Will I have to watch everyone I love perish, again, turned to ash before my eyes, expire in my arms like my sister? I grip the railings for support, the metal digging into my flesh. Short breaths come out, one after another. I wanted to live. But if everyone I know dies, what is there to live for in this world?

But I'm not alone. He's the same as I am.

And that just makes it worse.

"Does that answer your question? Are you happy, now you know you're not human anymore?"

"Stop it," I say, possibly too loud. I don't want anyone else to know this. "I thought none of us were human, anyway." I silently curse my shaking voice.

"Superhuman," he says. "If you want to use idiotic human terms."

"You really don't like people, do you?" I shake my head.

"They die," he says. "The fiends might be stupid, but they decimated the human race within a week. We're no threat to them." His fist clenches and he punches the rock wall with a force that makes the path above shake. "You still think of yourself as human, but you'll outlive every one of them. Even the Pyros. There's no point in forming attachments to collateral damage."

"That isn't..." He's so close to my own train of thought, it's almost scary. "That's not the point of living," I say, finally, as the silence becomes unbearable.

He looks away. Fragments of rock drop from his hand.

"I wouldn't know, since I'm not technically alive."

What can I say to that? I want to know more, about how they managed to create a person—using Pyro DNA or something, I guess, but I don't want to make him hate me again. I've never been good at giving advice, least of all when it comes to someone as volatile as... as a volcano.

"Whatever." He jumps onto the path in two leaps at the rock wall, something that would be impossible for a normal person. I curse myself for not being able to say anything to help. But I can't think clearly.

Who created him?

CHAPTER FOURTEEN

"You've got to be kidding me." Cas glares at Val. "I'm not working with her."

"Murray's orders," says Val. She's organising our patrol, trying to get everyone sorted, before we set out to search, once again, for the fiends that supposedly escaped. There are seven of us in total, and I'm the youngest, aside from Poppy. I don't know any of the others—except, unfortunately, Cas.

My eyes sting with tiredness. It's the crack of dawn and the few hours of sleep I managed to snatch weren't enough. My hands are clumsy as I check the position of the knife at my waist, ready for me to snatch at the first sign of danger.

"Come on," says Val. "We've got to make a move. There's a town a mile or so away, that might be their target."

"If it is, we're too late," says Cas bluntly. "This is a fool's crusade."

"Murray's orders," says Val, apparently unintimidated. "If you want to stay here and destroy our training dummy collection, that's your call."

Cas narrows his eyes. But he doesn't protest further.

It's a long trip down the mountain, made longer by the fallen rocks from the fiend attack. It's caused more damage than I thought, and I wonder at the ability of even a mountain to stand up to the fiends. If enough of them came here, they could pulverise our shelter and us along with it. I try to find cheerier thoughts, and instead concentrate on my steps. Crossing the ocean isn't as bad this time around, but it's hard not to think of those fiends with wings, and how they must have flown across the water to the base. What other mutations could they come up with? My thoughts land on artificial warriors and blades made of blood and ashes.

To distract myself, I get in some practise with my knife while waiting for the others to catch up. Without the constraints of the training room, I get free rein to swing at rocks and watch them crumble at a touch. The blade slices the air with a fiery light. Caught in the movement, everything else fades into the background.

"You okay?" Val asks, coming over to me.

"Sure," I say. "Just a relief to get outside."

"Yeah, we'll get to see real civilisation today," she says, with a smile. Though it fades almost instantly. "As long as we make it there in time."

A condescending snort behind us tells me Cas is listening in.

"What?" I say. "You might think humans are worthless, but I'll bet the feeling's mutual."

I deliberately raise my voice so the other Pyros nearby can hear, determined to wipe out any rumours we're buddies.

"It's human inventions that have kept us alive this long," Val adds. "Like the technology that keeps our base running."

"About that," I say. "Why don't you have any kind of transport? You have working lights, why not cars?"

"Up a mountain?" Now Cas is actually smirking at me. I clench my fist, wishing I could slam it into his face.

"Fine. What about air transport? Some of the fiends can fly. I saw," I add, and his expression becomes serious again. And angry.

"No, we don't," says Val, with a slight sigh. "Those of us who had cars lost them in the first attacks. Our base isn't a practical location for any kind of transport, and we have no contact with anyone overseas." She glances at the stepping stones, where the last of the Pyros has crossed. "We'd better move."

We take off to the west. This time we aren't heading for the divide, but to the empty road we walked down when I first joined camp and walked to the base. It seems a lifetime ago already.

"She has a point," I mutter to Cas—somehow we've ended up walking alongside one another. "Why're you going to the bother of coming with us if you think everyone's doomed, anyway?"

"None of your business."

Well, that's friendly. I side-eye him. "I'm not ruling out using the energy blast on you."

"You can't kill me," he says, but his tone isn't completely flat. Wait, is that *jealousy* in his expression? I suppose, from what he said last night, he's spent his whole life thinking of himself as a failed attempt at creating the world's saviour. Then I came along and turned out to be Transcendent by accident.

Hmm. No wonder he's pissed at me. I might find it almost funny, if not for the fact that the burden rests on *me* now. *I'm Transcendent.* But what does that mean? Cas's blood healed me… but at what cost to both of us?

A line of fire on the horizon grabs my attention.

Val swears. "That's the town."

For a moment, horror freezes me in place. Then, like the others, I break into a run.

I already know we're too late. The town's burning. Not an energy blast. Real fire reaches arms into the sky, a burning beacon that engulfs every building, growing larger with each passing second.

We don't need to enter to know nobody will have survived.

A choked sob from Poppy. "No," she whispers. "Who could have done this?"

The monsters, I think immediately. And then start when I realise Cas hasn't stopped, and continues to walk towards the town.

Despite myself, I follow. He stops a metre from the town's boundary, the wired fence that once formed a meagre protection against the monsters.

"I figured you'd come after me."

"Only to make sure you weren't about to walk into the flames."

"They'd have no effect," says Cas. "You know that."

Yes. It slipped my mind, stupidly. But now my eyes are on the ground, and the familiar outline of a symbol shaped like a flame. It's been drawn in the mud. With a stick, I'd guess.

"What *is* that?" I ask.

"Trouble," says Cas, finally turning back to meet my eyes.

"No shit." I wonder about shoving him into the flames until he tells me the truth. Last night only scratched the surface. But the smell of burning engulfs me as a nearby house succumbs to the climbing fire. I have to back away, old grief threatening to rise. *Focus. This means trouble.*

Cas watches me, his face tense. "It's a diversion. We have to get back to the base."

CHAPTER FIFTEEN

I've never run so fast. Dirt pounds under my feet. Wind roars in my ears. My coat streams back, like fire, and I wish I could propel myself forwards. I wish I had wings. Feet aren't fast enough.

The journey takes too long. I even forget to be afraid as we cross the water. My heart sinks to my feet when I spot the winged shape circling the mountain's tip.

Cas is miles ahead of the rest of us, but even he won't get there in time. Blood streaks the ground, the mud marked with claw-marks. The fiends have been here. But what about our defences? Questions war with one another in my mind. *I thought no one could get in.* But they're one step ahead of us…

The entrance appears intact. Cas leads the way, knife raised, ready to attack. It seems too quiet, with none of the usual bustle.

They can't all be dead!

A faint noise sounds from behind a nearby door—Murray's study. My stomach clenches.

Cas moves towards the door and pushes it open. I follow more slowly, heart beating a warning in my ears.

Elle crouches on the ground, a tall figure stooped over her. No sign of Murray.

"Who the hell are you?" Cas demands of the man. He isn't one of the Pyros, or at least no one I recognise. His dark red coat is similar in style to ours, and the knife in his hand is rust-red. Like Cas's.

The stranger looks up, his hood falling back. His head's shaved, and his eyes are piercing and grey. His gaze passes over me and locks on Cas. A smile curls his lip.

"You," he says. "I should have known."

For the first time since I've met him, Cas looks genuinely shocked. His hand actually slips on the weapon, but he manages to conceal it by catching the knife's hilt and pointing it at the other man's face.

"Jared?"

"Surprised to see me alive?"

"I'm surprised you'd show your face around here." Cas's tone is cold as ice, but the temperature in the room kicks up a notch. Smoke starts to rise from the knife in his hand.

"I came here to find you," says Jared. "I should have guessed they'd send their best warrior out."

"Then why were you threatening a defenceless girl?"

Elle whimpers. I move over to her, concerned, but she appears unhurt.

"Leah," she whispers. "Don't let him take Cas."

I blink, confused. Cas doesn't look like he's going anywhere. He and Jared stare at each other. I put two and two together—didn't Cas and Nolan ask that fiend if Jared was alive? Is he one of the other Pyros? The traitor, even?

I draw my own knife. The movement seems to break the two men out of their trance. Jared takes one step towards Cas, while I stand, my knife pointed at Jared's back. Before I can think about what I'm doing, the tip of my knife brushes his spine.

He tilts his head to look back at me. "And you are...?"

"Tell me who *you* are," I say, relieved when my voice doesn't shake. I don't know what powers this guy might be hiding, but for the first time it dawns on me that I'm not afraid. Not driven by adrenaline like in a fight, but genuinely unafraid for my life. Is this what it feels like to be Cas?

"I'm here to see Cas. And a girl." Something flashes in his eyes. "That wouldn't happen to be you, would it?"

"You don't know anything about me."

"I know the Pyros have found their Transcendent," he says. "That's you. Right?"

"I don't see what it matters to you." I move the knife, brushing it against his spine.

"I wouldn't do that if I were you," he says, quietly. "Do you want me to reduce this place to ashes?"

Can he do that? Who knows what powers he's hiding?

I lower the knife.

"Better," he says. "Now. We're going to talk. You see, Murray and I had an understanding. The last Transcendent caused a little accident that did some severe damage. I'm guessing by your age that you would have seen it on the news."

The energy blasts? The earthquakes? Or the coming of the fiends? My mind reels. *The Transcendent caused that? I thought she gave her life to close the door to the fiends' world.*

"Yes, I thought Murray would have lied to you. Shameful, really. But his daughter knows."

He reaches back and grabs Elle by the scruff of her neck. She yelps as he lifts her into the air.

"Yes, fortunate that I found you snooping around, isn't it?" says Jared. "What were you looking at? These old papers?"

He shoves a stack of documents off the desk. They're the papers Cas and Nolan found in the old house, I realise. I never got a close look at them.

"They're useless," says Jared. "Why do you think we left them behind?"

"I would have expected you to hide the evidence," says Cas. "The fiend told me you still lived, though I never would have believed it. I knew you were the one poking around the old labs, though you tried to pin the blame on the fiends. You forget I know you."

Elle sobs. Jared shakes her. "Pipe down. I don't want to hurt you."

"Uncle Jared…"

I freeze. My heart sinks in my chest.

Her uncle? Murray's brother?

"Quiet," he says, again. "You two—" he turns to face Cas—"Are coming with me. In fact, I'll bring little Elle, too. That ought to give Murray an incentive."

"I'm not going anywhere with you," Elle screams, thrashing around. Maybe she thinks her uncle won't hurt her. But I can't be sure of that. Suddenly things make a lot more sense. Murray's own brother betrayed him. That's why everyone avoided the subject. That's why Murray is so overprotective of Elle.

But what really happened two years ago?

"You don't own me," Cas says, quietly.

"I had more than a fair share in your creation. Doesn't that make me your master?"

Cas's words come out from between clenched teeth. "I'd be careful what you say."

"Such a *waste* of potential. You could really have been something great. Shame you were too weak to—"

Jared's voice cuts off in a gurgle as Cas slides his knife around the still-struggling Elle to point it at his neck. I can't breathe. One wrong movement from any of us and Elle could be impaled.

"Watch it," Cas breathes. "You created me to be a weapon superior to any other Pyros, including you."

"And you'd kill this girl to get to me?"

He throws Elle forwards, right into the path of the knife. My breath catches, but Cas's already pulled the weapon back, faster than I can blink. Elle lets out a squeak as she begins to fall, but Jared grabs her again.

Cas stands back, breathing heavily.

"Put the knife away," says Jared. "The same goes for you, girl. I need you to come with me. I need the Transcendent."

"What do you need me for?" I'm playing for time, trying to figure out how to get him to let Elle go.

"You're on the wrong side, girl. Both of you are. You have no idea what you could be. Murray's been feeding you lies. What's he told you, that you can defend humanity? The fiends are superior to the Pyros in every way. You can't win this fight with Murray and his pathetic hangers-on."

"Oh, really?" says Cas, one eyebrow raised. "And you think you can offer us a better deal?"

"You fail to see the bigger picture. But I suppose we did *make* you." He moves forward, Elle still dangling from his grip, and Cas's forced to pull his knife back.

"You were born to die, and you know it. How does that make you feel? Do you like being around these noisy, helpless humans?"

"What I think is none of your business. You're not welcome here."

"No," says another voice, "You aren't."

Murray stands in the doorway, wielding twin swords, the side of his head covered in dried blood. "Let go of my daughter, Jared."

"Or what? I hear you've grown soft. You wouldn't kill me, Murray."

"I wish you had died that day." Murray's tone is flat, but he can't keep a twitch of emotion out of his expression.

"Apparently one of our experiments worked." Jared laughs humourlessly. "Too bad just being indestructible isn't enough—as this one knows already." He gestures at Cas. "What's the good of not being able to die if you can't get what you want?"

"You fail to understand, as usual, brother," says Murray. "Turning yourself and others into monsters won't win you this war."

"And you think the Transcendent can?" There's a manic gleam in his eyes. "You might have abandoned experiments after our little *accident*, but I won't let things get out of hand. Let me take your Transcendent. And this one, too. Otherwise the girl dies."

"Jared," says Murray, starting to look nervous. "You don't want to do this."

Jared laughs. "You think I'm just going to walk out? I could destroy your people, but I've spared you. Maybe I won't be so generous next time. You're only safe because the fiends don't think you're worth destroying. Why should they sacrifice themselves when you're powerless to stop them from destroying humans anyway? How many lives have you even saved?"

"Stop." Murray's hands shake; sweat glistens on his forehead.

"Wake up, brother," Jared says, softly.

Elle chokes as Jared's grip moves to her throat.

Murray's eyes flicker from Jared to Elle. I feel so powerless, and a quick glance at Cas tells me he feels the same. If only there was something we could do to intervene without him hurting Elle.

"How did you know?" he asks, defeat seeping into his expression.

"About the Transcendent? My spies trailed the team who investigated the old lab. Killing one of my fiends confirmed her power. This girl is Transcendent: make no mistake."

"And what do you want with her?" For the first time, Murray looks at me.

Do something! But he's helpless as the rest of us, unless he's just stalling for time.

Jared opens his mouth to answer, and Elle elbows him in the face.

Somehow she's managed to move into an attacking position, and the blow knocks him back long enough for her to wriggle free. She runs to her father, as Cas steps in and presses his knife to Jared's throat.

"Enough," he says, other hand grabbing Jared's flailing wrist and squeezing, hard. "Enough, or I'll break every bone in your body."

"You think you can kill me? I created you."

"And I'll end you."

A trickle of blood runs from the edge of the blade. It's starting to smoke. Jared lets out a choked sound as the burning blade presses against his skin.

"Leave, Jared," says Murray, suddenly sounding incredibly tired. "Leave, and I'll spare your life. It would be easier if I killed you, but I don't want your blood on my hands."

"How pathetic," Jared spits. "For someone who claims to lead an army, you do an admirable job of staying in denial. We all have blood on our hands." He hisses with pain as Cas's blade burns his skin.

"Get out," says Murray, lowering his two swords. "Now."

Cas obliges, using the blade's position on Jared's neck to steer him towards the door. Jared's eyes blaze with hatred, but he has no choice but to move. Elle watches him with frightened eyes. I hold my own blade out, just in case, but he makes no sudden moves to attack.

A sound outside. Did someone hear what was going on?

Jared pauses, a flicker of a smile on his face. "Did you think I came alone?"

A moment's pause, everything frozen in the fragment of a second.

Then a roar shatters the silence. In a blur, Jared moves, ducking Cas's blade, and runs from the room. Swearing, Cas takes off after him. I run, my hand tingling on the hilt of my knife as it welds itself to me. Flames flicker along the blade.

I run out of the room to find Cas standing on the edge of the railing, swinging his knife at the attackers. Three winged fiends circle the corridor, too high to reach. My heart jumps to my mouth as Cas's feet wobble, dangerously close to toppling over the railing.

One of the fiends sees me and dives. I raise the blade, scoring a line across its leg, but its weight drives me back into the rock wall. The fiend staggers, dripping blood, its muscled form hunched on the edge of the platform. Hissing, it swipes with a claw, but I'm ready. I push its claw easily away with the side of my blade and quickly slash at its vulnerable face. Bright-red blood spurts from the cut. My skin tingles all over.

I'm not even hurt this time. Not now that I'm Transcendent. Indestructible.

I concentrate on the power, the bond between me and the weapon in my hand. Fire flares up, red flames dancing along the blade, and the smell of burning fills the air. The smell of being alive.

The weapon blurs in my hands. I'm fast enough to block the fiend's attack the instant it moves to strike. I knock the fiend's claws aside, but another pair of claws just miss my face. A second fiend hovers above the first, bat-like wings blocking the light. How many are there? For a second, the thrill of battle leaves me. I can't let the fiends hurt anyone. I can't let anyone die again.

The air lights up. Everything glows the fierce colour of sunset. The fiend screeches, tiny eyes screwed up as though it can't stand the brightness—but I can't risk my powers causing any damage in here. I falter, hand trembling on the weapon's hilt, and the second fiend dives without warning. I barely manage to lift the blade to meet its outstretched claws. Although the dagger doesn't break, I'm sent hurtling back under the fiend's impact. If not for the strange connection fusing my hand to the blade, I would have dropped it.

Momentarily stunned, I lift my head to see Cas in the act of jumping off the railing, kicking into the air. He rises two metres, maybe more—far higher than a normal human can jump—and even the other fiends pause to watch as his blade meets its target. He slashes the second fiend's wing, then starts to fall.

The breath catches in my chest. But he drops as fast as he jumps, and his feet hit the other side of the chasm. Safe. I breathe out.

Idiot. Get them while they're distracted.

The first fiend's still injured, leaving a trail of blood along the edge of the platform. It swings around as I attack it, so the blow glances harmlessly off its side. My second strike catches it in the face, but it only shakes its head like I stunned it. *How do I kill one of these?* Short of using my Transcendent power—and risking destroying my home—I don't know. This one's different. *Engineered,* I think.

"Come on, Transcendent!" a voice shouts. Jared.

He stands in the entryway, something tucked under his arm. And someone else is moving towards him, carrying two swords. Murray. Did he leave Elle behind?

I can't let him distract me. My blade scores another line across the fiend's bulging arm. Bat-like wings beating, it pulls back. But the second fiend's moved above me, and dives. Its fist catches me before I can dodge aside, and though I raise my knife, I'm sent head over heels into the dust. The impact shudders through my body and I gasp, the wind knocked out of me. As the two fiends soar at me, I roll over, kicking up at the nearest.

My feet connect and the kick sends it flying. *Holy crap.* I can do as much damage with my body as with my blade. *Of course I can.* Within seconds, the pain of hitting the ground fades and I'm on my feet again.

As if in response to my thoughts, fire flickers along my skin. The fiend expects me to slash with my knife, but instead I punch it in the side with my free hand. With a screech, the fiend beats its bat-like wings and retreats, letting its partner take its place.

They never used to work together. But they never used to have wings, either. These fiends are different, stronger. But I can take them down just as well as the others. I won't be beaten again.

I circle the other fiend as best I can on the platform. I get a couple of jabs in, which the fiend is too slow to block. Their advantage is brute strength, but it's nothing to a Pyro.

And even less to a Transcendent.

Another hit, this one to its face, creating a burn-mark on its stone-like skin. The fiend bares its teeth, a snarl building in its throat. I strike it again and again, leaving welts in place of bruises. Surely it can't last much longer…

That new, strange power's still there, beneath the surface. But I resist the desire to let the uncontrollable energy flood me in case I can't stop it.

The fiend falls to the ground in a heap of blood-red rock. I breathe in and out, swinging around to intercept the second one—but it's gone.

In fact, there's no sign of Jared, either. Or Cas. Did he get away, or did he make for other Pyros, who must be in their rooms, with no clue what's going on out here? I turn back to the fiend. Smoke rises from its skin. It's breaking apart, like the one I used the energy blast on.

I can't help watching in fascination. Its skin peels away, body crumbling to rock, to smaller rocks, to ash.

Find Jared.

I turn my back on the fiend and jump to my feet. Cas was fighting at the edge of the chasm, but there's no one there now. I run around the edge, but he's not below, either.

Where did they go?

I duck into the tunnel. The sounds of battle rise in my ears, and I quicken my pace. I run out onto the narrow path and nearly collide with Cas.

"Stay back," he hisses.

Yeah, I've heard that before. "Not happening," I say, peering round him, at the sheer drop into the valley. The sky is the colour of blood.

And Murray's further down, twin swords in hand, blocking Jared's path. No sign of the fiends.

"It's his fight," says Cas, seeing that I've moved.

The two brothers stand face to face. I can't see their expressions from here, but I wonder if Jared would stoop to killing his own brother. I know Murray wouldn't. Or do I? I didn't even know he *had* a brother.

"What did he take?"

"I don't know." Cas still has his knife out, in case he needs to step in. He could reach them in one jump; I know, having watched him take down that fiend in mid-air. Could I do the same?

"Don't," he says. "He's called the fiends off."

"Are there no more inside?"

"No."

Why would he just leave? It doesn't add up.

Not that he's going anywhere right now. Murray moves forward, and Jared laughs.

"You aren't going to hurt me with those sticks, brother." He raises his own weapon to match his brother's.

"You will return what you took," Murray responds. "Return it to me, and I'll let you go in peace."

"I'm afraid I can't do that. I need this information. If you aren't going to do anything useful with it, then I will."

"You're mad," Murray says, calmly. "What did you hope to achieve by coming here? Did you expect to just take two of my soldiers and leave?"

"I had a feeling you wouldn't be cooperative," says Jared, "so I left a prize for you. See if you can find it. If you're game, you can come and meet me at the place where this whole wonderful mess started."

A hand grabs at my ankle. I stumble, nearly falling over the edge—below, the sheer cliff tumbles down to nothing.

"Cas! Look out!"

He swings around, teeth bared in a snarl—but the ground shakes beneath our feet, the rock crumbling. I grab Cas for balance and he twists away, as though to yell at me to let go.

But suddenly there's nothing beneath our feet, and we're falling.

CHAPTER SIXTEEN

The air buffets me, sending my coat flying out, and my grip tightens on Cas's arm. Even though I should know the fall won't kill me, panic rises at the lack of control, of the ground approaching like a train at full-speed. A scream sticks in my throat, and before I can brace myself, the two of us slam into the ground.

The impact knocks the breath from my lungs and jars the bones in my body, but I roll over, unhurt, and turn to check on Cas. He's already on his feet, as though falling from a cliff is no big deal.

"Thanks," he says, glaring at me.

"What? That wasn't my fault."

I look up at the cliff, searching for Murray and Jared, but can't see them—the sloping cliff hides everything from view.

Cas's started climbing the cliff again. I reach up and grab a protruding piece of rock, using it to pull myself up. Rock-climbing without the fear of falling feels strange, but I keep hold of the knife, confident that it won't drop from my hand—just in case the fiends reappear. How many are there? Did they expect to kill us by knocking us down the cliff?

Finally, we reach the ledge, just as a fiend swoops down from behind. Its claws graze my head, but Cas swings his blade at it and decapitates it.

Holy wow.

The fiend's body crumbles, turning to rock before my eyes. I spot Murray, fighting another fiend. No sign of Jared. *Did he get away?*

Cas runs his knife through another fiend, then runs to help Murray. Not that he needs it—the two swords in his hands move in unison, leaving deep gouges. The fiend drops to its side, eyes blanked out, before crumbling into rock.

Murray lets the swords drop, breathing heavily.

"Where is he?"

Murray shakes his head. "Got away—should have expected a diversion."

"Idiot," Cas snarls.

I expect Murray to react to the insult, but he merely straightens, sheathing the swords. He looks strange carrying them. Strange, but somehow right. I've never seen him fight until now.

"So, what did he run off with?" Cas demands. "What did you let him take?"

Murray doesn't meet his eyes. "The research. And a weapon. He took it from the lab. I should have expected it…"

"*What* weapon?" Cas asks furiously.

"One we were making for the Transcendent."

My heart misses a beat. "What? How does that work? I thought *this*—" I hold up my own knife—"Was mine now. Like I bonded to it or something."

"We didn't expect that," says Murray.

I've no idea what he's talking about. "Shouldn't you be chasing Jared?"

"He flew away, on one of those fiends," says Murray.

"Great." Cas kicks viciously at a rock. "So you let the enemy get away, again. I want to know why he was so keen on taking me and the girl. As soon as you showed up, he ran off."

"He wouldn't have hurt me," says Murray, shaking his head. "And as to why he didn't take you, that may be because the weapon he stole will give him the power to overcome even a Transcendent."

"If he creates one of his own. You forget it didn't turn out so well last time."

He's talking about himself? His eyes are as unreadable as the rock wall. But suddenly, it makes sense. Murray's the leader, but I can't imagine him authorising cruel experiments. Cas said, *the Pyros created me.* Not Murray. No. Jared did, and now he's stolen one of our weapons.

"I fear he may have already succeeded."

My heart plunges. Another Transcendent? Like me, but created by the enemy—an enemy I didn't even know we had.

Cas's eyes narrow. "So why did he want to take me and the girl?"

"I have a name," I remind him. "And he said something about us being on the wrong side. What about that town? Did he start the fire?"

"Him, or his fiends." Murray shakes his head. "The ones that attacked were his genetic mutations. You knew, Cas, didn't you?"

"I figured," says Cas. "It spoke English. Nolan said the fiends might be making their own Transcendent, but I reckon that's what Jared wanted us to think, because we thought he was dead."

I look from one of them to the other. "So the fiends aren't making a Transcendent. Jared is?"

"He always has been," says Murray, running a weary hand through his greying hair. "That was the original goal. He used to capture fiends and experiment on them, too, trying to turn them against one another. He was convinced if we extracted all their secrets, we could create an army that could take down the regular fiends. Most of his experiments were dismal failures, but I begged him to stop, if just because he would have brought disaster upon all of us. I allowed him to continue in his cruelty when none of the other Pyros had any idea." His expression darkens. "After his death, I could have confided in a select few, but I didn't. I feared the consequences if someone took his ideas. They were well-meaning, in the beginning."

"They were madness," says Cas, his voice tight, "and you know it. Half the fiends out there in the wilderness are the monstrosities he lost control of when his ridiculous plans failed."

This is news to me. I stare at both of them. "The fiends are Jared's?"

"Some of them," says Murray. "He was desperate to find a way to out-manoeuvre the monsters before they exterminated humanity, and that's what almost destroyed us."

"Never mind that," Cas interrupts. "The real question is why he left his prize behind after going to all that trouble."

"He wanted the weapon," says Murray. "But... I don't know. He's supposed to be *dead.*"

"Clearly he's not," I say. "Did you *see* him die?"

"He disappeared when the breach closed," says Murray, and Cas shoots him a murderous look. *What—oh. The Transcendent died at the same time.* "There's been no sighting of Jared since, until now. Our focus was on the fiends—as it had to be."

"Jared's fiends? Or the others?" I've never thought of the fiends as anything other than purposeless killers, even now. But a *human,* or Pyro, giving them orders? A Pyro with resources like ours?

"Both," says Murray. "But I always saw the first fiend invaders as the main threat. We lost so many of our own last time, even the new recruits aren't enough to make up the difference. And if Jared provokes them…"

"Then we're screwed," says Cas.

"Pessimistic much?" I say, though this new information's changed the game entirely. The fiends have no limit, at least that I know of. Humanity's defence is reduced to a couple of hundred of us Pyros. The image of the monsters crawling out of the divide, knocking people aside like skittles, fills my head. Put an army like that in the hands of an enemy who has the exact same powers as ours and suddenly our training sessions look like nothing.

"We can still fight," I say. "We can stop him. Right?"

But neither Cas nor Murray respond, and we begin the long climb back up to headquarters in silence.

CHAPTER SEVENTEEN

As we reach the top, they start arguing. It takes me several attempts to ask an obvious question, as we pass by the boundaries.

"How did Jared even get in?"

Murray turns to look at me. "He knew about our defences."

"So why not use something different?" I say.

"Because he was supposed to be dead."

Murray doesn't speak another word until we reach the main chamber. Though the damage from the fight remains behind, the silence is eerie. Cas hasn't put away his weapon, and Murray carries his twin swords carefully as we make our way back to his office. *Elle,* I think, with a flicker of anger at Jared's nerve. He just walked in here.

And Murray *let* him. He really believed his brother was dead?

"Elle?" Murray calls, pushing the door open.

A whimper answers. My blood freezes, and I pull my knife from my belt with shaking hands. Elle wasn't injured. Murray made sure she was safe. Which means…

Someone stands in the middle of the room, a tall figure in red. A Pyro.

Nolan.

He turns to face us. A small body lies at his feet, twitching feebly.

"Elle!" Murray rushes forward, aghast. But Nolan moves in a blur, raising his blade to block Murray's path. The younger man's face is a mask of sadness, but he stares the leader down.

"I'm sorry, Murray."

Every tiny sound—from the dripping pipes to the hiss of smoke from the lava pool—is amplified in the hush that follows. My thoughts whirl. Nolan. A traitor. But why? Has he worked for Jared the whole time? Why would he hurt Elle?

"You." Murray chokes out the word. He hasn't drawn his own weapon, and leans on his desk for support. "Why?"

"I didn't have a choice," says Nolan. "I belong to Jared." He lifts his sleeve to reveal something carved into his wrist. A symbol leaps out at me, inked in red, bleeding as though recently sliced open.

A flame-shape.

"He marked all of his subjects," says Nolan, letting his sleeve fall again. "It's fiends' blood, another of his experiments. I never found out what he intended to do with me."

"That symbol," I whisper. "What is that?"

"A warning. Jared has my life in his hands."

Murray takes another step forward. "So you hurt my daughter?"

"Not everyone is as selfless as you," says Nolan, with the same hollow sadness in his tone, lifting his blade again. "I'm not the only one. There were a few more. I'm not sure who. But Jared told me. I met him on his way out, when I was patrolling outside. He told me he plans to pull a trigger that will kill all of us with the symbol. Those of us you let him recruit? We were meant to be the perfect soldiers. We have an incentive to obey, seeing as we can be killed at the touch of a button. And you'll lose your daughter, now, if you disobey."

I feel numb. The world's shifted on its axis. Nolan. The first to welcome me to the group. The first to make me feel I belonged. And now he's turned on innocent Elle, all to save his own life. It takes a minute to realise the buzzing feeling is rage. Pure rage. I want to hurt him.

Murray bends over Elle, shaking all over. "What… what have you done to her?"

"Just marked her, transferred some of my own blood." *That's why it's still bleeding.* "I didn't really have a choice. I'd rather die in battle with the fiends than suffer the death of the people with the mark. You can't imagine the pain."

"Elle." Murray's voice is little more than a whisper.

"There's a way out," says Nolan. "Jared himself has the cure. If Leah and Cas go to him, he'll deliver it himself."

"A likely story," Cas mutters. "I wouldn't have thought you of all people would turn on us, I admit. Have you and Jared been meeting up in secret all this time?"

"No, I haven't seen him in two years. It wasn't until the fiend at the divide told us he still lived. And that symbol kept cropping up."

The image of the flame symbol etched into the wall of that cave fills my head.

Nolan sighs. "I didn't know what it meant when I got it. I was supposed to be on the frontline in the war. All of us were keen to fight for him, until he betrayed us. I hoped he'd died."

"So, do you know what he's planning?" Cas asks. "Why reappear now? Is he in cahoots with the fiends?"

Nolan shakes his head. "Another invasion's coming. Jared's been watching the divide all this time, waiting to make a move. More and more are attacking. And the energy blasts are getting more frequent. He wanted to have a Transcendent to lead his army against them, but apparently he's failed to create one of his own. He needs Leah. And it won't hurt to have the invincible Cas on his side, too."

He failed? But that means…

I imagine another group like ours, concealed away. I thought the fiends would be enough to deal with. But people? Pyros? Could I really fight them?

"You're an idiot," says Cas. "You think you'll somehow be spared?"

"I told you, I want to choose my own fate. Jared showed me a taste of what awaits us if he kills us through the tattoos. It's unendurable."

"I couldn't give a damn about that. Get away from the girl. She's *human,* you pathetic excuse for a Pyro."

Murray's shaking Elle, over and over, but she's insensible. A lump rises in my throat. As Murray moves, I see a trail of blood leading to her bare arm, which has been carved with the same image as Nolan's tattoo. *Nolan* did that.

"Bastard," I whisper. The buzzing anger rises again, and heat rushes over me. A voice whispers in my ear, telling me he deserves to die.

Nolan saved me, helped me, made me feel like I could be human again. And now he's turned into one of the monsters.

I leap at him, dagger held high.

Nolan whirls on me, drawing his own weapon, and the two hit each other with a splintering crash. The impact jars my arm but I keep a firm grip on the hilt. Nolan's eyes narrow.

"Stay out of this, Leah. I'm sorry, but I can't help it."

"The hell you can't," I say.

"I wish I could say the same," he says. "I know you won't let me leave. But if you don't go to Jared within the next seven days, he'll order me to kill everyone at the base. At whatever cost. Do you want to risk that?" He addresses Murray.

Cas replies instead. "I'm all for letting you burn," he says.

"What about the others?" Nolan's expression darkens. "I'm not the only one marked by Jared. Everyone he picked out from amongst us Pyros bears the same mark. Jared will activate all of them at once, and your own people will turn on you. Including the girl." He glances down at Elle's prone form.

"You're despicable." I grip the dagger tighter, pushing forward, and as he pushes back, I strike him with my other fist. The cracking noise as I hit his jaw gives me a mild gratification. His head snaps to the side.

"Leah," says Murray. "Stop. It makes no difference now."

But fury has me in its grip. Fire rushes to the surface of my hand as I aim another punch. He ducks, but I anticipate it and kick at his knee. A sharp gasp escapes him and he drops his dagger an inch or two.

I deliver a right hook so powerful it sends him crashing into the desk. Nolan sits up, groaning. A deep red bruise marks the right side of his face. He's dropped his weapon, and Cas leaps in to retrieve it.

"Murray!" he snaps.

Murray looks up from Elle, his face creased with twice as many lines as before.

"Lock this bastard away somewhere before he can cause any more trouble."

Murray stays still, and I think he's at a loss at how to reply. Finally, he whispers, "The back room. It has a lock."

Cas nods, stalks over to Nolan, and grabs him by the scruff of his neck. Nolan scrambles for his dagger, but I kick it sharply, and send it spinning away across the floor. Cas drags him across the floor to the door at the back of the room.

"The key, Murray." Cas's furious expression never wavers.

Keeping his eyes on Elle, Murray fumbles in his pocket and withdraws a key, which he tosses to Cas. The throw misses, but Cas moves like a blur, still keeping a grip on Nolan, and catches it. He unlocks the door and throws Nolan inside. Slamming the door shut, he twists the key again, pulls it out, and puts it in his own pocket.

"Just in case," he says.

Murray lifts Elle onto the work bench. I move over to her, chest tightening at the sight of the ugly red mark on her arm. She whimpers. Her eyes are glassy, half-open, and I don't know if she recognises me.

"Sorry," I whisper, even though it's stupid to blame myself. Nolan had everyone fooled. Except it wasn't really him.

"That can wait," says Cas sharply. "Jared has his claws in us now. The only thing to do is as he says. Hand over the girl."

"Me?" I ask. "You'd give a dangerous weapon over to the enemy?"

"It's your life or everyone else's." Cas looks so calm, I want to slap him.

"I'll go," I say. "If it'll save everyone. But where? Whereabouts did he go?"

We look around as though expecting to see him hiding behind a rock. But of course he flew away—he could be anywhere by now.

"What if he wants both of us?" I ask, indicating Cas. "He was going to take Cas with him earlier."

"You're joking, right?" says Cas, eyebrows raised. "Who's going to act as a shield if I'm not here?"

"If we obey, maybe we won't need a shield," says Murray.

Cas's brows climb higher, incredulous. "You're joking. I go with her?"

"I'm not overly keen on the idea either, you know," I say. But the notion of being out there alone appeals even less.

"Whereabouts do we even go? If he's built a new lab, it could be anywhere. He has air transport now." He has a point. The old lab has turned to ashes.

Murray clears his throat awkwardly.

Cas turns on him. "There's something you're not telling us, isn't there?"

Murray hesitates a while before answering. "There is... our old base. He may very well have moved back in there. He did mention the place where it all started."

Cas's brow furrows. "Thought that place was destroyed in a blast?"

Murray shakes his head. "It was damaged, but not permanently. There were underground rooms. It's all I can think of."

"Well, we don't know for sure," says Cas. "If Jared can attack within the base itself, then the last thing we need is two of our fighters missing. Where's the proof that going to him will do any good? He's probably planning a surprise attack."

"The lab is only a day's journey away," says Murray. "I can send people after you."

"That won't be necessary," says Cas, though he still looks displeased. "But it's not my choice, is it?"

He studies me, and the intensity freezes me inside. I have to be the one to decide. And I suddenly know that I'll do anything to protect these people—even go out into the wilderness with Cas, perhaps to face certain death.

Better to die than to be the last one standing, alone in the world.

CHAPTER EIGHTEEN

Murray calls a meeting. It turns out Nolan locked the doors to the dormitories, and dozens of terrified faces greet us as Murray unlocks them. Everyone files into the hall.

My heart pounds in my ears. *I might never see them again. I might never see my home.*

Home. Strange that I think of this place as being akin to a home, after so long without one. And now I might be leaving it forever.

If it keeps them safe, if it spares Elle and the others, I'd do anything.

Murray's talking about an invasion. That word sparks panic even in the oldest, most experienced Pyros. They've been at a stalemate so long.

I follow Murray back to his office, along with Cas.

Murray turns to him, his face clouded. "Are you sure you want to do this?"

"Yes." Cas throws me a sharp glance. "I'll make sure we get there without any trouble."

"You'll need supplies, water…" Murray seems to snap out of a trance.

"Just give us what we need and make it quick," says Cas.

Murray sucks in a breath. "Be careful. There's no knowing what he's planning. If he's trying to create his own Transcendent…"

"We'll stop him," says Cas.

I nod. "We will."

He actually said *we*. As if he thinks I'm capable of helping. Who knew?

I still can't figure out what Cas *wants*. He's willing to throw himself into the path of danger without a second thought, but does he really expect to survive what Jared has planned? I don't think he's planning to sacrifice us himself, but if he throws us into the front of a battle against the fiends, then the odds of us making it out alive are pretty low.

It's what you're made for. You're Transcendent.

When he looks at me, his eyes narrow. "You. Go back to your dorm and get whatever you need. I'll stay here."

Typical Cas, I think at first. Then I realise that this is my last chance to say goodbye to everyone.

As I leave, I hear Murray ask, "Are you sure he'd do it? Sacrifice her?"

"You really don't know your brother that well, do you?"

Shivers run through me. Does he think I'm going to my death? *Not if I can help it.* The fiends have taken everything from me already. But the people here have shown me I can build a new life even in the ashes of the old one. I'm damned if I'll lose that now.

My chest tightens again when I hear voices from behind the door to the dormitory. Taking a deep breath, I enter.

All heads turn in my direction. I draw in a deep breath, my gaze travelling over the curious faces. People who've accepted me, when I thought I'd never encounter a friendly face again. I blink tears out of my eyes and force the words out.

"I'm leaving. I have to go."

"Why?" Poppy says.

Too late for regret now. I give a rundown of the night's events, but pause when I get to the part about the tattoos, not knowing how much I'm supposed to tell them. In the end, I don't, nor about Nolan's involvement.

The reaction's exactly as I expected: complete and total panic. Questions fly everywhere, and several people jump to their feet. I feel their fear, and yet, I can't stay and reassure them. Not when every second I waste makes it more likely that they won't get out before Jared makes a move. My one consolation is that none of them have the marks. That's the part I don't mention. I can't get a word in edgeways at this point. And the last thing I want is distrust and rumours to tear everyone apart, slow them down, when they're losing their best soldier. And as for me…

"Guys," I say, but my voice is lost in the general noise. I make my way over to Poppy and Tyler, who sit completely still, stunned.

"I'm sorry, guys," I say. "Cas and I have to go to Jared. It's the only way to stop this. You'll be fine, I promise."

"But what about you?" Poppy sobs, raising her eyes to meet mine. "You'll come back, right?"

I don't want to lie to her. Hell, I don't want to lie to any of them. In the world before, we might have been close friends.

"I'll try to," I say.

I meet Cas by the exit. He hands me a backpack, presumably containing enough food and water to survive outside for a few days. I peek inside and also find a sleeping bag. *Guess I'll be sleeping under the stars again.*

Murray hurries up to us. "Stay safe," he says, with a glance back to his room where Elle still lies. I wish I could say goodbye to her properly. *God, I hope she recovers from this.* What Nolan did was inexcusable.

"Bye," I say, and Cas gives a curt nod before disappearing into the tunnel.

Looks like I'll have my work cut out keeping up with him.

The collapsed path proves tricky to navigate, especially carrying supplies. When we reach the part where the fiend knocked me down, I stop.

"It wouldn't harm us if we jumped, right?" I say, looking down at the sheer drop. It didn't hurt the last time, and would save us precious minutes of scrambling down the rocks.

Cas stares at me and says nothing. It's a bit disconcerting.

"Just an idea," I mutter, looking away.

"No, it's a great idea. Hold on." He shifts the backpack so it's firmly on his shoulders and poises on the edge of the cliff.

He jumps, and my heart leaps into my throat even though I know it won't hurt him. Before I can start to doubt myself, I jump, too.

He said it was a *great idea*. I almost laugh as the adrenaline kicks in. I'm falling, falling…

My body slams into rock and I gasp, the thrill knocked out of me. I stagger, but I know nothing's broken, even bruised. Cas stands to the side, casually, raising an eyebrow as I try to regain my balance.

"You nearly landed on me, you know. Don't they tell you to look before you leap?"

"Sorry," I say, looking away. Then I stare. "Cas…"

"What?"

I just point. The ruin of a house stands nearby, tucked into the shadow of the mountain—I'd never have spotted it if we hadn't landed nearby. The roof's collapsed, but the walls are intact. The door lies open.

"What *is* that place?"

"Haven't we got more important things to worry about?"

True, but curiosity's grabbed me, all the same.

"What is it?"

"It was used for experiments," he says, already moving away from the cliff.

Despite myself, I move closer to it, curious.

"There's nothing there," says Cas.

"Who lived there?" I ask, peering through the cracked glass.

"If I answer, will you leave it alone? We don't have much time."

He's right, of course. We can't afford to stand around. I nod, turning my back on the house and instead in the direction of the path ahead. I can see the ocean swirling around the stepping stones ahead of the fields of heather.

"That house used to be home to the children of Pyros, or people who were deemed to have the potential," says Cas, as we cross the field. "It was like an orphanage of sorts. It's where Nolan grew up, actually."

Nolan. Hot anger rushes over me at the image of him standing over Elle.

Cas flashes me a look, as though expecting a reaction out of me.

"Is that where he learned to be a two-faced dick?" I venture.

He blinks; whatever he expected me to say, that obviously wasn't it.

"People will do things when they're desperate," he says. "What would you have done in his place?"

The answer's obvious. "I'd die before I hurt someone else."

"You say that, but how can you know for sure? Think what it's like to be in pain, real pain, so deep it swallows you up, reduces you to nothing. Wouldn't you say or do anything to get out of that situation?"

"Does it matter?" My voice cracks. I don't need him making me doubt myself now, not when everyone's depending on us already.

"It matters," he says, quietly, as though speaking more to himself than to me. "Bear in mind that if we get to Jared's place, you might well have to make that choice."

His words strike me at the core. We walk the rest of the way to the stepping stones in silence.

Now, of course, I have to endure the humiliation of him watching me struggle. He goes first, leaping across with a strange, careless grace. I push the thought away, wondering where the hell it came from. I need every ounce of concentration I have.

But my feet don't slip this time. In fact, I don't lose my balance at all. Maybe it's because I have enough to be scared of without worrying about falling in the sea—either way, I catch up with Cas easily. Once on the other side, I glance back at the hills. Nothing looks out of place—no clue that everyone back there could die at the whim of a lunatic.

Cas's looking at me again. Did he expect me to freeze up in terror at the thought of crossing the water? Does it matter? I force myself to meet his eyes.

"Where now?"

"We go to the divide and follow it inland." He recites it as though it's what Murray's told him, but I know he's been there before. He was… *created there*. I can't even imagine what that must have been like.

But his expression's closed, and I know if I press him, he'll take off on me. I just nod, looking out to sea.

We follow the coastline, spurred on by the invisible presence of a ticking clock. I don't think I've ever walked so fast. Before the sun's reached the middle of the sky, indicating midday, the divide is within view.

The newest Burned Spot waits for us, the place where the old lab used to be. My hands curl into fists. Maybe that power's exactly what I need right now.

Cas turns away from the coast before we reach the Burned Spot, leading the way through a field of dead grass. A dilapidated cottage lies ahead. I already know it'll be empty. No one would live this close to the divide. Apart from Jared, apparently.

The jagged line looks sinister even from a distance, and I can't keep from glancing in that direction every few minutes.

Finally, I ask the question that's been bugging me for hours.

"Is it really a good idea, walking this close to the divide?"

"No," Cas says bluntly. "But it's no less safe than anywhere else within a mile of here. We can't afford to deviate too much. Besides, most of the fiends roaming around were already here."

"What about that one we found last time?"

"It was obviously sent there by Jared. One of his altered ones."

"So how do we know which ones work for him or not?"

Cas gives me such a disparaging look, you'd think I'd suggested we take air transport.

"What?" I demand, determined not to be intimidated.

"Well," says Cas, "the ones that try to kill us probably don't work for him."

Oh, right.

"Unless," he adds, "he really intended to lure us away and then kill us."

"Real optimistic," I mutter.

"You have a better suggestion, I'd be glad to hear it. He intends to welcome us with open arms, perhaps? Like Murray did for you?"

I blink. "No, that's not what I expect. What's the problem?"

"You're too naïve."

"Naïve? Me? Just because I don't automatically assume everyone's an enemy?"

I'd pushed that instinct down, every day spent at the base making me feel more relaxed, more assured that I'd found something I thought I'd never have again.

And now Jared's destroyed that. Does Cas have to keep reminding me?

"I'd say that's a naïve position to take, yes."

"Okay, I just don't get you." I fold my arms. "What's the problem? And don't say it's because we're going to die. I don't intend to spend my last days on Earth arguing with a complete asshat."

Cas's been an asshat since birth. Nolan's words replay in my head, unexpectedly, and a blaze of anger surges through me. Why did he have to be the one to turn out to be a traitor? If he hadn't, I might have someone friendly to talk to, not the guy now staring at me like I've just started speaking in tongues.

"Tough shit," he says. "You're stuck with me."

"Did you just..." read my thoughts?

"You aren't very good at hiding your emotions," he says.

"You aren't very good at expressing them," I counter. God, I want to punch him. I know it wouldn't even hurt him, which is probably why I want to do it so much.

"I told you that you need to learn self-control."

"I thought that was about being Transcendent."

"It's the same thing. Your powers are linked to your emotions. You get angry, everything around you goes up in flames."

I pull my arms tight to myself. "Like you'd know anything about it."

Something flashes in his eyes. Anger. I hit a nerve.

"I know more about it than you," he says, softly. His tone makes the back of my neck prickle. Now the heat's coming from *him,* in waves. Even though logic screams at me that I'm more than a match for him, the sense of warning intensifies. It's like staring into the eyes of a lion seconds from pouncing.

I look away, curiosity evaporating. Exhaustion drags at my limbs, reminding me that I've not slept, and we've walked for miles without stopping. Normal people couldn't handle this. What's the limit for Pyros? I want to ask, but I refuse to admit weakness in front of Cas.

The divide continues alongside us, a jagged line on the horizon. Burned Spots mark the area around it, and I know that the further inland we go, the higher the chance of running into the fiends.

It's eerily silent, the sound of our cloaks whispering on the ground the only noise around for miles. I almost jump out my skin when a flock of birds passes overhead, at first thinking it's a group of those winged fiends, flying at a distance.

Occasionally, we pass a ruined farmhouse but that's the closest to human habitation we find. I wouldn't even recognise my own birthplace now. Towns stricken by energy blasts become nothing more than decomposing skeletons.

And we're approaching one now. The absence of a reinforced fence indicates that it was abandoned before the energy blasts started to strike. Houses lie derelict, and there are even a few cars sitting on the overgrown road or still in driveways. I haven't seen a moving car in what feels like forever. They stopped working when the power cut out, presumably a consequence of the first energy blasts. Besides, they'd draw unwelcome attention. One night at the camp, we'd chosen a spot by a country lane to settle down for the night, and I'd been awoken by a strange rumbling sound. Thinking it was an energy blast, I'd instantly jumped to my feet, only for Randy to shush me. Through a gap in the bushes, I'd watched, open-mouthed, as a car—an actual, working car—crawled past, bringing an achingly familiar smell of smoke and petrol. Ridiculous how that made me think of home.

I remember glimpsing the man driving the car through the window, envying him for having some means of escape. But that noise would draw the fiends like a magnet. We couldn't stick around to find out where he was going, or if he ever managed to get there.

Now, the cars have become part of nature, vines snaking through the shattered windows. I can guess what happened. These two cars collided when their owners were making an escape. One door hangs off its hinges.

Cas stops. "Want to look?"

I start in surprise. It's the first words either of us has spoken in hours, and certainly not what I expected. I'd resigned myself to a long, long day of walking ahead. Except it isn't day anymore. The sun's slipping out of sight, and before long, the stars will come out, twinkling in the ravaged sky.

"Why? We have everything we need."

"I just thought you…" He shakes his head. "Never mind. I just thought you might want to stop for a bit. I forget you're a Pyro."

"Thanks," I say, then bite the inside of my cheek to prevent myself saying anything more cutting. He was only being thoughtful, weird as it might seem, and starting another argument isn't what I intended.

"I recognise this place," he murmurs. "It's stupid. I never lived in a town, but it feels familiar."

"I don't know," I say. "I have no idea where we are. I might even have come here before, we moved around a lot."

But we never came this close to the divide. I don't know how Randy kept track of the direction, but he never led us astray.

Cas's eyes roam over the town—the sad-looking houses, the broken glass surrounding the wrecked cars—then he turns back to me. "You good to go? We can stop when the sun goes down, but I know we can cover more ground than this. If we want to make it within a week…"

"Got it," I say. I'm tired, but not to the point where it distracts me. And I haven't eaten or drank anything all day, either. Do Transcendents need to eat? Can we just... survive? Endure? Keep going even after dead?

Come to think of it, what do the fiends live on? I know they don't *eat* people, but I've never seen them scavenging, either.

More questions. I push them away, concentrating on the moment. Without warning, the world spins.

"Crap." I press my hand to my head.

"Are you okay?"

"Just a little dizzy."

"You should eat something. Did you even look in that backpack?"

I narrow my eyes at him. "Now you're being all parental on me?"

But I shift the rucksack onto one shoulder and unzip it. Most of the weight's from the water bottles stacked inside— the only food items I can find are slightly squashed energy bars. I retrieve one and bite into it. I glance at Cas and raise my eyebrows as he tosses a wrapper aside.

"No one teach you not to litter?"

"It's a bit late to save the environment now," he says.

Ha. Once again, he's confused the heck out of me. I stuff the rest of the energy bar into my mouth to avoid having to say something back.

Silence follows us along the road, but it's not a hostile silence this time. I wouldn't call it companionable, either, but at least we aren't snapping at each other. I don't have much energy left for that.

And it's getting dark. The pale shape of the moon hangs overhead, and the setting sun brings a chill that reminds me of the creatures that could be lurking out of sight. Maybe inside the divide…

A faint screeching sound, like someone dragging a heavy object along a wooden floor. I stop dead, hand going to my weapon.

Cas holds out an arm before I can move forward.

"That way," he murmurs. "If we get off the path *now*, we can avoid it."

"And if we can't?" My heart pounds. It sounds like only one of them, but the word *trap* screams in my ears. What if Jared sent it? What if it's one of his?

I can take it, I think, and as I rest my hand on the hilt of the dagger, a comforting heat wraps around me and confidence pushes away the fear.

"Then we fight. But I don't think drawing attention's our best bet right now. Especially so close to the divide."

There I was thinking Cas would throw himself into danger no matter what. Not that I'm one to talk, considering the giddy feeling the thought of fighting another fiend gives me. *Stop that.* What good is being Transcendent if it just makes me rush into reckless decisions that could get me killed? Though I suppose it's the fact that I *can't* die. Not easily.

Even Jared won't kill me. Or Cas, presumably. But the others? He'd blow them into oblivion to get to us. Why we're so important to him, I don't know. But I have a bad feeling it's not an altruistic mission, or even to put us at the head of his army. He didn't strike me as the soldierly type, and the idea of another army running around just doesn't add up. Not out here, in this lifeless wilderness.

It's like being back to square one, the day I first met Cas and Nolan. Now Cas is the last thing I have left.

He's right, so I follow his lead off the path, making for the hills—and hopefully, somewhere to shelter. Though that's probably too much to hope for.

Another cry echoes around us. It sounds closer. Cas swears under his breath.

Then the ground starts shaking.

CHAPTER NINETEEN

The earth shifts. I feel the motion in my feet, travelling up my body. A world-rocking tremor that knocks me sideways into Cas. He grabs my arm to steady me, and I start at the unexpected rush of heat. His hand's suddenly wrenched away, almost sending me sprawling.

"What—?"

"Are you doing that?" he asks, indicating the rocking ground

"*Me?* Of course not."

But that's what the shaking's like—the prelude to an energy blast. Like the very earth is alive beneath my feet, shuddering and groaning and tearing itself apart. Even my newfound sense of balance isn't enough. Nothing to brace myself against, apart from Cas.

And he's sliding away. This is more than an energy blast. For one thing, there's no tell-tale bright flare of light, no smell of burning. For another, cracks are appearing in the ground.

The earth really is breaking apart.

I jump over another crack as the ground splits beneath me. The line zigzags across the ground, cutting a deep trench in the earth. My feet stumble on the edge, and I move back, grabbing the nearest support—Cas's hand.

Heat. I gasp as light flares around me. Around both of us. Cas's wide eyes meet mine, and he tries to pull away, but our hands are locked together. Fire flickers across my hand, to his, and back again. The trembling earth rocks us both, yet I can't let go.

The temperature rises in the air. I can feel the power beneath the surface, but I push it down. My hand clenches tighter around Cas's, and he grips mine back. The disbelief on his face tells me he has no more control than I do.

The smell of burning rises, strong and insistent. Smoke rises from our clasped hands as the skin turns red and the flames jump higher, higher.

"What are you doing?"

Cas's words sound like they're coming from a mile away, beyond the shaking earth and splitting ground. I hold onto his hand, the only stable thing left in the world, and the power rushes to the surface again, overwhelming.

Another crack in the earth, right beneath my feet. I stumble back as the split widens—and the connection breaks. My hand slides out of Cas's as we're flung apart. My back hits the ground, knocking the breath out of me. Pain shoots up my arm, so intense that I scream.

Images flash before my eyes, some of places I recognise, some I don't. The base. Murray's office. The training hall, the lava pit—scenes pass by too fast for me to focus on any one of them.

Something heavy smacks into me, like solid rock. I gasp, but no sound comes out. I'm looking through someone else's eyes. And they're face to face with a fiend.

I stop breathing. The brutish, ugly creature towers over me, a growl slipping through its teeth. Bigger than I'm used to. Whoever I am, they're shorter than me.

I dodge a punch and retaliate with a swipe of my own, but my hands are small, clumsy. I have no weapon.

Chains dig into my ankles. My surroundings become clearer. A cage. I'm in a metal-barred cage. Sheer panic overwhelms me.

The monster lumbers forwards, and this time, it doesn't miss. Its blow strikes me across the face. Pain explodes behind my eyes.

The world becomes pain. A red haze blurs the fiend as it delivers the killing blow.

Dead.

Except I'm still alive. Barely, hanging onto some painful fragment of life, but alive.

Oh God… the pain…

My world's shrunk to my own mind, this tiny corner of sanity. I bury myself in it, as if I can turn my back. But the fog's slowly clearing, the pain's receding. Voices sound in my ears, fading in and out like a badly tuned radio.

"He's waking up."

"Has he Transcended?"

"Perhaps… almost ready…"

"Give it another minute." I know that voice. Jared. *What the hell is happening? Why can't I get out? Who am I?*

"Are you sure? We don't want a repeat of…" The words blur together.

"How else are we to get results?" Jared sounds angry, accusing.

My eyes flicker open.

"Cas. Cas, can you hear me?"

I don't recognise the other voice. But I'm Cas. I'm reliving something from his past.

The shock jolts me back to reality. I gasp, disoriented, as the world spins. I'm not on the ground anymore but in the air.

Hell, Cas is carrying me.

My mind spins. What did I just see? Was that really Cas's past? He was an artificial soldier, but did Jared really…?

The wind rushes over me as he runs, dodging the cracks appearing in the ground. I twist my head to look up at him.

"You can put me down." My voice comes out shakily.

Cas nearly drops me as he navigates around another crack in the earth. But the trembles have slowed down since I passed out. The world no longer feels like it's breaking apart, despite the new cracks in the ground.

But I feel like I'm breaking on the inside.

Something happened when we touched. Somehow, I relived part of his life, through his eyes. But why? How's something like that even possible?

That *pain*…

No human could endure it. Even a Pyro. And he was only a child.

Now I understand what the experiments were for. To make a regular Pyro Transcendent, they created one who could withstand anything, couldn't die even when bleeding out on the floor. Who could heal from near-death. I can't look at him. My mind's a whirlwind of confusion, memories that aren't mine tangled up with my own thoughts.

A final blast shakes the earth, and I stumble over the edge of a muddy hill. I land on my back with a gasp, the stars winking above me in the endless sky. A thud tells me Cas's landed beside me.

"Leah, move!"

When I just lie there, he grabs me roughly by the arm and pulls me back, under an overhang. Instinctively, I hold onto him as the last bone-shaking tremor rocks the world. But that's not why I'm trembling.

I lean back against him, still shaking. He doesn't push me away, and neither of us speaks. Seconds pass, turning to minutes, as we watch, waiting to see if the land's going to split open, if the tremors are going to come back.

Finally, he shifts position. I can feel him looking at me, as though waiting for me to speak first. I turn my head to face him and unexpectedly find his face so close to mine, we almost touch.

"Is it over?" My voice is hoarse.

"I don't know."

"That wasn't another energy blast, right?"

"I don't think so. But it wasn't natural."

"The fiends," I say. But those aren't the monsters I'm thinking of.

"Could have been. Or it might have been someone else."

"Not Jared?" I think of the man in my vision. Who the hell would do that to a child? What kind of monsters are these people?

And we're delivering ourselves into their hands.

"Jared never learns his lesson. Even after every mistake he's made, he still believes he can beat the fiends if he gets us onto his side."

In light of what I just saw, I can believe it.

"I don't understand him," I whisper. "He…" My voice chokes up. How can I tell Cas what I just saw? I don't even know how it happened.

"Welcome to the club," says Cas. "If you'd been here two years ago, you'd know. His stupidity was what drew the fiends out—made them launch an all-out attack on humans—in the first place. If he hadn't provoked them, they might have gone crawling back into the divide. We won the first fight, you know. It was only when we lost the Transcendent that things got really bad." He stops, abruptly.

"Jared said..." I hesitate, not sure if I want to know the answer. "Did the last Transcendent destroy the world?"

"We were manipulated," says Cas, through clenched teeth. "By Jared, of course. He turned on us during the fight, when she was supposed to close the bridge. He killed her before it fully closed, and her powers set off the first energy blast." Cas's tone never wavers, but bright anger gleams in his eyes.

Murray said she never harmed anyone intentionally. She didn't do it on purpose.

But that means...

"He manipulated both of us." Cas's voice is tight. "Just like he's doing to the two of us. I don't know if he has a plan, but either those earthquakes are his, or they're coming from the other side."

"From... the fiends' world?"

He nods. "The invasion. Jared's been in hiding for two years. He must be making a play for a reason. He always did have a more in-depth understanding of the fiends than Murray did."

Given what I just saw in Cas's memories, I believe it. My mouth is dry, my hands still trembling. *How can he still live with the Pyros like this?* But he was created to be one. He's known no other life.

"So Jared expects the invasion to happen... now. And that's why he needs us." I'm voicing the obvious aloud, but I can't stand to listen to my own thoughts any longer.

"Their leaders must be coming back. It's the only way."

I glance sideways at him. "Their leaders? Who?" My mind conjures up an image of monstrous super-fiends. "Murray mentioned a name—the Fiordans."

"They're shape-changers," says Cas. "After the last invasion, they were stranded back in the fiends' world, leaving half their army over here on *our* world. Any of us Pyros can take down a fiend, even an army. But their leaders... no one but a Transcendent would stand a chance against them."

I stare. *"That's* my purpose? Not—not to close the breach, or..."

Cas's eyes narrow. "Purpose? You can do whatever the hell you want. Kill the fiends, stop the Fiordans, even run away."

"I'm not running," I say. "But are we walking into a trap?"

"We've come too far to go back now," he says.

I nod. We can't go back anyway, not if we want to save Elle. Not to mention whoever else has those marks from Jared. *He's twisted. We have to stop him.*

"How much further?"

"I don't know. I hope we aren't too far from the divide, but it's hard to tell."

"I'm not all that keen to go back that way," I say. "Those tremors came from the divide."

The thought of the last world-wide earthquakes splitting the earth open, fiends swarming the streets, fills my head. We only got away so easily because we're Pyros. What happened to the normal people, camps like the one I used to live in? Did they think the end of the world was happening again?

The ground above us shakes. I start upright, thinking the tremors have begun again—but it's only the overhang that's shaking, as though something heavy has landed above us.

It keeps shaking. Soil rains down. A familiar screeching sound chills me to the bone.

There's a fiend standing above us.

I roll out from under the cliff, with Cas on my heels, and we turn to face our enemy. *Hell.* There's more than one of them. Three ugly, brutish fiends face us. They knew we were there.

My hand flies to my dagger, and I pull it out the sheath, fire flaring up my arm. The power makes my body rock, and I remember losing control when Cas and I touched. I can't afford that to happen again.

The fiends jump at us. I dodge, rolling on the ground again, as Cas catches one with the edge of his blade. Another lands beside me, and I leap to my feet, slashing with my dagger. I miss, but the fiery edge glides along the fiend's arm, and it hisses at me.

Heat rises as I strike its other arm with the side of my hand. The fire consumes me, and I throw myself into the fight gladly, giving into the rush of power. The fiend shrieks as I slash it across the leg, leaving a deep burn in its rock-like skin. It staggers back, swiping with its meaty hand, but I catch its hand in mine. The size difference is ridiculous, but fire rushes to my palm immediately. The fiend screams again, pulling its blistering hand from my grip.

A heavy weight slams into me from the side, and I stagger back. Its partner's arrived. I feint a couple of times, caught between two fiends, stalling while I work out a strategy. My fist flies out. I know I've telegraphed my attack when the fiend dodges, but it gives me time to get into position to attack its partner.

The second fiend, however, has a different idea. Before I can strike, its wings have carried it up out of range, and I have to duck its clawed feet as they grab at my head. I catch a glimpse of Cas battling the other, sword flashing, as I roll in an undignified heap to avoid the grasping claws. I stick my dagger into one then pull it free in a spray of blood, forcing the fiend to retreat out of range.

Hardly out of breath, I get back on my feet, and two huge arms fold over me from behind. I choke, kicking out as I'm lifted into the air. The fiend's grip tightens, squeezing the air from my lungs. *The power.* I imagine fire, blasting the monster to dust, and the fiend hisses at me. *Come on.*

Red light flashes before my eyes, flaring from my arms, my shoulders. The fiend lets go, bellowing in rage. I have no chance to brace myself before my back hits the ground, but it barely winds me. I'm on my feet in a second, dagger still in hand, heat melding it to my skin. Fire still burning.

The fiend's smoking all over, standing back as though unsure whether to lunge at me again. But they're stupid, and they can't override the instinct to kill anything that looks human.

I thrust with my dagger as it runs at me, burying the weapon to the hilt in its chest. Blood pours over my hand,

and I pull my weapon free, moving aside as the fiend staggers. It drops to its knees, and the ground shakes like the tremors have started up again.

The second fiend, the one I wounded, jumps in to take its place, causing another mini-quake. It's easily twice my size and its palms could crush my skull like an egg, but it knows I'm no normal opponent. Blood streams from my dagger, but the hilt remains firm in my hand. I duck the fiend's swinging fist and stab its uninjured arm, but misjudge. The side of its hand hits my head and my teeth rattle in my skull.

Shaking my head, willing the dizziness to pass, I spin to face the enemy again. *Fire. Come on. Fire.*

Flames fan out from my arms and my dagger as I raise it to the sky. The fiend's eyes follow the motion, unable to resist the bright light.

I leap forward and sucker-punch it in the face with my other fist.

The flames consume the fiend, head to toe. Its skin blackens and crumbles, breaking apart and turning to ashes. At that moment, gravity catches up with me and I drop to the ground—I jumped six feet into the air, maybe more. *Oh my God.* I've never taken out a fiend with one punch before, either. Unless Jared's are easier to kill, and somehow I doubt it.

I'm stronger than before. My powers are stronger.

A sudden jolt of pain shoots up my arm from the dagger, and images flash before my eyes—images of barren land under burning sky, lava flowing across the ground, hot enough to melt the skin off bones. Fiends crawling out of cracks in the ground…

I blink. The world comes back into focus. Cas stands over the crumbled remains of the third fiend, breathing heavily.

Clapping echoes in the silence.

"Congratulations!" calls a voice from above, on the cliff.

Jared.

CHAPTER TWENTY

A smirk crosses Jared's face. "I knew you'd come."

Cas moves closer, blood-stained blade held out. "What have you done, you fool?"

"Me, a fool?" Jared laughs again. "You should look closer at your own transgressions, Pyro. Look what you did to that girl."

Cas's gaze flashes back to me. I blink, nonplussed. What he did to me? Jared can't know about any of that. *He's lying. He has to be.*

"Well, this is nice, isn't it? It could have got very messy, with your friends back at Murray's little hidey-hole. I'm glad my brother was able to see reason. It certainly makes things easier for me."

"I thought you were waiting for us at the lab," says Cas, tonelessly.

"Didn't anyone teach you not to interrupt?" Jared jumps down from the cliff, feet slamming into the ground. "As a matter of fact, I was on my way there when I spotted some wayward fiends behaving rather unusually."

"Wayward?" Cas echoes. "Meaning they're not yours?"

"Don't trifle with me, boy. If I didn't know my brother to be a coward, I would accuse him of unleashing this himself. Somehow, the fiends on the other side must have found me out. Or is one of you in contact with them?"

"I have no idea what you're talking about," says Cas. "I don't know, maybe they're pissed off you've been experimenting on so many of their kind. Perhaps they know you're planning to throw Leah and me into battle with them."

Jared lifts an eyebrow. "Is it so hard to believe that I have your best interests at heart? I would never put you in danger like that. You're too valuable."

"So why do you need us so badly? I might not agree with Murray, but he's preparing us for the invasion better than you ever did."

"By hiding? Fool, the fiends were never going to stay away indefinitely. As long as the divide exists, they will always find a way to break through, and their leaders will not stay down. Mark my words, they'll attack soon, if they haven't already."

"Yes, I think we've established that," says Cas. "What I want to know is: what was the point in threatening to kill two hundred other Pyros to get us to fight a battle we intended to fight in the first place? Or do you just like making enemies?"

Jared's face is brick-red. "I warn you, boy, you'll regret those words. You have no choice but to come with me, and you'll find I have little mercy left for the likes of you."

His tone brings me out in goose bumps. I don't want to imagine what could be worse than what he put Cas through as a child.

We can't go with him.

"Well, if I die before I get to battle the fiends, it'll be a shame, won't it?" I'm impressed at the utter indifference in Cas's tone. I couldn't have managed it if I'd been in his place.

"You know better than anyone that death is often a welcome relief."

"So, anything else you want to tell us?" asks Cas. "Like how to stop those tattoos from killing people?"

I look at him. So it isn't just about his own life. He's genuinely concerned for Elle and the other victims of Jared's experiments. *Yeah, he might be an asshat, but he's better than this guy.*

"Is that truly all you want to know?" Jared's eyebrow lifts again.

"Preferably before you send us to our deaths, yes."

"I told you, I have no intention of sacrificing you."

"And that earthquake was just for show?"

"You don't believe me." Jared's voice is coloured with disbelief.

"I can't imagine why," says Cas. He still hasn't put the blade away, and it gleams crimson in the moonlight.

"That attitude of yours won't help you. You're going to come with me now. Do you think you have a choice?"

"As a matter of fact, I do."

"You think so little of me." Jared's attempt at a wounded expression falls flat.

"Yes, but Leah and I are more than capable of killing you ourselves. If you die, have you left explicit orders behind for someone else to set off those magical tattoos of yours? I know you don't like sharing." He spits the last sentence out.

Jared's eyes are noticeably wider. *He didn't think of that,* I realise—and we actually have leverage over him. Now we just need to use it to our advantage before we lose it.

Cas's plainly got something in mind. He moves over to the now-frozen Jared, raising his knife to point it at him.

"I think we could come to an *agreement,*" he says, his tone mimicking Jared's earlier confidence. "If you'd be so kind as to cooperate, I might not have to skewer you."

The gleaming blade is reflected in Jared's eyes as he looks down at it.

"You mistake me, boy," he whispers. "I didn't want to have to do this, but you've given me no other option."

He snaps his fingers. For a few seconds, nothing happens. Cas's blade's inches from his neck, but Jared doesn't look fazed.

The sound of wing beats fills the air. I look up to see a dark shape silhouetted against the sky—no, three of them, moving closer fast. The winged fiends. They were hiding nearby all along. Of course.

Cas moves with lightning speed, but Jared anticipates him and draws a weapon of his own, a dagger around the same length of mine. The side of his blade blocks Cas's.

A stalemate.

Cas's eyes narrow. The dark shapes in the sky are getting bigger by the second. We can't afford to waste another minute.

As I move, something holds me back, a voice whispering in my ear, asking if I can really kill another person. *I have to stop him hurting us*, I tell the voice. *I have to stop him killing the others.*

I lunge with my dagger, but Jared whips out another blade with his free hand. The weapon shakes—and a scream rises in my throat as sudden pain hits me, deeper than anything I've felt before—a horrible, wrenching pain that feels like I'm being pulled apart from inside. Burning, everywhere, searing, consuming every part of me. I can't see Jared or Cas. Every sensation given over to agony. The screams rip my throat apart, but the only sound is a roaring in my ears. Trying to fight it is like swimming against an impossible current.

I'm pulled back, vividly, to a family holiday in Cornwall. Mum and Dad chose a bad moment to take their eyes off four-year-old me, and before they knew it, I'd swam out to sea—too far out. The current took hold of me and tossed me like a discarded doll. Choking on salt water, I saw my own death approaching, cruel and merciless, and had no power to prevent it.

And then the lifeguard pulled me out.

This time, there's no lifeguard, and soon, even that memory fades. I can't think. Everything fades away, piece by piece, until nothing's left but the pain.

Time disappears. Every second burns, every minute passes without relief. I've lost all sense of self.

I can't even remember my name.

***

Bright light fills my vision, so intense it hurts. The blackness in my mind fades, and it takes a minute to realise I can feel anything besides pain.

Everything hurts with the memory of it, every inch of me, inside and out, feels as though it's been dipped in burning lava. Thoughts trickle into my mind, from a time I still had senses, still had memories. *I thought nothing could hurt Pyros like this, let alone Transcendents.*

It takes another minute or five to process the flood of words in my head. Pyro. Transcendent. Phoenix.

Leah. Me.

Memories return in a dizzying rush, and I feel like some of them aren't mine, though I couldn't say which. They fade in and out as I lie… somewhere. I know I'm lying down, but it hurts too much to take it in. I retreat back into my own head, running through the reel of images again. One person keeps returning, sparking emotions back into my ravaged body. Mostly anger. A tall, scowling guy, wielding a long knife and a bad attitude.

Cas.

Another image appears: a boy in a cage with a terrible beast. Horrible sadness rises, bringing tears to my eyes, hot and stinging. I'm not burning anymore. But I still feel the echo of it. I shudder, my body arching. *That pain.* Never felt anything like it. Never. What the hell happened back there? Jared moved as I lunged at him, but I don't *think* he stabbed me. There's not a mark on me, anyway.

I blink the tears away, slowly gaining awareness of my real surroundings. I'm in a bedroom. Small, nothing in there aside from a chest of drawers and the bed I'm lying on. The softness is a welcome relief against my burning skin. Someone's removed my coat, but I'm still dressed in the plain black combat outfit I wore underneath it.

I sit up, looking around. My boots lie at the foot of the wooden bed. Light spills into the room from an open window which looks out onto a courtyard. A brick building faces it.

More importantly, there's a door behind me. I stand, but just as the thought of escape enters my head, it opens and someone comes in.

Jared. He sweeps into the room, red cloak flying. The echo of pain burns again, and my hands curl into fists. I picture my fist flying out, his head snapping back... but I'm here for a reason.

A girl's face flashes before me. Heart-shaped, kind, young for her age.

Oh, God, Elle.

I'm here for my friends. This madman has their lives in his hands, and is willing to kill to get me on his side.

Now I'm his prisoner.

My hand jumps to my belt, and I curse myself for not noticing I was missing my weapon. The dagger's gone.

Jared closes the door behind him and studies me, a pitying expression on his face. It doesn't fool me for an instant.

We study each other, neither breaking the silence for a minute. Finally, he says, "I'm sorry, Leah. You gave me no choice."

"What the *hell* did you do to me?"

He shakes his head. "I'm not about to give up all my secrets yet, Leah. Are you?"

I say nothing, hoping my blistering glare speaks for itself.

"You know," he continues, "It's a pity none of us realised how the last Transcendent came to be. If we had, we might have won the war already. As it is, you'll both be most valuable to me."

"I'm not fighting for you," I say, quietly. "Never."

"You won't be fighting yet," he says. "The two of you alone can't hope to stand against the forces of Fior. But your blood will be enough for me to complete my task. I need

Transcendents, and only you and Cas have the ability to create them."

"What—me?" *I should have guessed.* I have the same healing power as Cas, after all. *Oh God. He'll never let me go, now.* He didn't just want one Transcendent. He wanted an army.

And now he can make one.

Jared smiles at me, like he knows what I'm thinking.

"Cas was your experiment before," I say. "I'm betting he won't want it to happen again."

"Actually, he was quite compliant after you were taken. He followed me without a fuss, I'm glad to say. Wouldn't have wanted him to wander off alone and run into the fiends."

What? That can't be right.

"I thought all the fiends were yours." I cough. My throat's so dry, my skin itches all over. I feel, for the first time in a long while, human.

And I don't like it.

"It was necessary for me to keep some of the fiends here, yes. I needed their blood for my experiments. Cas himself carries it within him, and that same blood now resides in your veins. You are part of one of the monsters you so despise, Leah."

I shake my head. "No."

"You feel it, don't you," he says, softly. "When you fight. The power in your blood, the raging fire that nothing can quench. You're a soldier, Leah, but you're more than that. You're more than a Pyro. You'll never be free of the fire." He pauses. "When Cas healed you, do you think he knew that?" he asks. "I admit, I'm curious. I was there when he was a child, but even I didn't guess the potential of his healing power. He refused my requests to experiment. He was always stubborn."

"Yes," I say, hot anger suffusing the word. "Yes, I imagine he was. You forced him to fight to the death, repeatedly. You knew he could heal himself. *What was the point of that?*"

I'm on my feet by now, screaming in his face.

Jared draws in a breath, slowly. "It's started, then," he murmurs.

I pause, anger still thrumming through my veins. "What?"

"The visions. The dreams. I don't believe Cas would have confided in you willingly about his past. Am I correct?"

I grit my teeth. He's right, of course. But that means…

"That is why the first experiments all failed. That's why he vowed never to heal again. I'm sorry, Leah." He stops, shakes his head, then asks, "Wouldn't you like to see Cas? I was surprised you didn't ask about him right away."

"Is he a prisoner, too?"

"Prisoner?" Jared gives me an unconvincing smile. "You're not a prisoner here, Leah. This is a sanctuary for you. It can even be your home, if you like."

"No thanks." I might not know exactly where I am, but I can hazard a guess. "What were you saying?" I hate asking him anything—hate even being in the same room as him, but right now, he's the one with the answers. "How did you know I'm seeing... visions? What happened to the other people Cas healed?"

His silence sets alarm bells ringing, but I hide my sweaty palms.

"I will take you to him, if you promise not to run away."

Fine. I'll ask Cas, then. One thing's for sure: I'll get my answers. Even though I know I won't like them.

He beckons me, and I get to my feet, wincing as my body protests. Every movement brings a whisper of the pain, and it's not something I can shake off. But I won't let it distract me. I'm here for a reason. I need to find a way to save Elle and the others, to prevent this madman from destroying the base. Once I'm sure they're safe, Cas and I can escape.

The corridor outside is painted white and carpeted in blue. Bright fluorescent lights gleam overhead, and as we turn a corner, daylight streams in through an open window. Confused, I glance out at the field of dead grass outside, which looks like it belongs to a park or school.

"Where are we?" Much as I'd rather not speak to this bastard, I figure asking questions is the quickest way to figure my way out of this place.

"I thought you knew. Did Cas not tell you? This used to be the base for Pyros until the regrettable tragedy two years ago."

A screeching noise interrupts him, raising the hairs on my arms. *Fiends!*

"They won't hurt you," Jared assures me.

"They're your lab experiments?" I ask. "How many of them are running around killing people?"

Jared's face pinches inwards. "You still don't understand the necessity of what we do. We alone stand against the fiends, Leah. If it wasn't for our using the fiends, we could never have created that remarkable weapon you use."

The dagger. I can't make a run for it now, without my weapon. Not that there's any way out. We passed several other windows before, and it looks like the whole building's surrounded by high brick walls.

He catches my expression. "Not to worry, your athame dagger's quite safe." He's almost smiling now, the sick bastard.

Wait. "What about *your* weapon?" I ask. "How—what did you do to me?"

Our blades touched, and that intense pain made me pass out. Like… *Nolan*. The tattoos. Is that what Nolan meant when he talked about pain? Was that how Jared tortured him, the reason he would hurt Elle to spare himself?

Jared's stare pierces me, giving me the uncomfortable feeling he's guessed my thoughts. Sure enough, he says, "I suspected you'd be susceptible, Leah. You haven't fully reached your potential yet. Once you awaken as Transcendent, even my power won't be able to subdue you."

Why's he telling me this? I narrow my eyes at him, and he half-smiles. "I kept your dagger safe, Leah. You and the weapon are conduits for energy. Just like the Fiordans. Those are our true enemies," he says. "People used to mistake us for them, as they were able to take on the form of humans. Surprised?"

I don't say anything.

"Cas told you, I imagine. I doubt my brother would have been as forthcoming. After all, who's to say who really committed the murder of so many humans? It was a clever idea, very clever. The apocalypse has ended the world, and mysterious figures in red are walking around, like a cult ... but I digress. You and Cas have a link to the Fiordans—he, because he was born of their blood, and you, because you were reborn with *his* blood. In short: the perfect gift for me. Firstly, I need to check that your blood functions in the same way as his. You're going to have to heal someone for me, Leah. Can you do that?"

Is he serious? I say nothing, biting my lip. *No,* is my instinctive answer. But I doubt he'll accept it.

He nods, as though he expected that reaction. "Stubborn, Leah. You'll see, however, that you have no option but to comply."

Somehow, I know what's coming before I see it, before we round the corner and come to a metal door very much like the ones at the base. Jared unlocks it with a key he pulls from his coat pocket, and he pushes it open.

Cas lies on a bed, unmoving, face stained in blood.

CHAPTER TWENTY-ONE

I choke on a scream, my hand clapping to my mouth. The pieces of the scene fit together again, one at a time. Cas on the bed. Long claw-like slash marks crisscross his torso and face, so deep I wouldn't recognise him if I didn't *know* it was him. His eyelids are closed, brushed with blood.

"Cas," I whimper into my hand. *God.* Tears come thick and fast. Forgetting all about not showing weakness in front of Jared, I reach the bed in one stride and drop to my knees beside him.

"I am sorry, Leah."

I whirl to face him, furious tears flying from my eyes. *"You said he wasn't harmed! You said...* you said I'd be able to feel it if he... he..." I can't go on. My hand moves by itself to stroke his ravaged face. A sharp pain pierces me from the inside, but not a physical pain.

"I'm sorry. I did wonder, but though his blood flows in your veins, it seems the connection isn't deep enough yet for actual physical pain to transfer over."

He speaks like a scientist discussing hypotheses—a cold-hearted, ruthless monster. Fierce rage rises from the pain in my chest, and I feel the temperature climb.

"Watch out, Leah. You don't want to hurt him, do you?"

I can't hurt him. Can I? I don't know enough. Jared has us at his mercy, and knows it.

"What do you want me to do?" My tone comes out flat.

"Use your blood to heal him. If it works, it's proof that his gift transferred to you. Of course, he can heal on his own, but the process takes longer and is rather more painful. It's your choice."

"I don't have a weapon." It's like I'm listening to someone else speak from a distance. Like I've locked that horror somewhere inside, too deep to reach.

Jared steps forward, holding out a knife. I don't feel anything, only numbness, and it comes as no surprise when he doesn't hand it to me, only gestures that I hold out my hand. I do so, and he slices me across the palm.

I don't even feel it.

The blood drips onto Cas. I direct it into the gaps in his shredded uniform, the crimson stripes which could only have been caused by a particularly vicious fiend. Tears drip onto his chest and mingle with the blood. *I'm sorry. I'm so sorry.* My hand shakes, and I grip my wrist to hold it steady. There's no way to tell if it's working.

What if it doesn't? Would he… die?

Cas stirs, and I jump, heartbeat rising. His eyes snap open and he sits up so fast that I shoot backwards, almost tripping over.

"Cas."

"What are you doing here?

Relief washes over me, so strong it makes my knees go weak.

"You're okay. I thought you were—"

"The girl healed you," Jared says. He's been so quiet, I'd almost forgotten he stood there in the corner. Now he moves towards Cas, an expression of delight forming on his face.

"It seems you've transferred your gift to the girl after all. Good. That'll make things much faster, with both of you ready to work."

"You're joking," says Cas. He flashes me a pained look, and I blink, confused.

"It's a risk we have to take," says Jared, with an unconvincing sigh. He snaps between serious scientist and lunatic with a disconcerting speed, and I wonder whether the madness started before or after the war. *Stupid,* I tell myself. *He tortured children. He was always a madman.*

"What?" I ask. "What's going to happen to me? Am I going to die?"

Strangely, the idea doesn't scare me, not as much as being used for one of Jared's experiments. Not as much as that awful, all-consuming pain. But I can't die before I stop Jared from hurting the others.

"No," says Jared. "You won't die—at least, not at first. But over time, the longer the two of you are connected, you'll become insensible, little more than an empty shell, stripped of your own emotions. Taken over by..."

"Mine," Cas says, flatly. "And you can't blame anyone but yourself for that, Jared."

"The visions have started already," Jared tells him.

Cas looks away, but I see another flash of pain in his eyes. Does he feel guilty for what's happening to me?

"They'll get worse," Jared continues. "I've never seen it happen to a fully-active Transcendent. Perhaps it's because Leah's not a child. I did wonder about the effects on an adult

Pyro, but I never could find any willing volunteers. But what Leah's experiencing—every other Pyro who succumbed to the visions died within a few weeks."

My heart lurches. *Dying?* Am I really—? I look at Cas, but his gaze remains on the floor. Jared's expression is more like pity. More of a condescending sort, not like he *regrets* his experimental subject dying.

"You're sick," I say, shakily. "You hurt kids just to see if Cas could heal them, then let them live visions of him being tortured until they went crazy and died? Is that it?"

Cas's head whips up and his eyes narrow in pure rage as he stalks towards Jared. "I'm not doing *anything* else for you. Never. You'll have to kill me first."

"And the girl? What about her? And what about Murray and your friends back at the base? I have the means of destroying them in this very room." He looks at me.

"I'm not interested in any more of your sick experiments," I say coldly. My insides hollow out. *Dying. I can't be.*

"So you aren't curious about the link between a Pyro and their weapon? Why you feel such an attachment to this particular one?"

He reaches into a pocket inside his coat and withdraws a long dagger—*my dagger.*

My hand shoots out automatically, but he pulls it out of range.

"Made of the ashes of fallen Pyros. It's one of my proudest achievements." His gaze darts between Cas and me, as though expecting a reaction. I refuse to let one show, but my heart's beating fast again. *He made the weapons, too?*

"But they have an inbuilt weakness. Ashes and blood—that was to be the original end of it, but as you know, Cas, blood can be used as a different kind of weapon."

"The tattoos," says Cas flatly. "So you want to have us heal people so you can bind them to your command. They disobey, they get blinding pain. I know how your mind works. But isn't a bit excessive? Aren't the tattoos enough?"

"There are other advantages. Well, if you've quite recovered from your injuries—I see the girl's taken care of that—then we'd better get to work."

"Not on your life."

"No," I say, quickly. "I want to see proof that you haven't harmed my friends."

Jared meets my eyes, curiosity sparking. "Have you no regard for your own life?"

"Are you going to show us or what?" Cas folds his arms. It's amazing that he can still look so intimidating, even covered in blood and in the company of a lunatic who has both our lives in his hands.

"It won't make any difference," says Jared. He pushes open the door, and Cas stalks out.

Before I can follow, a loud screech echoes down the corridor. I start at how close it is.

"Where the hell did you put that fiend?" Cas demands. "Don't tell me you locked it in your office."

The one that attacked him? Anger rushes over me and it's all I can do not to leap at Jared.

But he's frowning. "No, of course not. It's outside, with the rest."

Another screech. Definitely close by. And there's another sound too, quieter, background noise. The rumble of ground moving.

A scream. Human.

"We're being attacked?" Cas asks of no one in particular.

"No." Jared shakes his head. "No, of course not. It can't be."

But that scream…

"Tell me what you did with my weapon," Cas says. "Now."

Jared's still shaking his head. "No one can get in. *No one.*"

"Yeah, well, we're supposing they can. Do you have my knife?"

"In the lab, but..." Jared starts walking again, fast. Cas strides alongside him, close by, even though he's unarmed. I rush after them, wondering if I can somehow steal my knife back from Jared. He's not looking at me...

Then we round the corner, and a brutal sight hits my eyes.

Bodies. Several red-coated men and women lie motionless in the corridor, bodies marred with terrible wounds, even worse than Cas's. Slash-marks, like the claws of a modified fiend.

Boom.

The walls shake. Plaster dust rains down, and the fluorescent light flickers and dies. An explosion shatters the left wall, and the biggest fiend I've ever seen shoves its way into the corridor.

It's taller than the ceiling, twice my height and ten times my size, a creature of pure muscle. A boulder-like fist slams into the opposite wall, and bodies are trampled by its boat-sized feet. The giant turns to face us, as though it's slow to realise it has living company.

"Hell," Jared whispers.

"What have you done?" says Cas, backing away. I've never seen him run from a fight before.

"That's not one of ours—never!" Jared turns tail and runs, and I follow, feet flying, one thought reverberating in my head—*get the knife*. As he halts at a dead end, I tackle him. Instinct takes over, and I lunge for the knife sticking out of his belt—*mine*. It melds to my hand almost instantly.

But can I kill that thing even with a weapon? I don't know, and I'm not about to stick around and get cornered.

"Come on!" Cas lifts me to my feet and pulls me alongside him—I can barely register the shock that he's not leaving me behind—but he's weaponless, and the lumbering giant is on our heels.

We're faster, though, and Cas knows where he's going. He pulls me through corridor after winding corridor. It's quiet, apart from the faint rumbling sounds and occasional fiend's cry, but we don't stop to check anyone's alive here. Escape's the only thing that matters.

Skidding around another corner, we almost run right into a barricade. A group of pale, terrified faces hide behind all kinds of weapons, and suddenly there are a dozen knives pointed at us.

"Get out of the way," says Cas. "And if I were you, I'd get the hell out of here."

"There's no way out," one of them says. "None."

"Yes, and there's a giant rampaging right behind us," says Cas. "Can't you hear it?"

The clatter of weapons falls into silence, and as if on cue, a tremendous *boom* makes the walls vibrate.

"I want my knife back," says Cas. "So if you don't mind, *get out of the way.*"

And they do, quietly, without a fuss. Half the group flees in different directions, but I'm already running alongside Cas. He pushes open a door at the corridor's end, and we run into a gigantic laboratory.

No time to take everything in. Cas gives the room a cursory glance and strides over to a table where his dagger lies flat, immersed in some kind of liquid. He pulls it out, sending the liquid flying everywhere.

"God knows what that is," he mutters. "He could have tortured me with it, but decided to set his fiends on me instead. We can't go out that way." He nods to a door that I belatedly realise leads outside into some kind of yard. "That's where he keeps his experiments." He frowns, as though thinking. Urgency pulls at my feet, but I don't know this place, and that monster's still out there.

"This way," he whispers, pushing open the door we came through, and I follow him into the corridor again.

How big is this place? I can't help wondering, as we run through corridor after corridor, seeing no signs of the destruction over the other side of the building. We run across a courtyard, and my heart lurches when I glance up and see winged shapes up in the sky.

"Come on."

And finally we come to a pair of glass-windowed doors leading out into what looks like a junkyard. A high wall surrounds it, but Cas approaches it all the same.

"This is going to have to be fast, and we'll need to run as soon as we get out. We'll attract a bunch of attention, but there's no other way."

"What's the plan?" I glance up at the sky again, but the dark shapes are behind us. They haven't spotted us—yet.

"We're going to bring the wall down. Both of us. On the count of three—you ready?"

I nod, hand gripping my dagger, though I know it won't be much use for this, and readying myself to run.

"One… Two… Three."

We run, hitting the wall at almost the exact same second with a *crash*. I reach inside for the power and feel the energy blast extending outwards, turning the brick wall to dust—but Cas takes my hand and the surge recedes, bringing me back to reality. I cough as I inhale brick dust.

"You okay?"

I nod, and we run.

Cracks spread out over the ground, and it vibrates beneath my feet. Whatever's happening isn't over yet. Cas makes for a patch of trees, shelter. Running alongside him, I keep glancing up at the sky, but it doesn't tell me anything about what's happening back there.

Or where that giant fiend came from.

We slow down as we reach the trees, turning back to the building. It looks deceptively calm, bar the destroyed wall we escaped through, but the shaking under my feet and the dark shapes in the sky tell me something's very, very wrong.

"What now?" I ask. "We can't go back there, but I don't know how to get to the base. How can we stop him from hurting the others?"

"With luck, he's dead," says Cas. "If not, then he has bigger problems."

"So where now?"

"This path leads to the main road. If we follow it, we can find out what's happening over the other side. But I don't want to leave you alone."

"What, you think I want to stay behind?"

"Look, whatever's out there isn't something we can beat. *Nothing* gets past Jared's security. He's always kept this place protected. Which means the fiends have found a way to breach it. They'll be coming for us, but they don't know we're here, which gives us a head start. If you run, you might reach Murray and the others in time to warn them, if they've got far enough away from the base."

"But we're miles away, right?" I was unconscious, but I'd assumed the winged fiends had carried us here.

Cas shakes his head. "For a Pyro, it's walkable within a day."

"So is that your plan? We go join Murray again?"

"I don't know about you, but I have no intention of fighting for Jared, and I think this place is a lost cause. With the others, we'll have strength in numbers. He doesn't have as many of those fiends as he used to—not enough to make an army, anyway. I had a look," he adds in response to my expression of confusion. "While you were unconscious. Of course, he wanted me back in his lab, so I pretended to go along with it. I know that place too well; it hasn't changed much in the past few years. So I had a look at his latest experiments. Pretty much the same as before. Failed attempts at creating artificial Transcendents. But he's not quit messing with the fiends, either."

He reaches down to a knife-sheath on his boot and pulls out a test-tube of a thick, glistening reddish-brown liquid.

"I stole this. Not much of it left. He was playing around with DNA, too, but that was in the part of the building which that giant fiend rampaged through. There probably won't be anything left now. That's how he engineered the winged fiends, but judging by the ones we met on the road, I'd guess they weren't as easy to control as he hoped."

He flings the contents of the test tube at a nearby tree. The thick liquid splatters across the bark.

"He can't use it now."

Without his coat, the gaps in his black uniform stand out, slash-marks across his arms and chest. I realise I'm staring and quickly look away, back towards the building.

"That's how the tattoos work," he says, moving away, further into the woods. I hurry after him.

"Pyros share some kind of DNA coding that's different from regular people," he explains, "And he found a way to separate it and use it as a torture weapon. Anyone inked with one of those tattoos of his can be controlled at any time. He took blood samples from everyone when they arrived, so it was a simple matter of putting our blood into an object. It's how he convinced so many Pyros to fight the fiends the first time around. You know, there were once at least five hundred of us."

I feel dizzy. "Five hundred?"

"Or more. We lost half of them when the divide opened. Then Jared played his hand. He'd inked everyone in his secret inner circle. Then if anyone argued, he could convince them to do as he told them or suffer unbearable pain. Amazingly effective."

I just gape at him. Even knowing what I do about Jared, the thought of him controlling that many people... *he's a sadist. A genuine sadist.*

"He only revealed it after the first attack, when it became clear the Fiordans' weapons had us outmatched. We lost half our army. The Transcendent didn't want to fight. I was the shield," he says, dispassionately. "So I survived."

"I..." I whisper. "He's..."

"Yeah, he's something else," says Cas, his mouth pulled down in a grimace. "You might say being so close to the fiends cost him his sanity. He's tried injecting himself with their blood before—if you haven't guessed, he's determined to create an invincible warrior. Seeing as his army failed the last time, he knows the key is the Transcendents. Like you."

"Yeah, but I'm not exactly invincible," I say, thinking of how easily he brought me down when our weapons touched. "So he was planning to make me into a monster, or just use my DNA? What about that giant? Is that his, too?"

More to the point, I can't hear it anymore, which strikes me as ominous. Why is it so quiet?

"I'd say no. Even he has limits. It's new, and I have a feeling it came from the divide. There's no other way."

Silence settles between us, and I become aware that we've unconsciously moved closer to one another. Without his coat, he looks... almost vulnerable. He blinks his pale blue eyes—why have I never noticed they were blue before?

"What?" he says, breaking the trance. I look away, my face flushing.

"Just wondering." I scramble to remember what we were talking about. "About where that giant came from. Do you think there might have been another bridge opened?"

Cas's eyes narrow. "No, because freaking giant fiends are a normal occurrence in our world."

The sarcasm startles me. I didn't even notice we'd gone for so long without him belittling me in some way, and the reality-shock reminds me just how dire our situation is. That moment of vulnerability feels like I imagined it.

"Okay, you're the expert," I say. "So, are we just going to hide in here bickering, or do I get to take down that giant monster? It's not immune to Transcendents, is it?"

I'm only half-serious—the idea of tackling the beast isn't exactly an appealing one, and I'd be happy to leave it to destroy what's left of Jared's lab. But at the same time, there are innocent people in its way, and if there *is* another bridge, then God only knows what other monsters are out there.

"I have no idea," Cas says, coldly. "If you really want to die here rather than saving everyone back at the base, go right ahead."

A pang hits my heart for Elle, for all of them.

The trees around us start shaking, and a tremendous roar sounds from the building. The ground vibrates with heavy footsteps, and Cas pulls me out of the way as a gigantic shape crashes through what's left of the wall we broke through, sending bricks and dust flying everywhere.

The giant roars again, and we run.

CHAPTER TWENTY-TWO

We don't get far before the trees start falling down. Branches fly everywhere as the giant shoves its way through, and several times, I'm hit by falling limbs which would stop a normal person in their tracks. Cas and I run flat-out, dodging amongst the trees, but we haven't a hope of out-running this monster.

The forest ends abruptly at the edge of a cliff. Cas grabs my arm and pulls me back, just in time. It's not a cliff. It's a deep trench in the ground, so deep you can't see the bottom, like it reaches the core of the Earth itself.

The divide was closer than I thought.

Oh, hell.

Trees fly, and the giant explodes out of the forest in a flying leap. Cas grabs me roughly and pulls me to the ground, and I'm so surprised I drop automatically to my front. The giant sails over our heads and right into the trench. I expect to see it falling, but the trench is suddenly a river of lava, and I can't see anything for the thick, swirling fiery liquid. The giant has gone.

I breathe out, gripping the cliff's edges with my hands. That was too close, far too close. I turn to Cas, biting back a whimper. Maybe I'm not ready to die, after all.

Cas's wide eyes meet mine; for the first time since I've known him, he genuinely looks stunned.

"It's a bridge, all right," he says. "Right into the infernal gulf. I've not seen that place since the first time…"

I start as I realise I've grabbed onto his hand without even knowing it. Was it when he pulled me down? I unfurl my fingers. He doesn't even look at me.

A deep, horrible sadness pulls at me—so sudden and out of place that tears well up in my eyes. *Dammit.* I blink furiously and turn away. What's the matter with me?

An image flashes before my eyes. A person kneeling at the edge of a gulf—looking into the lava—

"Leah!"

I blink again and my vision clears. *Crap. Not again.* Am I seeing Cas's memories? Now's not the time to get distracted.

"What's happening to me?" I ask, in a whisper.

"I'm sorry." Is it just me, or is that devastation coming from his own voice? Or is it my own emotions influencing what I think I hear? I shake the feeling away, but it clings on, relentless. Pushing myself to my feet, I stare at him.

"When?" I ask. "When will I... go mad? Is that what's happening?

"I don't know. I never saw any of the others."

Oh, God.

"Never mind." My own voice sounds oddly distant. "We need to go..."

But my vision's blurring again, faster than I can blink.

***

My vision clears, and I'm in a field of scorched ground. There are people all around me, wearing red. Faces blur past, but one stands out, and it takes me a moment to realise it's Cas. He stands apart from the group, in front.

I can hear voices but not understand them, like they're speaking another language. I watch, an outsider, as Jared pushes his way through the crowd to the front. Like a camera zooming out, now I see the whole scene from above—

Oh. My God.

Now I can see the divide, and there are fiends swarming over the edge, more than I can count. From here, the small group of people look like tiny insects, organised into a formation with Cas at the front. But it's too far to make out any other faces. My vision blurs again.

The scene changes. Bodies litter the ground. A few survivors are scattered, weapons in hands and determination etched on their faces, but there are far more fiends, too many. The scene zooms out again. Now I can only see tiny dots moving around.

Far away from the divide, another confrontation's taking place. The camera zooms in, and once again, I'm dragged along with it. A small group of people stand at the top of a hill, surrounded by fiends on all sides. Cas is one of them. Jared's another. All hold daggers up to the sky, which is now an angry red. By the way they stand, I can tell the earth is shaking.

A flash of light. Screaming so loud—the earth shakes—bodies fall…

Without warning, the scene changes again. Now I'm inside a lab. Someone sits across from me. Murray. My arm's held out in front of me, not my arm but someone else's—male, muscular, and with a dark red symbol carved into the wrist. A flame.

Murray's voice fades in and out, like a radio with a bad signal.

"Nothing I can do… it won't fade, but Jared's gone. It won't hurt you."

But who am I? I try to move, but I'm not in control of my actions. Just a bystander watching the scene from the view of the person in the chair…

"I get it." Cas's voice.

I'm Cas.

And that tattoo means he belongs to Jared, too.

***

I snap back to reality with a gasp. Cas hasn't moved; he stares at me, looking almost helpless.

My hand reaches out and pushes up what's left of his sleeve. The ugly red mark is the same as Nolan's.

"Surprised?"

Cas and I both start at the other voice coming from the forest. A smooth, impossibly familiar voice.

Jared steps out of the trees. His coat's torn and he's covered in dust, but otherwise looks unharmed.

"You," growls Cas.

"Me," says Jared. "I hoped you both got away unscathed. I expected you to, but you can never be sure of anything."

"How did you escape?" I ask.

"I have a trick or two up my sleeve. It looks like you had a close call," he adds, indicating the still-flowing lava river below us. "Fior has opened, and the first bridge is already in place. Pity Murray and the others... they have no idea. The fiends will catch them unawares."

My chest tightens. *No...*

"How are *you* alive? Why did the giant run away?"

"Because it's weak," says Jared. "All fiends are. They were never warriors, certainly not at first. The two of you are to come with me, *now.*"

I raise an eyebrow. "You're joking." My heart drums. I want to kill him—but I can't risk the others.

"I'm serious, Leah. I need you both. You're immensely valuable to my research."

"There's a bridge to the fiends' world on your doorstep," says Cas. "I'm pretty sure your *research* can wait."

"We need soldiers. Too many lives were lost, but if the two of you can create more Transcendents..."

"Not happening." I fold my arms. "I'm not working for you."

"I'm not dying because of the likes of you," snarls Jared. "The invasion's started already, don't you understand? If the two of you die, then that's it." He snatches up a branch, and I tense into a fighting pose, ready to defend myself, but instead, he throws it over the edge of the trench. It soars over and into the lava—except I never see it land. Instead, it ignites, dissolving into ashes.

"That's what we're up against," Jared hisses. "Our world versus theirs, and in case it's escaped your attention, we're at a significant disadvantage. Even if you survived the journey back to Murray, you'd be on the losing team. He might have the numbers, but none are Transcendent."

"Neither are yours," says Cas. "And I told you, I'm never being your weapon again."

"Apparently, you need a reminder." Jared sighs, theatrically. "I always liked you best, Cas. I never wanted to hurt you."

Cas raises an eyebrow. "You had a strange way of showing it."

"Discipline is a necessity," says Jared. "Always. But it hurt me to hurt you, Cas. You could have been so much more."

"Yeah, if I didn't have a useless healing power," he snaps. "I'm *not* doing it. And yes, I do remember the pain. But the answer's still no."

Another sigh. "So be it," says Jared, pulling something from his jacket. A knife, almost identical to Cas's. He lifts it to point the tip at the sky, lifting his other hand to stroke the edge of the blade. Cas makes a strangled noise.

I don't think, just throw myself at Jared, my own dagger in my hand. I barrel into him, knocking him off his feet, and we crash to the ground with a solid *thump*. He gasps.

My dagger-free hand reaches for the blade crushed between us, trying to grasp the edge. It's wet and slippery, and I can't get a grip on it. Jared gasps again, going limp beneath me. Warmth soaks my front.

Wait… no! Heart thrumming in my ears, I pull back.

My dagger's buried in Jared's chest.

I back up further, my breath coming short. I killed him.

His blood soaks through my clothes. Bile rises in my throat. I let go of the dagger, but it stays attached to my hand, and slides out of his body as I fall back.

Dazed, I can only lie there, stunned.

"Leah! Come on!" Cas tugs on my arm, pulling me to my feet. "We have to go," he says.

"Is he…?" I can't look at him.

"He's dead. Come on."

I'm shivering despite the heat radiating from the dagger in my hand.

Go back to the others. Make sure Elle is safe…

He's dead. He can't hurt them anymore.

Relief battles disgust and shock. Cas and I run through the forest, and I hope he knows where he's going, because my mind's a blank at the moment.

"Jared's dead, he can't hurt them," Cas says. "They'll know we're at war, but if another of those giants got through, there's nowhere for them to run. Even the base won't hold."

"Damn." I can't see a solution. All I can do is keep moving, keep running.

Keep fighting.

I can't lose them.

We run until another part of the divide cuts off our path. Cas pulls me back from the brink of a cliff where the forest ends abruptly, trees tumbling down the cliffs into the trench.

"Damn," Cas says. "They're still breaking through. If the bridge isn't closed, then what's left of our world will be wiped out."

"Hell," I whisper. "Is there anything we can do?"

"Close the bridge," Cas says. "We did it once before, two years ago. This isn't a full invasion like last time. But we need to find where the bridge *is.*"

He sounds so calm. I glance back at the deep scar in the ground as we turn away and try to find another path. My mind whirls. I killed Jared. His blood is still soaking into my skin. *He deserved it,* a voice whispers in my ear, but it doesn't make me feel any better.

Fallen trees bar the way, and the smell of burning grows so intense I have to cover my mouth. Eyes watering, I look up at the canopy and see smoke pouring from somewhere nearby.

"There's a fire!" says Cas. "Crap. We'll have to get out of the forest, it'll spread fast."

He doesn't say it, but the forest is the only thing giving us cover from the fiends. Whenever there's a gap in the canopy, I see dark shapes too big to be birds. Jared's twisted creations are still out there. Smoke pours onto the path, obscuring the way, almost blinding. I keep my eyes open at a squint and we run, ducking under tree limbs and hacking through undergrowth with our weapons. Finally, we reach a gap in the trees and push our way through, out of the forest.

Hell awaits us. The scarred ground is cracked and small fires have sprung up everywhere. Cas and I look at each other.

"Which way?" I ask, my voice hoarse from the smoke.

"Right over..." He trails off. "There."

The divide cuts a deep trail out of the forest and towards a line of hills, closer than I expected. Rising up into the red sky, the tips of the mountains look like they're ablaze.

But that's not what draws my attention. A colossal shape is rising through the divide—even from a distance, it towers over everything but the mountains themselves.

The giant is back.

"No way," I whisper.

"We have to move fast," Cas whispers. "It's slower than we are. If we run, *really* run, we could make it back to the base."

He's pointing at the nearest mountain, but the silhouette of the giant looks a lot closer than we are, its back to us, moving in that direction.

"Come on."

But as we take our first step onto the rocky, torn-up ground, Cas drops to his knees, his face a grimace of pain. I crouch down alongside him.

"What's wrong?"

Cas's hand moves slowly, his teeth gritted together, sweat beading on his forehead. I've never seen him in so much pain, and it scares me to death.

He lifts his arm, and I see the tattoo on his wrist is pulsing red-black. Veins stand out on his arm as another spasm of pain rocks him.

"No—no!" I bend over his wrist, push up his sleeve. Pressing my fingers to it, I feel the pain pulse through the connection and quickly let go. Shame hits me almost instantly—but what can I do?

"He's alive," Cas gasps, between spasms. "There's—no other way."

"No!" My dagger's still coated in Jared's blood, but I don't hesitate to press it to my own hand. Blood healing—will it counteract the effects of Jared's poison?

"That won't work." Cas's back arches and he grits his teeth.

"I have to do something!" I look wildly around, desperate for a way out. The giant's got smaller even in the last minute—closer to Murray and the others.

"There's—nothing." A painful smile curls his lips. "I'm sorry, Leah."

Pain rocks him again, and he stifles a cry. "This was always going to happen," he gasps. "I'm Jared's—always. I wasn't made to live. I was made to die."

"No. He doesn't own you!"

"He's the master of pain, Leah. That's enough."

He curls up against the wave of agony, and I almost feel it myself in the echo of the horrific pain Jared inflicted on me. I'm amazed he's still conscious. I bow my head over his face, tears burning my eyes.

"You have to help the others," he says.

"I'm not leaving you!"

"I'm not worth it, Leah." His eyes half-glaze over.

"Cas…"

"Don't be stupid. Go. Only you can close the bridge. You'll know it when you see it."

His eyes roll back in his head, his body spasming in pain. Tears spill from my eyes, and my throat closes up. *Cas… no.*

"Please, Leah. Go."

Another glance up. The giant's moved even further. Can I hope to outrun it now?

"Go…" His voice is faint now; I can only hear it because I'm so close.

Something inside me is screaming. Fury and grief battle for attention—fury at the sheer injustice of the universe, at Jared, at everyone. I feel the gap where something could have been, like the echo of pain, but somehow worse than anything Jared can inflict.

"GO!" Cas screams, and the fight seems to go out of him. His hand clasps mine, and images burst behind my eyes—images of the last fight, dead Pyros everywhere, people falling, mowed down by fiends. Then he lets go, his hand dropping to the ground again.

It was an underhanded move, but God, he's right. I can't stay.

I straighten, trying to lock my feelings behind a barrier, wiping my eyes.

And I run.

CHAPTER TWENTY-THREE

I move faster than ever before, the ground flying away like I'm airborne. The cracked earth and other obstacles barely slow me down, and the hills get closer by the second.

But so does the giant fiend. Even from a distance, I can see it knocking trees and rocks aside, its sights set on the hills. I might not be able to warn the others, but maybe I can intercept it first—maybe, as Transcendent, I can beat that thing.

So I change course and run towards the fiend. The divide gets closer until I'm running alongside the trench. Lava flows below, and I know I'm looking into another world entirely. The air above it shimmers.

A roar echoes ahead. The giant's stopped moving. *Tell me it hasn't found the others!* My heart pounds, and I run so hard it's like I'm trying to escape from my body. *No. Don't let it reach them…*

But it's turning around, slowly, huge feet skimming the edge of the trench. Then I see something that almost stops me in my tracks.

Another giant fiend is coming out of the divide.

And I'm running right at them.

It's too late to divert my path. I swerve slightly to the left, away from the divide—and glance back at the mountains.

The sight hits me like a punch to the chest, knocking the breath from my lungs. Fire engulfs the divide. So close to the base.

To my home.

First I lost Cas, now everyone else is in danger. The giant fiends turn to face me, and rather than fear, all I feel is rage.

My hand grips my dagger, my skin heats up, and I welcome the rush of power.

The fiends look at one another, as though startled to see me running towards them. I'm nothing in their eyes, a tiny human, easy to crush.

I'm going to kill them.

A scream rips from my throat, and I raise my dagger to the sky. Fire flickers up my arm to the blade and red tints my vision. The fiends react slowly, but they begin to lumber towards me, huge feet creating dents in the ground, crushing rocks. I almost lose my footing as the edge of the divide crumbles away, making the trench wider, but I outrun it.

Power rushes to the tip of the blade, and bright, piercing, flame-like light streams from it, reaching into the sky like a beacon.

The fiends stagger back, momentarily… blinded? Stunned? I don't know. But I still can't stop running. The ground rocks under my feet with every step, ripples flowing outwards. Am I doing that?

My feet leave the ground, though I don't remember jumping. The heat rising around me is so intense it numbs all other feeling, and I'm propelled forward, through the air, right at the nearest fiend.

It moves its huge arm to strike me, but I'm more than ready. My blade strikes, bringing an arch of flame with it, and the giant screams. The ground buckles as I land, and the giant falls back, crashing into its partner. Its severed arm drops over the edge of the divide.

The dagger vibrates in my hand, and I raise it once again. The two giants stand side by side, blotting out the sky, ugly faces bared in snarls.

"I'll kill you," I whisper, unafraid. Pure power pulses through my veins, washing away everything. Even my grief stays behind the barrier.

The second fiend kicks out without warning, but not at me. At the ground. Dirt and rocks fly up, like a wave crashing over my head, and I choke on soil, momentarily blinded. A blow sends me flying, and suddenly there's nothing underneath my feet.

I'm falling.

A blinding flash of light envelops me. I can't see anything—not the giants, not the hills, not even the river of lava which I should be falling into. But I'm suspended in the air. Wind buffets me, a hot breeze, but I can't tell where it's coming from. I blink, trying to clear my vision.

I'm not suspended in the air, but on a semi-transparent bridge. The small hairs on the back of my neck stand up as I feel eyes on my back, something watching me. I turn around slowly, dagger lifted.

I don't expect to see Jared.

He looks the same as when I last saw him, including the red stain on his chest where I stabbed him. Horror chokes my throat as questions explode in my mind. *How—how?*

"You," I whisper.

No. Not him. The original fiends could take on human form—that's what Cas told me. There's no way Jared can be here. Or so I tell myself.

A smile curls his lip. "You dared to try to kill me, Transcendent?"

I can do nothing but gape at him.

"Have you nothing to say to me?"

Honestly? Plenty of things. But I just want to fight until there's nothing left of me. Nothing left to feel.

"You're no fun."

Jared reaches up to his face and rips the skin away. Beneath is the red, raw skin of a true fiend. I watch, almost in fascination, as his outer skin collapses, and the fiend emerges, right there on the bridge between the worlds.

In a way, I'm disappointed. This fiend—Fiordan, whatever—barely comes up to my shoulder, and is far less muscular than the monsters I've become accustomed to. It almost looks… human.

"You will die, Transcendent," growls the Fiordan, the words rolling from its tongue in a way that suggests English isn't its native language. "You are not supposed to exist. Jared might have tried to get around human limitations, but the end result will be the same. Your world will fall. We will win this war."

I lift my dagger again, feel the rush of power. Whatever abilities this fiend has hidden, I can take it. I have to. If there's no one left to fight for our world, then I'll do my damned best to make sure this monstrosity never gets to take it.

For everyone the fiends took from me. For Lissa. For my parents. For Murray, Elle, everyone at the base. For Cas.

I run, letting out a scream, and the dagger answers my call. Fire flares around me, and I leap at the Fiordan.

The inferno envelops both of us. I scream in pure fury, and the buzz of power is like a physical presence, guiding my every move. I can't hear anything over the roaring in my ears, but I'm almost positive my opponent is screaming, too. White light folds over us, and the ground rocks under my feet with the energy blast.

A red hand grasps my wrist. Through the light, I can make out the outline, and snarl, trying to push it away. The grip's weak, barely there, and a finger drops from the hand, then another, crumbling to ashes.

I let go of the power, and the light recedes. There's nothing left of the fiend. It's gone, turned to dust and ashes, like…

A human caught in an energy blast.

I stumble back, suddenly on solid ground again, which rocks beneath me, like when the energy blast struck the camp, and everyone around me was consumed. Everyone but me.

Even the fiends couldn't stand against it.

The energy fans outwards, rippling above the divide. The flame-like patterns recede, the semi-transparent view of the burned-red landscape fading away.

I drop to my knees.

Somehow it sinks in that I'm on Earth again. I didn't fall through the breach. And the others are out there, still alive.

Staggering to my feet, I walk alongside the divide. My uniform survived the blast, incredibly. Of course it did. It's indestructible, like me.

I look to the divide again. The bridge is *gone,* like it never existed. Does that mean the fiends can't come back? No. The divide is still there, which means…

A tremendous roar almost causes me to lose my balance. *Oh, shit.* The giants are still fighting, the uninjured one pummelling its companion into the ground, and the one with the severed arm is barely a metre away from being pushed over the edge of the divide. I guess the first one couldn't resist an easy target. They're just brutes. But thanks to me, they're stuck on this side of the divide. I have to kill them.

Neither notice as I sneak up on them, dagger at the ready. Body aching with tiredness, still trembling with the echo of the energy blast. I feel like collapsing, letting the shock, and grief for Cas, take me. *No. I can't. Not yet.*

The fiend finally spots me, but it's too late. I leap up and slash with my blade, leaving a trail of fire in its wake. Distracted, it starts to turn around, but the other giant kicks it in the shin. As the two start grappling again, I dodge in and out, slashing at their flanks.

Finally, I reach within for the fire and it shoots upwards from my blade, vibrating outwards. Once again, the fire and light consume me and the giants along with me. The sound of heavy objects falling fills my ears, and I know it's the two fiends falling to pieces, crumbling like stone.

I'm left, shaking, amongst ashes.

Breathing heavily, I look up, my vision clearing. The divide still gapes before me, the air shimmering above it, but on the other side, on Earth, I can see the sun rising.

I fall to my knees, consumed by exhaustion and a dozen other emotions. Pain and grief rock me, and guilt, and terror, and I gladly let the world fade away.

***

"Leah! Leah!"

Someone's shaking me.

I groan. The hard ground presses against my face, and my eyes sting with dust. Energy blast. Everything around must be dead…

But there's someone else here.

Slowly, it all comes back, one painful piece at a time. I open my eyes.

Elle blinks at me, concern etched on her face. "Leah. I couldn't carry you back on my own. My dad's coming."

"Elle." I cough, my throat dry as ashes.

"What happened to you?"

Too much. Too much to say. I merely whimper, too worn out to talk.

"Don't worry, you don't have to tell me now. You're going to be fine. My dad's a genius. You know, he found a way to stop the tattoo from hurting me? Whatever Jared did to you, you're going to be fine."

Jared. Cas. Oh, God.

I screw up my eyes, hot tears spilling over.

"Leah, you're scaring me."

"Sorry," I choke out. "Is everyone at the base okay?"

"I thought *you* were dead!" Elle's crying now, her arms wrapped around me. "You and Cas left and then there were earthquakes and… I thought it was the end."

"It almost was." Smiling's painful, but the corner of my mouth lifts all the same. "I'm so glad you're all right. All of you. But what was that about the tattoos?"

"My dad made up some kind of substance to counter it." She lifts her sleeve. The red mark's still there, stark and vivid, but no longer bleeding.

"What…?"

"Um. Leah, this might sound weird, but he used your blood."

My blood? When did he even get that? The nurse, Sandra, did take a sample of my blood when I first arrived at the base. My blood is more than human. It's Transcendent. Because…

I think of Jared's experiments with fiends' blood and suppress a shudder. I can't tell her about that. Not now.

A cool breeze drifts past, making me shiver. Elle looks at me curiously. Her innocent expression twists the knot in my chest.

"My dad's coming."

The outline of a figure's walking towards us. Murray. I glance back at the divide, my chest knotting again. What do I say to him, knowing his brother's still out there, and Cas...?

Despite everything, I know what I have to do.

I wasn't made to live. I was made to die. I don't believe his words, not for an instant. There's no question. I have to take the fight back to Jared. And I have to save Cas.

Sunlight bathes the earth, filling me with a new surge of hope.

I will save him.

Thank you for reading!

I hope you enjoyed *Indestructible*. If you have a minute to spare, then I'd really appreciate a short review. For independent authors, reviews help more readers discover our books. I'd love to know what you thought!

About the Author

Emma spent her childhood creating imaginary worlds to compensate for a disappointingly average reality, so it was probably inevitable that she ended up writing urban fantasy and young adult novels. When she's not immersed in her own fictional universes, Emma can be found with her head in a book or wandering around the world in search of adventure.

Visit http://www.emmaladams.com/ to find out more about Emma's books, or subscribe to her newsletter (smarturl.it/ELAnewsletter) for new release alerts and a free short story.

Printed in Great Britain
by Amazon